D1326056

CAPTAIN
BULLDOG
DRUMMOND

CAPTAIN BULLDOG DRUMMOND

By

GERARD FAIRLIE

following

SAPPER

THE BOOK CLUB

121, Charing Cross Road, London, W.C.2.

THIS EDITION 1946

THIS BOOK IS PRODUCED IN COMPLETE CONFORMITY WITH
THE AUTHORISED ECONOMY STANDARD

MADE AND PRINTED IN GREAT BRITAIN
BY C. TINLING AND CO., LTD. LIVERPOOL, LONDON AND PRESCOT

CONTENTS

CONTENTS

THE GREAT MAN AND THE SOLDIER MEET

THE Great Man left that part of Whitehall which, although apparently just an unassuming street, has for so long harboured those who have lived the joys, the tragedies, and the thrills of the story of our Commonwealth. He walked fast, an absorbed expression on his fine, strong face, as if anxious to reach his destination before the light failed for that day and darkness took perilous charge of the blackout. He looked neither to right nor left, nor did he appear consciously to notice the many passers-by hurrying homewards. He walked straight, and others avoided a collision with him rather than he with them : he did this quite unconsciously, in no autocratic spirit, lost to the world all round him in his own troublous thoughts : but many of those who hurried past would have paused a moment, and willingly made way, had they recognised him in the gathering gloom.

The Great Man turned to the left in Trafalgar Square and made for that part of London which houses so many of the well-known clubs. As he arrived at the imposing doors of one of the most famous, he turned in and nodded a greeting to the hall porter. That worthy, his ribboned chest a silent tribute to his service for his country, smiled back. The Great Man pursued his way, hung up his hat and his coat in the convenient passage-way, and then mounted the wide stairs to the first floor. As he went, fellow-members murmured a good evening, but contrary to habit the Great Man scarcely noticed them : he walked straight to a door facing him.

As he opened this door, the lively sound of many voices greeted him. The club, ancient in history and tradition but modern in thought, provided for its members a most attractive and rather unexpected bar, and it was to this room that the Great Man had immediately made his way. He looked around him, smiled to one or two acquaintances,

7

but continued apparently to search for someone. Finally his face lightened, and he smiled broadly with evident satisfaction : he walked over to a small table in the corner of the room, where a middle-aged man, resplendent in the red tabs with a strip of gold which indicate at least a major-general, was sipping a pale yellow drink with obvious pleasure.

As the Great Man approached him, the Soldier looked up.

" Hullo, Frank ! " he said. " Have one ? "

" What is it ? " asked the Great Man, pulling up a chair and sitting down.

" You won't believe it," said the Soldier, " but it's sherry, old chap ! Real honest to goodness dry sherry ! Where on earth they've discovered it heaven only knows, but this is a great day in my war-time life ! Think of it . . . *real* honest to goodness *dry* sherry ! Have one quick, before it's all gone ! "

" I will," said the Great Man with decision.

The wine was procured, was tasted, was approved with acclamation, was consumed, and a second glass for each made it's appearance before the Great Man suddenly looked up at the Soldier.

" Can I have a few words with you ? " he asked. " In private ? "

The Soldier leant back in his chair, and looked at his friend enquiringly before replying.

" In private ? " he repeated. " How exactly do you classify this desired conversation ? Most frightfully secret ? Awfully personal and confidential ? or just don't scream it from the house-tops ? "

" Don't tell anyone at all."

" Oh, I see . . ." The Soldier looked regretfully at his glass of sherry, still more than half-full. " So I suppose this is no place to conduct this conversation ? "

The Great Man laughed.

" You're incorrigible, Dick. However, there's no particular hurry . . . finish your drink in peace."

From outside came the urgent wail of the air-raid alarm. There was a sudden momentary hush in the room : then general conversation was resumed, a few jokes were cracked, a few ruderies pronounced at the enemy.

"Dash!" said the Soldier, "If they drop one within a mile of me while I'm drinking, I get hiccups." He swallowed his drink, and beamed. "Fooled 'em!" He rose to his feet. "I'm ready for you . . . Where shall we talk? The Library is usally pretty empty at this time of day . . ."

It was. They were the only two members in the great, dark room as they made themselves comfortable in armchairs.

"Cigar?" suggested the Great Man.

"What have you been doing?" said the Soldier as he took one. "Filching from Winston when he wasn't looking?"

"I bought these myself," stated the Great Man with mock severity.

"Blinking plutocrat!" The Soldier grinned. "Out with it!"

But in spite of this encouragement there was a pause The Great Man seemed to be marshalling his thoughts: the Soldier waited quietly, even if he did feel a trifle impatient. He was more than merely interested: when his friend asked for a few words in private, it was his experience that those few words were worth a great deal of attention. The Great Man was not at all free with his confidences—in his position he could not possibly be—and what he said was always of the utmost interest.

At last he started:

"I'm worried . . ."

"Sorry to hear that . . ." said the Soldier encouragingly. "What's on your mind?"

"France," said the Great Man simply.

"Eh?"

"More accurately, the French."

There was a pause.

"As I remember it, and of course subject to correction, the French were in a pretty poor state in thirty-nine and forty," said the Soldier slowly. "They were overrun by the Huns, in far too many cases they failed to fight as they should have, and then they hurried into a disgraceful armistice and just . . . gave in. I grant of course that they were up against superior forces and overwhelming enemy air power, but . . . so were we, and we didn't give in. Far from it. As a matter of fact, we're going to win this war in spite of all the enemy advantages in the face of which the French surrendered. A fair statement of fact, or not ? "

" Very nearly, but not quite . . . " The Great Man paused, then continued thoughtfully. " Both nations were horribly unprepared to meet such armament as Germany had amassed, and through our own faults. The French did agree to a disgraceful armistice, but they hadn't got the channel between themselves and the enemy . . . "

" True," said the Soldier, leaning forward, " but they could have put the Mediterranean . . . "

" Gone to Africa and left the whole of their mother country . . . Yes, they could have and they should have. Some of them see that now . . . "

" de Gaulle and his Free French ? "

" Yes, and others actually within France . . . "

The Soldier looked round carefully before replying, as if to satisfy himself that they were still alone. Outside, the ack-ack guns broke into a roar. He waited until they were satisfied, and when he spoke, he lowered his voice perhaps unconsciously.

" Now look here, Frank, we all know that we've got fellows working in France, just as we have fellows working wherever they can inconvenience the blasted Huns. I've no doubt they use Frenchmen to help them, but . . . there are mercenaries everywhere, in every nation, and I imagine the job is well paid . . . "

" You have more faith in the Treasury than I have, and apparently less in the patriotism which you will also find everywhere. The thing is comparative ; a great nation is a nation with a high percentage of patriots, that's all. Do you think the spirit animating the Free French is totally absent inside France ? "

" Well . . . "

" Dick, if England were overrun by a ruthless, barbarous enemy, who take a pleasure in shooting women and children, you'd be careful not to let your real feelings become too obvious, wouldn't you, even if only for the sake of your family ? I know I would."

" Well . . . yes, I suppose so . . . "

" But that wouldn't mean that you'd lost your patriotism, would it ? or that, given the chance, you wouldn't take risks to worry and harass the enemy and perhaps help in his final defeat ? "

" Personally, I'd like to do that . . . if he overran England . . . "

" Quite."

The one word seemed to finish the conversation. The Great Man puffed at his cigar, leant back in his chair, almost closed his eyes. There was quite a long pause, with the Soldier watching his friend covertly. Then, suddenly, without changing his position, the Great Man spoke again.

" The point is, how many Frenchmen are thinking . . . and acting . . . that way now . . . in this month of November in the year of our Lord nineteen hundred and forty-three ? "

" Don't ask me ! " said the Soldier. " Always ready to oblige, and all that, but . . . "

" Yet," said the Great Man, leaning forward abruptly, " the answer to that question is of vital importance. We are planning—and you will know it, Dick—an invasion of Germany through France which has to succeed, or the war will be prolonged for years. It is absolutely essential, therefore, that the mind and soul and muscle of the French in France be appraised. And what do we know of the French now ? Do you realise that here in England, just a few miles from France, we simply do not know what to think ? Certain French elements are singing one song, other French elements in North Africa are singing another, isolated Frenchmen escaping to North Africa or here are telling stories that seem fantastic and sometimes incredible, Washington and London are certainly agreeing in public—

but are they in secret ?—and yet this operation must succeed, because if it doesn't we might even lose the war ! "

" Don't frighten me ! " said the Soldier. " What can I do about it ? "

" I want you to wrack your memory," answered the Great Man quietly, " and unearth someone from among your innumerable friends capable of doing a really big job."

" You want to find out about the French ? "

" Yes."

" But surely," said the Soldier, " you've got your own means ? " The Great Man smiled a trifle ruefully.

" Of course I have . . . we have. But there is always the possibility of . . . shall I say ' bias '? The Americans have a bias, we have a bias, on a lower level our organisations may have a bias . . . an independent investigation would perhaps be invaluable . . . "

" Is this to be an . . . official investigation ? "

" As official as such an investigation ever is. I wouldn't dare start such a thing without approval ! "

The Soldier let out a soft laugh.

" You're a liar Frank, but I see what you mean. Why not ask the Free French ? "

" The Americans would say they are more biased than anybody ! and they are plainly open to such an accusation."

" I take it back," said the Soldier. " That was a stupid suggestion."

" Not more stupid than most military interference in political or diplomatic matters," remarked the Great Man mischievously, but he went on at once : " Listen, Dick, I have approval to set in motion the impartial investigation which we need. It must be absolutely secret—there are of course both British and American organisations responsible for advising their Governments on just such matters, and they would be . . . shall we say hurt, if they were to hear of it. Quite apart from that, the safety of the man—the men—concerned in this investigation requires the most complete secrecy. That is why I stipulated before we started talking that what we said was to be repeated to nobody at all. I came to you because I was stumped to think of a man who was capable of undertaking this mission—this most important mission—and I knew that in you I could ask the advice of the one man in London—perhaps in the world . . . "

" Is this flattery, Frank ? "

" . . . who was most likely, out of his immense circle of friends, to be able to suggest a name to me."

The Soldier smiled.

" Thanks. Qualifications ? "

The Great Man thought for a moment.

" Whoever it is," he said slowly, " must certainly have courage, both physical and mental : he must be the soul of discretion : he must be able to think, and draw conclusions, entirely objectively without any fear of his taking sides : and . . . and . . . oh, yes . . . of course some knowledge of the French language would be highly desirable . . . "

" Would it matter if he could also see like a cat in the dark, could move as silently as a panther in spite of his great size, could hit like a horse and drink like a fish ? "

The Great Man sat upright.

" I'm sorry, Dick," he said stiffly, " but I cannot regard this as a laughing matter."

" And, Frank, I am not doing so." The Soldier grinned.

" I wish I hadn't said ' drink like a fish,' it's made me thirsty."

He rose to his feet : the Great Man followed suit.

" You want time to think it over ? "

" Oh, no ! " The Soldier laughed gaily. " Would the—er—qualities I have described prove any ban . . . ? "

" Of course not," smiled the Great Man, " provided, of course, that—as in the case of the fish—the drink had no effect . . . "

" That goes without saying. Poor Hugh ! I wonder how he's getting on with only war-time beer ! "

" Eh ? "

" Nothing. Now listen : the man I'm thinking of may be a little rusty : I haven't seen him since the war. But I think I could find him and find out. Then I'll let you know. He has all the qualifications you mentioned—except possibly the French—as well as the qualities I recited."

" Who is this man ? "

The Soldier smiled, as if at some pleasant recollection.

" He was in my regiment in the last war : we were subalterns together . . . "

The Great Man spoke with a trace of impatience.

" Dick, who is this man ? "

" Hugh Drummond."

" Who ? "

" Captain Hugh Drummond, D.S.O., M.C."

" I don't think I know him . . . "

" No ? " said the Soldier softly : then he laughed. " Oh, yes, you do ! I'm talking of the man they used to call Bulldog Drummond . . . remember now ? "

A slow smile spread on the Great Man's face.

" I knew I could rely on you ! " he said.

" We haven't got him yet," said the Soldier. " Old Hugh's a fussy individual : he likes to believe in the cause before he thrusts out his neck . . . not like us poor soldiers who just have to obey the politicians' orders ! Come on, I've talked too much : I need something for my throat ! "

" With soda, presumably," said the Great Man, as he followed his friend from the room.

As they passed through the hall, the shrill and steady wail of the ' All Clear ' sounded.

" Bad for the pubs," said the Soldier, " people will hurry home now ! "

" Maybe an omen," said the Great Man, but to himself.

II

A FISHMONGER SUFFERS A SHOCK

THE hedge looked perfectly innocent from the slope which overlooked the valley. But the man whose job it was to keep an eye on all that bit of country was by no means perfectly at ease. To be frank—one of his favourite

piping times of peace, when I came in one summer day and asked you for a Dover sole ?   Perhaps you meant to forget, as you hadn't got one."

" He never forgets a face ! " said the thin man.   " Most awkward, sometimes."

" Shut up, Algy : you talk too much on active service. Now then, let battle continue . . . you're the last one we've got to deal with, Mr. Deacon, so Algy, get out your smoke bomb and give the signal . . . "

It was then that the worthy fishmonger really did get his surprise.   One moment his two captors were with him, but the next they had disappeared off the face of the earth, or so it appeared to him.

" Cor ! " remarked Mr. Deacon, rather enviously shocked.   " At his age, too . . . ! "

But he was not left long to ruminate : from the wood on his left there suddenly emerged a lighted smoke-bomb, belching forth its densening white cloud from a position where it could readily be seen from all the front.   Almost at once, too, the sharp sound of blank ammunition, mingled with realistic explosions, violently shook the quiet of the wood.

" Ah ! " thought the fishmonger, pleased.   " I said they'd attack through there ! "

An identical thought cheered his platoon commander. Bulldog Drummond was no doubt a splendid leader—he had been nervous about his redoubtable opponent ever since he had been told that this exercise was to take place— but the ground was ideal for his defence and he had massed practically all his men by that wood . . . it was the only danger spot.   He had posted look-out men elsewhere, of course, just in case Drummond was mad enough to try to cross the open country on the right.   In fact, from what he was told, Drummond was mad enough for anything ; but he would be duly warned if such an attack took place, and his men could move quickly to their alternative positions. As it was, his positions to defend the wood were admirable : had not the Chief Umpire, as important and knowledgeable a man as the Major, congratulated him on them ?   Good :

the battle was practically over already, the much-feared Captain Drummond was defeated. It was a great feather in his cap, specially with that brass hat around . . . wonder who he was, no less than a general, someone had said.

In the wood, extravagantly firing blank and throwing with reckless abandon crackers which went off with loud reports, Hugh Drummond was encouraging Algy Longworth to still greater similar efforts.

" Keep it up, Corporal ! Make 'em think we're all here !"

" Aye, aye, sir ! " Longworth grinned. " Oh, sorry, that's naval . . . very good, sir ! Where's Peter . . . he ought to be showing by this time . . . "

" There he goes ! " laughed Drummond happily. " The Sergeant at the head of his merry men ! By jove, they're scampering beautifully . . . what a lovely surprise for the enemy ! "

It was a surprise all right. The attackers, coming in unobserved from the left under cover of all the excitement and noise from the wood, fell on the defenders from the flank and rolled them up. The Umpires were unanimous on the point. It was not until much later, that the defending Platoon Commander really understood why he had not been warned.

. . . .

On the march home, Peter Darrell came alongside his officer.

" Leave to speak, sir, please ! "

Drummond grinned.

" Yes, Peter ? "

" Did you notice a brass-hat around the place to-day, Hugh ? "

" Yes." Drummond smiled at the recollection. " He was hanging around when Algy and I dealt with the look-out men . . . heard some very unmilitary talk, I'm afraid !"

" Who was he ? "

" Oh, just some busybody from the War Office, I suppose. Tell the chaps there's a pint apiece to-night, in the local, to celebrate the victory, will you, Peter ? Oh, and remind Algy it's his turn to pay . . . "

III

HUGH DRUMMOND TALKS TO A VISITOR

MRS. HUGH DRUMMOND—Phyllis to her friends and, behind her still slender back, to practically everyone else including the inhabitants of the nearby village—met her husband as he entered the house and deposited his Sten gun in the umbrella stand.

" Nice fight ? " she asked, as she gave him her cheek to be kissed.

" Very pretty ! " There was relish in Captain Hugh Drummond's voice. " Went entirely according to plan, just as we discussed it last night."

Phyllis smiled : it was her Hugh's habit, the evening before these exercises, to hold a council of war with his life-long pals, Peter Darrell and Algy Longworth, now masquerading as his sergeant and corporal, and she was a frequent and frequently fascinated listening member of the group.

" Poor old Deacon ! " laughed Drummond gaily. " He was nearly frightened into a jelly ! When we let him loose he goggled at us like one of his own cods ! "

Drummond relieved himself of his equipment, and hung it up on a coat-peg.

" Lunch nearly ready ? "

" Yes," said Phyllis.

" Good."

" Wash that stuff off your face, Hugh, and come to the library. I'll be having a short one there . . . "

Hugh Drummond looked at his wife with immediate suspicion : he saw her smile faintly, and leave him. What the devil did she mean, the library? That room, comfortable though it was, was only used since the war on what might be described—if anything could be so described in the Drummond house—as formal occasions. And what had she said ? A short one ? With the scarcity of gin, and total absence of French, such a description was a hollow mockery except on very special occasions when the reserve was brought out. Then that mildly guilty smile, and the sudden flight . . . ?

Drummond played the game : he did not creep to the library door and listen. But on his way upstairs, he glanced into the dining-room, and there saw his suspicions confirmed : the table was laid for three.

Drummond wasted no time in removing the camouflage from his face and hands, and throwing off his battledress. More comfortably attired, he went down and entered the library.

A very distinguished military gentleman, covered in red tabs and medal ribbons, rose to greet him.

" Hullo, Hugh . . . "

" Good lord ! " said Drummond, taking the other's hand. " Don't tell me it's old Dick ! Heavens ! Were you the brass-hat hanging about the place this morning ? "

" Hope you didn't mind ? " said the General, almost apologetically. " I came down here to see what had become of you, but when I heard you were out on an exercise, I just couldn't resist coming to look at you . . . and was it worth it ! The old Hugh up to all his games again ! "

" They asked me who you were, and I described you as some busybody from the War Office ! "

Both men laughed.

" By the way," said Drummond, " is that what you are ? "

" It'll do as well as any other description ! I've been in the War House for a year now, for my sins ! "

The lunch, cooked and served by Phyllis who had developed a talent for the art with war-time necessity, passed very pleasantly in reminiscence. The two wars were compared, the Regiment toasted, stories of old friends were exchanged. After they had washed up, and Phyllis had disappeared on some errand to the village, the two men sat down in armchairs before a wood fire, and Drummond produced a box of cigars.

" I say ! " said the General, " real Havana ! "

"The last box," laughed Drummond, "but you're welcome to one, old man. All I ask is, don't slip an extra one in your pocket!"

"I am honoured!"

They lit up and settled down.

"What are you up to now, Hugh?"

Drummond paused before replying. He blew a ring of smoke into the air, and then looked across at his companion.

"In many ways, not nearly as much as I should like to, Dick. Of course I do Home Guard—we're pretty good round here, and keen as anything, as I hope you were able to observe—I help Phyllis with her prisoners-of-war stuff, and . . . well, I till the soil for all I'm worth. All this small place is turned to producing food, as you may have noticed when you came in. But . . . it's not awfully satisfactory. When the war started, I tried to join up . . ." he leant forward. "Do you know what they told me, blast 'em? They were all honey, and said of course they'd be delighted to have me back, and they really would try to find me a nice station. Station!" he snorted. "R.T.O.! *Me!* Can you beat it!"

The Soldier murmured sympathetically. Drummond suddenly laughed.

"I kept my temper, but only just. I said I wasn't an old fogey, which they seemed to think, and that I was extremely fit. I invited the interviewing officer outside to prove it."

"Oh, lord!" gurgled the Soldier, "what did he do then?"

"Turned a pretty shade of pale green, and spoke most awfully quickly. Said-it-wasn't-his-fault, all-regulations-and-all-that-but-he-himself-couldn't-do-a-thing. That was obvious, of course, the measly red-taped little rat! He ought to have been out with a squad and not sitting in an office! At least, that's what I thought at the time . . ."

Drummond paused.

"Well?" the Soldier encouraged.

"Of course I turned it down flat. But, when I tried elsewhere, I found, much to my surprise, the same story. And since I just had to be an R.T.O. or grumble at home,

I decided to be unselfiish and leave the Station jobs to the real decrepits, and do an able-bodied job on the farm. But how beautifully I grumbled ! "

The Soldier laughed.

" I'll bet you did ! "

" Then came Dunkirk, and the L.D.V.'s. That was plainly the only cup of tea left to me. It's . . . been fun !" There was wealth of longing in the voice, which the Soldier was quick to notice. " But it's taught me something . . . I now realise that the powers-that-be were quite right at the beginning of the war. There was no point in cluttering up the vestibule with chaps of my age, no matter how fit we thought we were. Because, Dick, we don't last the pace like the youngsters—I've noticed that in the Home Guard. We can do all they do for a day or two, but not for week after week . . . and failure to do so would be dangerous in an officer. So I've got to accept the fact that my contribution—and that of others of my generation, like Algy and Peter—is in the things we are doing. Algy's actively on a farm, and Peter's a foreman or something in a factory . . . you'd scarcely believe it of either, would you ! But we would have given the Hun a good smack in the eye if he had dared to invade . . ."

" From what I saw this morning," said the Soldier, " I have no doubt you would."

Hugh Drummond laughed.

" I'm afraid we weren't as good as that in nineteen-forty, but he'd have been picking shot-gun pellets out of his tum-tum all the same. Now it's your turn . . ."

" Nothing to my story," smiled the Soldier, " they gave me a Brigade after Dunkirk, and a Division in North Africa. Then they pulled me back for this armchair job."

" Which no doubt it would be indiscreet to ask about ? "

" It would."

" Bad luck," grinned Drummond. " You must find it terribly difficult not to talk about yourself ! "

" That," said the Soldier grimly, " will cost you one more glass of that excellent brandy."

Drummond laughed, and went over to a side table.

" I hoped you would say that ! " he said, " it gives me my excuse."

The telephone bell rang sharply.

"Help yourself, old man," said Drummond, turning towards the instrument, " and don't be mean with mine ! " He lifted the receiver, " Yes ? Yes, this is Hugh Drummond. I beg your pardon ? " He was silent, listening, for a few moments, " Just a second . . . who are you ? Oh, I see." Once again he listened, but this time most attentively. Then : " Well . . . thank you very much. What number shall I ring when I get there ? Eh ? But then how . . . oh, I see. Not at all . . . good-bye . . .

Slowly Drummond replaced the receiver on its hook. He paused for a moment, apparently deep in thought. Then, throwing off his preoccupation, he turned back towards the fire. He found the Soldier smiling to him.

" Good health, Hugh ! "

Drummond picked up his replenished glass.

" Skin off your nose, old top ! "

The Soldier leant forward.

" Hugh," he said seriously, " I'd better come to the point, because my car will be fetching me any moment now. I've got a confession to make . . . as a matter of fact, I didn't come down here to-day solely to renew an old friendship . . . "

" Or to inspect the local Home Guard ? "

" No. I came down . . . to see whether Hugh was the old Bulldog . . . "

Drummond smiled.

" Verdict ? "

" I'm . . . don't think I'm being patronising . . . more than satisfied. I gather you would welcome a chance to . . . to increase your contribution . . . ? "

Hugh Drummond laughed.

" You bet I would ! " he said.

" Right. Will you come up to town and lunch with me at the club . . , soon, as soon as possible ? There's somebody I want you to meet . . . "

" I should be delighted. But I warn you it will be expensive . . . "

" I only wish it could be ! Still, they may have kept some of the sherry. And in the meantime, I think it better be mums the word . . . when'll you come ? "

" To-morrow ? "

The Soldier laughed.

" The same old impulsive Hugh, and thank the lord for it ! To-morrow it is . . . "

Hugh Drummond rose to his feet as the sound of a car drawing up by the front door became audible.

" Dick," he said, and the other looked at him sharply, for there was a sudden serious tone in the normally cheerful voice, " you say this is very hush-hush ? "

" Yes."

" Who are you sharing the secret with ? "

" One other man."

They reached the front door.

" Give my love to Phyllis," said the Soldier, " and thank her so much for the lovely lunch."

" Of course," Drummond remained for a moment without opening the door, but with his fingers on the handle, deep in thought.

" I wonder . . . " he said, half to himself.

" What ? "

" You said only one other man ? "

The Soldier looked surprised.

" Yes. I'm positive of that."

" I wonder . . . " observed Drummond quietly, opening the door.

" What on earth do you mean ? " asked the Soldier, rather alarmed in spite of himself.

" You look lovely in your red hat ! " grinned Drummond. " Never mind, I'll tell you to-morrow . . . "

And with that the Soldier had to be satisfied, for there was something in Hugh Drummond's expression which forbade further questioning.

There was also a light in his eye which would have frightened Phyllis, but brought joy to the restless hearts of Algy Longworth and Peter Darrell, could they have seen it. For it was the same light that used to spring to life when something—something usually rather exciting—was in the wind.

IV

A COUNTESS GIVES ORDERS

IT was really a very lovely suite. Of course, the hotel was one of the most famous in London, and known not only in that city but throughout the world. You would have expected to find that at least one of its suites was luxurious in the extreme. But this one, perhaps because of the restrictions of war-time to be seen everywhere else, struck someone entering for the first time a scented blow, brought to mind immediately and irresistibly some scene from the more romantic of the Hollywood films.

In the first place, it was very feminine. You came in from the passage into the sitting-room, all pink and white. The thick carpet was a darker shade of pink, perhaps, than the silken covers to all the furniture : the curtains matched the carpet. The walls and the ceiling were white, and the chromium fittings and fender round the real fire added a silvery lustre which was rich if inclined to be cold. But it was the quantity of flowers which really characterised that room : a multitude of pink and dark red roses in one squat vase, a bunch of white carnations in another tall and slender, and in yet a third a combination of the two which dominated the room from the centre table. The whole impression was one of lightness, of delicacy, of cleanliness.

The woman sitting by the desk suited the room to perfection. She was tall and thin,. austere a little in her dress which contrasted with her very fair hair, delicate of feature. She was certainly beautiful, but more by general effect than by any more searching criterion. One false note she displayed, or else a tremendous advantage : considering the fairness of her hair, her eyes were very dark indeed . . .

She was busy with her correspondence, which was voluminous. A casual observer might have been surprised that one so plainly blessed with so much money did not employ a secretary to relieve her of such a tedious occupation. Had that observer looked over her shoulder, he would have seen that most of her business lay in charitable organisations connected with the war : true, there were also many social invitations demanding replies, but these were only a fraction of the total. The casual observer could also have noticed, had he really been observant, that the lady—clever, undoubtedly, in the art of making up— yet could not wholly hide the tell-tale lines in a woman's neck which indicate, not necessarily middle-age, but the approach to it.

She was interrupted by the telephone. The instrument, cream to go with the rest of the room, was by her side on the desk. She spoke quite softly into it, but her deep voice had a quality of resonance which on first hearing was attractive : but afterwards there was something, some doubt which might have come to a critical listener's mind. Resonance, yes : beautifully produced so that there was no difficulty in hearing the soft tones, undoubtedly : but, in spite of its softness, an underlying autocratic quality which might be a threat to any difference from her opinion ?

" Yes ? . . . Very well, I will see him now . . . please send him up."

She did not bother to put away her correspondence, nor even to complete the letter which she was writing. She rose and stood by the fire, falling naturally into a pose which admirably suited the gracefulness of her figure already well set off by the straight lines of her dress. She took a cigarette from the box on the mantelpiece, lighted it with a gold lighter, and placed it carefully into a longish black cigarette holder.

She had not long to wait : there came a knock on the door.

" Come in . . ."

A short nondescript little man came in, dressed quietly in a dark grey suit.

" Good morning . . ."

" Good morning . . ."

He shut the door behind him, perhaps with unnecessary care, and then advanced into the room. They did not shake hands, but she motioned him to a chair. He sat down : neither smiled. She continued to smoke, watching him all the time.

" Well ? "

" I came up with him by the early train," said the little man, and suddenly laughed, although the sound was unnaturally mirthless.

" *With* him ? "

Her voice was curt : the question appeared to be a criticism, and he was quick to reply.

" Not in the same carriage, of course. By the same train, that's all."

" When did he arrive ? "

" About three-quarters of an hour ago."

" And then . . . ? "

" He went straight to his club. Couldn't get a taxi, so went by underground. I travelled by the same train again."

There was a short pause.

" He is rather good at knowing when he's followed," she said quietly. " At least, he used to be . . . you're quite sure he did not notice you ? "

The little man laughed again.

" Don't worry, lady. He's never set eyes on me in his life."

" Not when you were listening yesterday by the window ? "

" Not he ! "

For the first time she smiled, but it was no comforting expression for the man sitting in the chair.

" For your sake," she said, " I sincerely hope you are telling the truth."

The little man shifted his position awkwardly : he would have liked to have said something in his own defence, but the words she had used, and her tone of voice, had been ambiguous : he was not at all sure whether she had uttered a personal threat to him, or whether the man he had so skilfully followed was the danger. In any case, he reminded himself, one did not argue with the lady . . .

" Is that all ? "

" It's all you asked me to do, isn't it ? "

She looked at him disdainfully.

" Yes," she said, " it's all I asked you to do. Thank you. Report as usual . . ."

" Very good . . ."

The little man rose to his feet, but he stood for a moment undecided. Was this a suitable opportunity to ask for a little cash ? The temptation always assailed him when he entered those rich and luxurious surroundings. He looked up at her face, and for the hundredth time asked himself how it was possible for such a beauty to be so hard and close with money, when he saw her suddenly smile. He decided to take a chance . . .

" I'm a bit short at the moment . . . isn't that what you are going to say ? "

Her voice belied the smile. Shaken, the little man rushed into a denial.

" No, lady . . . good gracious, no . . . "

" I'm glad of that," she smiled again. " I must confess that I do not approve of employees who perpetually ask for advances . . . it makes me doubtful of their efficiency . . . is that quite clear ? "

" Perfectly clear."

" You are all very well paid, or I am wrong ? "

" You are not wrong, lady . . ."

" And you have another reason for liking your work ? "

The little man drew himself up very straight.

" I have."

" Splendid ! " She was almost purring. " You can go now . . ."

The little man went : he went a good deal faster than

was compatible with dignity : he even forgot to shut the door. It was only when she had shut the door behind him that she really smiled.

But she did not waste any time : she returned to her desk, and, sitting down again, took up an address book. Quickly she turned up a name, found what she wanted, and picking up the telephone asked for a number. She had to wait a little time before getting through, and a frown of impatience came over her face, but at last she was connected.

" Is Captain Hugh Drummond there, please ? "

The answer was evidently in the affirmative, for the frown disappeared and she waited again with a faint smile playing about her lips. Suddenly she leant forward :

" Captain Hugh Drummond ? I hope I haven't dragged you away from the bar . . .? You must be thirsty after your journey . . ."

Her voice, as she spoke, was startlingly different to normal. It was high, but not forced : it had no resonant quality : it was, in short, completely disguised. Yet she produced it as naturally as that in which she had spoken to the little man, and with no apparent special effort.

" You had time for a pint before I rang up ? I am so glad, I must have judged it just right ! "

She paused, evidently listening.

" Yes, I see you've come to London against my advice." She spoke in the soft, reproving tones a woman might use to a wilful child. " Well, that was . . . shall we say a little silly ? You see, I always give good advice . . . to my friends, that is . . . Still, I am also of a forgiving nature, and so if you decided not to keep your luncheon appointment . . . well, I don't think anything will happen to you. Anything unpleasant, that is to say. Why not have a real beano all on your own ? Or, if you're not afraid of Phyllis, why not ask one of the lovely ladies that dear Algy has so often introduced to you, out for a *tête-à-tête* ? Wouldn't that be fun ? Eh ? Oh, you really mustn't be so ungallant ! Anyway . . ." her voice changed almost imperceptibly, but there was just a suggestion of a threat

as she continued, " that is my final advice to you. Good-bye,
Captain Drummond . . ."

She rang off. She rose to her feet and moved gracefully to the fireside. She suddenly burst out into laughter,
loud and long.

Hugh Drummond kept his luncheon appointment, and
was glad of it, because the Soldier went out of his way to
be an impeccable host, and fortunately—as he himself said—
there was some of that sherry left. Drummond fervently
agreed : such sherry had become as rare as a valued jewel.
There was another guest present, a man with whose name
Drummond was very familiar and whom he found a pleasant
and interesting companion. All through lunch Drummond
had the impression that he was under observation : he
was not altogether surprised, after the conversation which
he had enjoyed with the Soldier on the previous day.
But he did not speculate as to what it might mean : the
explanation would come all in good time, and in the meantime the food tasted admirable, the beer was less watery
than usual, and undoubtedly there was some excellent
port to look forward to . . . if he had known how to
do so, he would have smacked his lips.

After the port—it was just as excellent as he had hoped
it would be—Drummond found himself addressed by the
Great Man.

" Could you spare me a little of your time this afternoon,
Captain Drummond ? "

Drummond thought he noticed an almost imperceptible
sigh of relief escape from the Soldier.

" Certainly."

The Great Man turned to the Soldier.

" In that case, if you don't mind, Dick, I'm going to
drag my fellow guest away to my office . . . thank you
very much for lunch."

They walked, for it was no great distance. Conversation
is always difficult in a crowded street, but they talked of
this and that. The Great Man was in cheerful mood, rather

as if a weight had been lifted from his mind. His principal anxiety seemed to be to get to his office quickly, but Drummond ambled along beside him, was in fact frequently half a yard in front. Now that the time had come, he found himself very anxious to hear what the other had to say.

It took over an hour to say it.

"As I understand it," said Drummond quietly, when the Great Man had finished, "you want me to find out just how much we can rely on French assistance, from within France, in the event of an allied landing in that country?"

"Precisely."

"And the task is complicated by the necessity for secrecy, in order not to disturb the equanimity of those already on the job?"

"Brutally correct."

Drummond thought for a moment.

"What guarantee," he asked abruptly, "have you for supposing that my findings, whatever they may be, will be acceptable to our friends the Americans?"

The Great Man coughed. For a moment he was tempted to be diplomatic, and say nothing committing in a great many pleasant phrases. But then he looked at Drummond, and he laughed: such a course of action would obviously be useless with this rugged, direct individual.

"None."

"Wouldn't it be better if . . . if they would believe me?"

"Obviously. But I don't see how . . ."

His voice tailed off: he looked troubled.

"It seems to my simple mind," said Hugh Drummond pleasantly, "that if you make friends with somebody, and take him in as a partner, you trust him totally. It seems therefore, that when you are engaged in the grim business of a world war, and you have a great ally like America, you must trust that Ally totally . . . otherwise there's no reason for the thing, from the point of view of a lasting peace after the victory has been won. Your secrets must be his secrets, except perhaps some small domestic secrets which are not worthy of the word." Drummond suddenly grinned. " Pardon my lecture ! "

But the Great Man was serious.

" There's something on your mind," he said. " Go on . . ."

Drummond accepted the invitation, but he spoke unusually slowly, carefully choosing his words.

" I read the papers," he said, " and I sometimes see the American press as well. It is quite clear that, close though we may be on every other point, we do not see eye to eye with official America on France. You believe that the French, in spite of their defeat, can still help us considerably under General de Gaulle. President Roosevelt does not wholly share that view, and is flirting with other possible leaders for France. It is to bring independent evidence to support your view that you wish me to undertake this investigation . . ."

" Stop ! " interrupted the Great Man sharply, he paused for a moment, and then continued slowly, " You mustn't put it that way, Drummond. I . . . we . . . are not asking you to collect evidence to support a view : we are asking you to make an independent—you used the right word there—investigation in order to assist us—British and Americans in coming to the right conclusion about the military value of resistance to the enemy within France. It may be—mark you, I am not saying so—but it may be that our British and American expert advice on that subject is conflicting and confused. When experts disagree—and I can promise you British experts are just as much in conflict with each other as with our Allied experts—what better than to call in a sound, impartial opinion whose only qualification is plenty of common-sense ? "

" Sorry ! " smiled Drummond, " I sit corrected."

" And, while I am about it," went on the Great Man, " you mustn't imply that there are secrets between the Americans and ourselves. Far from it. Our secrets and discoveries are bandied to and fro across the Atlantic in an almost alarming manner, to a man who simply cannot pin complete faith on to codes ! "

"Good!" said Drummond quickly. "That means this investigation will be no secret to them . . ."

"Eh?"

"You heard!" Drummond grinned. "They know of my proposed future activities."

"I can't say they do, at the moment . . ." smiled the Great Man.

"But they've obviously got to," laughed Drummond, "because they've got to appoint my confederate . . ."

"You're going rather fast . . ."

"Not really." Hugh Drummond was very serious again. "It stands to reason they must, so that they will believe what I . . . what *we* . . . say when we're through, doesn't it?"

"It would add weight . . ." conceded the Great Man musingly.

Drummond rose to his feet.

"All you've got to do," he said, "is to find the man who is to be my American buddy, give us a good deal of the ready . . ." he smiled, "that's cash to you . . . give us a perfectly free hand and power to add to our number if we feel so inclined, and then provide us with certain travelling facilities when we give the word . . . and of course your unlimited confidence. Simple, isn't it?"

The Great Man rose as well.

"Those are your conditions?"

Drummond smiled, and nodded.

"Those are my conditions. But I would like to say this: I hope to high heaven you succeed in persuading—whoever you have to persuade—to accept those terms. The whole thing sounds like fun to me . . ."

"It's not my idea of fun," said the Great Man drily, "I have much too great a respect for the Gestapo . . ."

"It's all right for you," laughed Drummond, "you've been in harness all the war . . . but I've been nothing but a blinking cabbage. I tell you, I'm champing at the bit . . ."

The Great Man did him the honour of seeing him to the door.

" Where shall I find you ? " he asked.

" Nowhere for the next hour or so," smiled Hugh Drummond, " but after that in the country . . . here, I'll write it down for you . . ."

He did so. They shook hands.

" Presumably, in the next hour or so, a female visit ? " said the Great Man, with an unexpected and rather unbecoming smirk on his face.

" Quite," replied Drummond drily, " only I have an idea she'll be as difficult to find as a butterfly on Christmas Day . . ."

V

INSPECTOR MCIVER ASSISTS THE ENEMY

HUGH DRUMMOND walked to the famous hotel ; everybody seemed to walk in London, or wait in a queue for a bus. He strode along briskly, and it did not take him long to cover the distance. He entered through the great swing doors, and advancing into the lounge looked about him ; a man, sitting in a secluded corner, made a sign to him. Drummond smiled a greeting as he went to him, and sat down beside him.

" If it isn't the famous Inspector McIver of Scotland Yard ! "

" How are you, Captain ! " McIver did not appear to resent Drummond's bantering tone ; in fact he seemed thoroughly pleased. " Glad to see you after all these months . . ."

" So am I. Having a nice war ? "

" So-so. And you ? "

Drummond smiled again.

" I believe it's improving . . . well, seen any old pals yet ? "

" Yes." McIver was pleased to notice the sudden interest reflected in the attitude of Drummond. " This seems to be an oddish place, in spite of its luxury get-up.

A woman I arrested some years ago for bigamy has just cut me dead : can't think why, because from the look of her furs it doesn't seem to have done her any harm."

He spoke perfectly seriously, and Drummond, watching him out of the corner of his eye, was uncertain whether or not McIver was indulging in a minor leg-pull. He decided to exercise as much patience as possible.

" Anyone else ? "

" Yes," went on McIver without a change of expression. " A man I failed to arrest for blackmail because his victim was too chicken-livered to take the stand when it came to the point. I shouldn't be surprised if he were still paying, and that's why this fellow can afford to come here . . ."

A short pause.

" Anyone else ? " asked Drummond resignedly.

" No." McIver looked up. " That's enough for one afternoon, isn't it ? "

" Not for *this* afternoon," Drummond smiled. " Not even a glimpse of one of *my* old friends ? "

" Not even a smell . . ."

" Now don't be rude," Drummond noticed the twinkle in Inspector McIver's eye. " Some of *my* friends— particularly the ladies—were scented rather pleasantly, and the word ' smell ' is a coarse, misleading word for such an aroma. Remember, it's a lady I'm interested in . . ."

" When did she ring you up ? "

" Yesterday afternoon in the country . . . and this morning just before I rang you. You're sure the call came from here ? "

McIver frowned.

" Not absolutely," he confessed. " There were three calls to the club almost simultaneously, and one of them— maybe yours—may have been from here. The other two are untraceable. But the check-up doesn't work on this side. There's no note of local numbers kept here . . . the only chance was that one of the operators might have jotted down the club number on her pad. None did, and not one of them remembers being asked for it, although one girl is not sure but in any case has no idea what room asked her for it, if she ever was asked for it. I'm afraid it's as vague as that ! "

" You're slipping, Mac ! "

Drummond spoke banteringly, but there was disappointment in his voice. McIver replied apologetically.

" It's the war," he said. " Tracing telephone calls was always a chancy business, unless we had warning ; now, with amateurs on the job all round, that sort of finesse isn't to be found very often. One can't blame anyone—it's just the war ! "

" I'm not blaming you or anyone else ! " Hugh Drummond realised he had almost offended the Inspector, and he spoke pleasantly. " Matter of fact, I don't understand how people get away with as little as they do, what with your difficulties . . . I daren't even try for an extra pat of butter . . ."

" Still," said McIver, mollified, " it may have come from here . . ."

He looked round the lounge : so did Drummond. Both had in their mind's eye the vision of a tall, dark woman, pale of complexion, with a crimson mouth, beautifully if rather exotically dressed, very attractive even if obviously as hard as the blade of a rapier.

" Not a smell of Irma . . ." murmured McIver——

" Aroma. Or perfume. Possibly scent . . ." corrected Drummond.

But, as he looked round the room, he could not but agree with the Inspector. Allowing for her remarkable powers of disguising herself, powers which Drummond was forced to admit had on more than one occasion fooled him completely, there was surely no one there who could possibly be the dark beauty no matter how much transformed. At a table next to them, two old ladies were engaged in animated conversation liberally interspersed with " and believe it or not, my dear . . ." somebody's reputation was being torn to shreds. A little further along, an extremely fat full Colonel—whose tabs shone brightly somewhere round the back of his neck, and whose war armchair must have been specially reinforced—was making eyes at an attractive woman even when his mouth was full of tea-cake. Drummond let his eyes rest for a few moments on this woman; she was very fair, her hair shone almost silvery in the artificial light; that proved nothing, of course, in these days of constant changes. But she was . . . somehow too graceful in her carriage, not austerely severe; and her whole expression was too soft and gentle . . . really too soft and gentle to appeal to him. Besides, her nose was straight and delicate; that had not been so of the colourful Irma, whose nose had perhaps been her one slight blemish . . .

There were, of course, plenty of young guardsmen with their pretty little things. But all of these were much too young and fluffy. And there were rather too many apparently perfectly fit youngish men about the place . . . Drummond had to remind himself of the total mobilisation in order to avoid thinking uncharitable thoughts . . .

"You've made enquiries, of course?" suddenly asked Drummond.

McIver understood what he meant.

"Oh, yes. The Hall Porter here is one of my friends . . . he's often been rather useful. I gave him as good a description of our friend Irma as my vocabulary would allow, and he said to me that sort of person had disappeared to neutral countries in September, thirty-nine. As a matter of fact, he's probably about right."

There was a pause.

"Why," asked McIver, "do you think it was Irma?"

Drummond laughed.

"The whole thing reeks of her. No one knew . . . somebody of importance was coming to see me yesterday. I didn't myself. But she did, and she rang up—when he was actually there, mark you—to suggest a quiet Home Guard life was probably the pleasantest . . . and safest, and hadn't I much better not come to London. When I implied I didn't know what she was talking about, she said she'd ring me at the club if I came up. She did: merely to warn me off keeping a luncheon engagement, an important luncheon engagement, which I don't see how she could have known about. And, Mac, she knew all about Algy . . . and his life-long weakness for blondes . . ."

" H'm ! " said McIver.

" Eh ? "

" Only h'm."

" Oh."

" Yes," said McIver. " H'm."

Hugh Drummond thought for a few moments more of the woman—that tigress with all the cunning and the cruelty of the cat and the appearance to create desire even in a saint—whom he had known as Irma Peterson. He had no doubt that Irma Peterson was not her name ; he was doubtful whether she were really the late and certainly unlamented Carl Peterson's daughter, as they had claimed she was. But even as he thought of her he was conscious of a thrill ; what a tremendous prospect it would be if only he were privileged once more to match his wits against her ! And somehow Hugh Drummond felt quite certain that even if she herself had not been his mysterious caller on the telephone, her will had been behind the calls . . .

Drummond laughed to himself ; what had she said ? Made him sort of a threat, hadn't she ? Well, he could thank her for putting him on his guard . . . He looked up at the despondent Inspector.

" I'm afraid it'll be a shock to your system," he said, " but as far as I can see there's nothing for it but to have a cup of tea . . ."

" No, thanks . . ." said McIver with alacrity.

" Sure ? "

" I've never been so sure of anything in my life." The Inspector looked at his watch ruefully. " They don't open till half-past five."

" Can't wait till then, got to catch my train," Drummond rose. " Sorry to have dragged you out on a wild-goose chase, Mac."

" That's all right. No trouble when it's for you, Captain."

38

Hugh Drummond smiled : it was not often that the dour Inspector McIver paid a compliment.

" Nice of you to take it like that. But keep your eyes open, Mac ; and tell your boys to look out for anything even vaguely resembling the elusive Irma."

" I will."

They were walking towards the door. Directly they had passed her, the fair lady with the very fat Colonel looked up sharply after them. The Colonel, had he been an observant man, might have caught a glimpse of a momentary gleam in her eyes which might have made him revise his entire estimation of her character ; but he missed it. She was not looking at them as they approached the door, but beyond them towards a tall thin man who was lounging by the flower-stall. He smiled, a very faint smile, and nodded almost imperceptibly. As he quickly left the hotel, the fair lady turned, all sweetness, back to her gross cavalier.

Drummond, with McIver beside him, moved through the swing doors, and stood for a moment undecided. The walk to the station was possible in the time still available before Drummond's train was due to start, but he felt that he had exercised sufficiently for one day on London's pavements.

" No use waiting for a taxi," said McIver, " I should take a bus."

" Somebody must turn up in a taxi in a moment," thought Drummond.

As if divining his thoughts, the Commissionaire addressed him.

" Sorry, sir. I've got a waiting list inside if a taxi does turn up."

" Take a bus . . ." urged McIver. " Hullo ! what's that ? "

As he spoke, Drummond saw it too : a taxi with its flag up ambling at a peace-time pace down the street, and no glove or rag over the flag either ! They both started off as if one man, but long before they could attract the driver's attention a tall, thin man hailed it : the taxi drew up beside him.

" Dash ! " said Drummond, slowing up.

But McIver did not slacken pace.

" Maybe you can share it with that bloke," Drummond heard him say as he went on. " It's the only way to get one nowadays . . ."

By the time that Drummond, slightly self-conscious, reached the taxi, McIver had successfully concluded the negotiations. Yes, the tall, thin man—who seemed quite pleasant—would be only too pleased to share the cab, he was going that way anyway. Would the gentleman mind dropping him at the entrance to the Park, and taking on the taxi . . . the driver had no objection . . .? good.

" So long, Mac. Thanks for the lesson ! "

" So long, Captain. I'll let you know if anything turns up."

Drummund was smiling as he entered the cab : the thought of the glamorous Irma's reaction, could she hear herself described as ' anything ', struck him as amusing.

It was the last coherent thought he could remember until he opened his eyes and found himself the centre of interest of a little group composed of one policeman, two porters, and the taxi driver ; and, as soon as he tried to move, quite obviously the possessor of a truly remarkable headache.

VI

A BLONDE WRITES A LETTER

THE pink and white suite looked as beautiful as ever, but the luxurious setting did not suit its present occupiers nearly so well as it did the very fair lady. They themselves seemed to feel this, and to regret her absence.

" Where the devil is she ? " asked one man petulantly.

" Downstairs," replied the other, " ogling yet another fat boob into a big cheque for one of her darned charities."

They were an ill-assorted pair. The first speaker was extremely well dressed, although to the more fastidious members of one of the older clubs, his taste might perhaps have been criticised for being on the loud side. It was difficult to tell his years : he might have been much older than the youngish middle age into which class a first glance would have placed him : or yet younger than his face might indicate, for he was slim and well-built, holding himself upright and square almost in a military manner. His expression at that moment clearly proved that he was of an impatient nature; or perhaps merely disliked the company of his companion, the short nondescript little man, dressed in dark grey, who had already visited the suite that morning.

The subject of charities seemed to rankle with the latter.

" Charities ! " he repeated with a wealth of disdain, " Wonder what she does with all the money ! Wish I was one of her damned charities ! "

" If you really want to know," remarked the other, " she hands on the money to the organisation for which it is intended." He paused only for a moment. " No doubt subtracting fairly heavy expenses, of course . . . what else would your small imagination conjure up for her to do ? "

A flush came over the face of the little man.

" I wish you wouldn't pick on me . . ." he spoke bitterly. " I may not have had your education, but we're all in the same boat now . . ."

" Oh, shut up ! "

" . . . and you don't do your work any better than I do mine."

" You bore me."

The little man rose belligerently.

" And what if I do ? " he asked. " Isn't what I say right ? "

" My dear man," the dandy spoke cuttingly, " what you say is presumably perfectly correct—until you are caught out."

" That goes for you too."

A voice, sharp and imperious, spoke from the door : " Can I never leave you two alone without quarrelling ? "

The effect of her voice, and the unobserved entrance of the very fair lady, was totally different on the two men.

The dandy, with scarcely a pause to adjust his tie, turned towards the door with a smile and the suggestion of a bow, apparently quite oblivious to the reproof she had just uttered. But the little man very nearly went to pieces: he literally cringed, a not particularly pleasant spectacle.

The fair lady was, however, clearly in no mood to suffer her subordinates lightly : nor, apparently, now that she had arrived, had she any intention of wasting time.

" Tom," she spoke to the small man, " you will go back to the country at once—by the very next train—and keep your eyes skinned for any Drummond movement. Where-ever he may go, I want to know . . . specially if he shows any signs of staying away from home for a period. Is that clear ? "

" Yes, lady."

She surveyed him for a moment, her eyes expressionless : the small man shifted uncomfortably under her gaze : he particularly disliked that look of hers, because you simply could not tell what was in her mind . . . abruptly she turned to the dandy.

" As for you, Major . . . I think you'd better become a hussar again."

The dandy flushed : clearly she had touched on a raw spot ; and judging from the faint derisive smile on her lips, certainly with intention. The tall man recognised that his employer was in an ugly mood, if such a term could be applied to so attractive a woman, and try as he might he could not help hoping that the interview would be short. When she was like this, he had found by bitter experience that the best place to be was a long way away from her, in fact the farther the better.

" A gallant hussar ! " she laughed mirthlessly, a dry harsh sound. " Do you think you can manage that ? "

" None better ! " replied the dandy.

He was rather surprised to hear himself speak : he knew he was blushing, but he knew the cause of it was a throttling anger. Why must she always pick up his past and throw it in his teeth, specially in front of little rats like that nasty man Tom. And he hated himself for being unable to prevent himself reacting : it was so undignified. After all, it was nearly ten years ago now since he had been cashiered, and nearly eight years since he had completed his sentence. The famous regiment which had so unceremoniously thrown him out, had no doubt forgotten all about him : and he had contrived largely to forget all about that period of his life. He would have succeeded entirely, had it not been for these displeasing reminders which came with monotonous regularity from this woman whom they called the Lady . . .

" You will proceed to the village which has the honour of calling itself Hugh-Bulldog-Drummond's home—not with Tom, of course : in fact, if you should see him about, you can give yourself the pleasure of ignoring his existence entirely—and there you will contrive to make the acquaintance of a certain Algy Longworth and a certain Peter Darrell, who live in the vicinity and share the same public house with Drummond. They are cronies of his . . . of long standing. Concentrate on Algy . . . unless he has changed considerably, his tongue was specially designed for careless talk. What I want to know is this . . ." She paused, and then continued slowly, enunciating each word carefully, " What is Drummond up to ? He has been visited recently by a very hush-hush major-general, and . . . I think he's about to be up to something. I have encouraged him . . ." She suddenly laughed, less harshly than before. " Far better that one should know with whom one has to deal, know him well and know his weaknesses . . . so I want him to take on . . . the job I am fairly certain he has now been offered. Besides, I have a personal account to settle . . ."

The man whom she had addressed as the major abruptly shuddered : she had, for a flash of time only, just while she had uttered those last eight words, revealed something of her feelings about this man Drummond, and the dandy would not have stood in Drummond's shoes even for a most considerable financial reward, conscious though he might be, more than most, of the advantages of money. A personal account to be settled with the Lady—which moved her at the mere recollection to such a disturbing extent—was something he fervently hoped would never be experienced by him.

" Have you got the idea ? "

" Yes, lady . . . "

" I feel fairly confident Hugh Drummond will not embark on any new . . . shall I say, adventure . . . without the collaboration of Longworth and Darrell: he never has, and there's no reason for him to change at his age. Drummond and Darrell are like oysters . . . but Longworth shares two weaknesses with you, major . . . beer and blondes. The first, you can supply, and he might be indiscreet."

" I understand."

The dandy understood very well : this might prove rather an amusing job : but he did wish she wouldn't aim those little poison barbs in nearly every sentence she addressed to him . . .

" Good. I shall need progress reports from both of you and independently. And of course anything new, anything which might prove of the smallest interest must be reported at once. If I am not here, then use the Hampstead number."

It was their dismissal, and both men recognised it. As they moved to the door, she spoke again.

" First reports to-night," she said.

The door closed behind them.

The fair lady took a cheque from her bag : she looked at it and smiled : that ridiculous Colonel had really been too easy ! For the hundredth time she marvelled at the stupidity of men, specially elderly men, all the same and continually hoping to buy her favours by continually subscribing to the charities she gave the impression of so greatly cherishing. She added the cheque to others in a small drawer in her desk, and locked it. As she put the key back in her bag, someone knocked at the door.

" Come in . . . "

A tall, thin man entered, closed the door with exaggerated care behind him.

He smiled. She smiled.

" Took it like a lamb ! " he purred, in a curiously low and gentle voice. " Thanks for warning me, but this great

man of yours must be seriously out of practice ! Never had
an easier job in my life . . . I'd put on the dope extra thick,
of course, after what you said, but practically as soon as
the cloth hit his face he went under . . . no embarrassing
noise, and better still no strength required. I got out at
the corner of the park, and waved him off. Most friendly,
I wish he could have seen it ! "

" The envelope ? "

" Slipped it into his inner-pocket, with his wallet . . ."
She looked at him sharply.

" You took nothing ? "
He laughed.

" Not even his return ticket ! "

" All right, Darwin. Thank you . . ."

" Not at all," said the tall, thin man. " You would have
laughed ! It was that ass McIver who practically pushed
him into the cab—old Sam, the driver, was a bit nervous at
that moment, because the Inspector was the chap who
first pinched him and set him on the road to ruin—but
McIver was much too keen to get Drummond a lift to the
station to notice Sam ! "

She did laugh, quite genuinely, this time.

" Thought it would amuse you," smiled Darwin. " So
long. Anything to oblige at any time. May I have the
evening off ? "

She looked at him with unusual indulgence : there were
not many of those who worked for her from whom she
would have tolerated such an attitude : but the tall, thin
man was a favourite, partly because he was magnificently
ruthless, partly because he was always so cheerful.

" You may."

" Thanks. I want to go to a concert . . . "

He left the room. The odd thing about it, said the lady
to herself, was that he probably meant what he had said.

.   .   .   .

It was less than an hour later that she entered the drawing-
room of a private house. An elderly man, and another no
longer in the first flush of youth, rose to greet her.

" We were wondering if you had forgotten," gently reproved the older of the pair.

The blonde lady made herself comfortable.

" Do I ever forget ? " she remarked as she sat down. " I have been busy . . . "

" Drummond ? "

" Yes."

The younger of the two spoke for the first time. His voice was low and harsh, and his words were pronounced with a very faintly guttural accent. He was not English, obviously to anyone with a sensitive ear : but his nationality would have been difficult to place exactly . . . central European, perhaps . . .

" What is the importance of this Drummond ? "

" Just this." The fair lady lighted a cigarette, and placed it to her satisfaction in her long holder before continuing. " You will admit we have been getting a little out of touch lately . . . not really producing results ? "

" I will admit that we have been asked for more than we have been able to supply . . ."

" I would have classified those requests as rude messages," remarked the lady drily. " Drummond, I hope, will lead us back to something hot. I have kept my eye on him, ever since we have been planted in this . . . this dreadful country. Alaric here has thought it a waste of time and money, but I hope soon to prove that it was not. Why on earth these otherwise reasonably efficient people have allowed a man of his adventurous spirit and—although I hate to say it—successful record to potter away his time in the Home Guard is beyond my understanding ! but they seem to have recovered their senses now . . . just in time for us, I hope. I have no idea for what purpose he has been approached—although once again I hope to find out soon —but he has been approached, officially. I was taking no chances—that spineless wife of his might have exerted her totally incomprehensible influence over him and made him stick to the wild excitements of running his village platoon, or whatever they call it : so I offered a little bait . . . am I interesting you ? "

The elder of the two men nodded : the younger spoke quickly : " Very much."

" Good. Drummond has two weaknesses, both youthful beyond his present age : the first, that if anyone dares him to do anything, he will almost certainly do it, and the second . . . " she smiled, ". . . . an over gallant interest in me. By that, I do not mean to claim that I arouse in him any sentimental dreams—he knows me far too well for that—but I flatter myself that he considers me a worthy opponent for . . . shall we say, a game of chance. In those circumstances, and thanks to the watch on him of which Alaric has always been so doubtful, I was able to ring him up and play on both his weaknesses in order to try to influence him towards taking whatever offer is in the wind. I issued a gentle verbal threat over the telephone against his acceptance of such an offer, and I did it in such a manner that he will recognise the technique, although," she laughed drily, " certainly not the voice."

" Over the telephone ? "

It was the older man, the man to whom she referred as Alaric, who interrupted her.

" Why not ? " She spoke indulgently, as if to a child, " You should know that a big hotel, specially in war-time, is the safest place to telephone from. To continue, only an hour or two ago I arranged for him to have a small lesson, one which will do him no harm but will—unless Hugh Drummond has changed unrecognisably, and that I have reason to doubt—infuriate him to no small measure : it will seriously hurt his pride. If anything is needed to sway him to the job, that will : because I ask you to remember that all this is connected, in his mind, with whatever they have offered him. It looks as if I . . . or at any rate someone with a certain power . . . is trying to prevent him doing it."

She paused, and looked at the two men : they were smiling admiringly at her. She was pleased : she was one of those few women who preferred admiration of her brain by clever men to the normal feminine attraction exercised by her face or figure.

"However," she went on seriously, "I do not wish you to under-estimate this Drummond: that is a mistake which has been made before, with disastrous results. He will lead us to something, and something important—that is certain, for they will not call him out for anything small—and heaven knows we need a coup at the moment: we cannot deny that our masters are becoming justifiably impatient. True, we were planted here for quite a different purpose, but . . . perhaps we were too successful early on. A close attention to Drummond himself, and perhaps even more to his intimates, will yield results. You must leave most of that to me. Is there anything else you would like to know? because if not I must be on my way: I have a committee meeting to attend."

The two men rose. The elderly and benevolent Alaric helped her on with her mink coat.

"How are the charities?"

She looked at him and smiled.

"Flourishing."

He laughed.

"I congratulate you, my dear. Only you would have thought of doing so much good to so many—and to your charming self at the same time. A great idea, Irma . . ."

She turned on him in a flash, her eyes blazing.

"A great idea . . . who?"

Involuntarily he recoiled.

"I beg your pardon . . ."

"That name," she spoke imperilously, acidly, "must not be pronounced."

"An oversight . . ."

"One not to be repeated."

She swept from the room.

.   .   .   .

In a first-class carriage, his head still aching an accompaniment to the rumbling of the wheels, Hugh Drummond drew once again from his pocket the short typewritten note which he had found there on getting his ticket from his wallet. He looked at it ruefully.

"*You're slipping, Hugh,*" he read. "*You wouldn't have been caught so easily only a few years ago. I hope the headache isn't too bad, but you know you really asked for it . . . and you can't say I didn't warn you! Now don't you think it would be wiser to forget all about your visit to London, and just continue your peaceful life down in the country? Your village is very fond of you, and what about Phyllis? You'd be missed dreadfully if anything happened to you . . . and this was just a warning. The next time, something will happen to you . . . unpleasant . . . unless you are sensible.*

I hope, for your sake, this is good-bye.

P.S.—I really am sorry you're slipping so badly."

Hugh Drummond looked out of the window: his eyes watched a field of ruminating cows go past, but he saw nothing. *Slipping!* That had been the very word he had used on Inspector McIver . . .

"Damn it!" he said abruptly, and the only other occupant of the carriage, a clerical gentleman, jumped perceptibly. It was perhaps fortunate for his peace of mind that Drummond completed the sentence to himself. "I know that tempus fugits, and all that, but . . . Hugh my boy, you're rusty, and it won't do . . . hell, what wouldn't I give for a real stoup of ale!"

VII

ALGY AND PETER CLAIM RINGSIDE SEATS

THE 'Bull and Bush'—that typical country inn which relies for its attraction more on the excellence and quantity of its beverages than on any structural beauty or architectural design—was not very full that evening. Most of its regular clients had already left for their homes, perhaps because it was a dark and dirty evening and one's own particular fireside held a more than normal attraction. But two regulars lingered on.

" I'll match you this time," said Algy Longworth.

" Call . . . " invited Peter Darrell.

" Tails."

They glanced at their coins.

" Three in a row," complained Darrell. " Alf, two more bitters, please . . . "

The proprietor obliged.

" What took Hugh up to London ? "

Darrell paused a moment before replying.

" I don't know. But, Algy, did you notice something . . . something about him, I mean ? "

" Can't say I did. Here's how."

" Good health. He seemed to me . . . sort of elated."

" Elated ? "

" Yes."

Algy Longworth considered the point.

" Funny elated or excited elated ? "

" Er . . . I should say excited elated."

A thought struck Longworth.

" Not blonde elated ? "

Darrell laughed.

" Don't be ridiculous. Not in our Hugh. Now, had it been you . . . yes, if it had been you, I should have said blonde elated."

" Odd," said Longworth.

" May be nothing, of course. May be just my imagination. But I got the distinct impression that old Hugh was up to a piece of something . . . took me back years, it did. What did he say he went up for ? "

" Shopping."

" Shopping ? "

" Shopping."

" Odd," decided Peter Darrell.

They consumed their beer in silence for a few moments.

" I had a short one with Phyllis on the way down here," volunteered Longworth.

" Did you ? "

" Yes. Asked her why Hugh had gone off to London."

" What did she say ? "

" Shopping," said Longworth.

There was another silence. It was broken this time by the sudden opening of the bar door, and the advent of the man under discussion. The faces of the other two lit up, and they greeted him in unison.

" Hullo, Hugh ! Had a nice time ? "

" Hullo, Hugh ! Enjoyed yourself ? "

Hugh Drummond spoke deliberately.

" Evening, boys. I have had a nice time. I have enjoyed myself. Evening, Alf . . . set 'em up, please."

The proprietor was already drawing three bitters.

" Mine's a pint," stated Drummond emphatically, " Halves for the children, of course. And how I need it . . . "

Longworth was sniffing the air : the light of understanding dawned on his face.

" My goodness ! " he exclaimed, " you've been to the dentist, and had gas . . ."

" Do I still smell of the stuff ? "

" Do you still smell of the stuff ! " remarked Darrell, drawing away.

" That's what did it," said Drummond with conviction.

" Did what ? "

" There was a man in the carriage with me, a reverend gentleman," said Drummond, " at least he stayed with me until we were near the junction. Then he suddenly rushed out and staggered away down the corridor . . ."

" Some people," said Longworth seriously, " can't stand gas. Careless dentist, I call him, to let the beastly stuff get all over your clothes." Then, suddenly, " My goodness, gracious me ! "

" What's happened now ? "

" But," said Longworth in horror, " you went up to London *elated*, Peter said so. You actually went up to London elated at the prospect of going to your dentist with the distinct possibility that he would sales-talk you into a covey of gas. Possibility be damned ! probability is the word for a man who'll spill it all over your clothes ! My goodness, gracious me ! "

" It wasn't quite like that . . ." said Drummond quietly. " Now look here, chaps . . ."

He paused : a sound had come to his ears. He was not wrong : the door opened, to admit a middle-aged man of distinctly military appearance. The newcomer, who was carrying a suitcase, approached the bar.

" Good evening," he said affably.

" Good evening," responded Longworth.

" I wasn't really talking to you," said the stranger pleasantly, " but good evening all the same." He turned to the proprietor, " Have you by any chance a room to let ? "

Alfred looked the stranger over with a practised eye in a very few seconds. Alfred prided himself as a judge of men and as a man of quick decisions.

" Well, sir . . ." he said, " I'm afraid this isn't the Ritz ! " he giggled : it was his stock remark. " We're a bit rough and ready round here nowadays . . . how long would you be staying ? "

" Oh, a few days, I expect."

" Well, sir, if you'd like to have a look at all we've got . . ."

" If I could just see one room . . . thank you very much . . ."

He followed Alfred from the bar. As he passed through the door, he smiled to the trio.

" Good evening to you," he said pleasantly.

" Good evening," responded Longworth.

The stranger disappeared.

" Sensation ! " remarked Drummond.

" Eh ? "

" A visitor comes to our forgotten village." Drummond laughed. " The gossips will have a lovely new topic to-morrow."

" You were saying," said Darrell quietly, " that it wasn't quite like that . . ."

" Yes," said Longworth, " did the dentist chap approach you from the rear, struggling with his gas tubes, under cover of a beautiful female assistant ? "

" It wasn't quite like that either," Drummond thought

for a few moments, seemed to be coming to a decision. He suddenly appeared to make up his mind. " Listen, you fellows . . . I'm regrettably sure Phyllis hasn't got enough in the house to feed you, but could you come up after dinner for a chat ? I think it might interest you . . ."

Darrell looked at Longworth. Longworth looked at Darrell.

" Any beer ? " asked Longworth.

" Fortunately, lots."

" That settles it," said Darrell. " We'll be there."

. . . .

Longworth and Darrell let themselves into Drummond's house without ceremony. Since the irreplaceable manservant Denny had disappeared to work in a factory, and was irreplaceable, Drummond had made no attempt to replace him. He himself did the heavy work, Phyllis looked after the cooking and the house, and a woman from the village spent an hour or two in the mornings in helping her. The result was that neither really approved of bells rung by old friends, and the consequent trot to the front door, and Darrell and Longworth were definitely on the list of those who walked in without ringing.

They went straight to Drummond's den, which by those not on the list would have probably been referred to as the library. A large jug of ale and three tankards met their gratified gaze, but the room was empty. Darrell promptly helped himself and Longworth, and took a deep taste before making their presence known : he went to the door, and called :

" Wotcher, Hugh ! "

The sound of someone descending the stairs became audible. Hugh Drummond entered the room, attired in pyjamas and a very old silk dressing-gown.

" Welcome," he said, with a grin.

" We've welcomed ourselves," remarked Darrell, " Shall I pour out yours . . . ? "

" Thanks."

Algy Longworth approached Drummond with over-evident caution, ostentatiously sniffed the air around him, and then turned with relief to Darrell.

"It's all right," he said, " he's decontaminated himself." He turned back to Drummond, "Where's Phyllis? I supposed she swooned when you embraced her, and hasn't come round yet?"

Drummond smiled.

"She's gone to bed," he said, " and asks to be excused. Had a tiring day . . ."

"Have *you?*" asked Darrell meaningly, handing him his tankard.

Hugh Drummond made himself comfortable in a big armchair before replying. He lighted a cigarette with deliberation, as carefully as if it had been one of his rare and precious cigars. He looked at his two friends, and a sudden thrill struck them both simultaneously. There was an expression on his face which they had not seen for many— far too many—years, an expression which perhaps would have meant nothing in particular to anyone else but which might, to them, precise the most splendid tidings that could possibly be given them. Longworth and Darrell—perhaps particularly the irrepressible and ever-youthful Algy—had resented just as much as Drummond their relegation to the land and the Home Guard, and would have grasped at any straw which promised a more active contribution. Years ago, when something spiced with danger, something perhaps a trifle adventurous was in the wind, that same expression had found its way on to Hugh Drummond's face : could it be—could it possibly be—that something rather exciting was in the wind now?

Longworth drained his tankard, filled it up again, and sat down anxiously beside Drummond. The less optimistic Darrell filled and lit his pipe quietly. Neither made any attempt to prompt or hurry Drummond: they knew only too well, from long experience, that their friend and leader would speak when it suited him, and not one minute before.

Drummond stirred. Longworth jumped. Darrell leant forward.

" What would you say," at last said Drummond slowly,

" if I told you that, after being duly warned, I had just quietly put my head into a noose and practically pulled the plug myself ? "

He evidently required a reply : Longworth provided it.

" I would say that you were taking too much water with it."

" Yes. Rusty," added Darrell.

" Well, I did just that very thing this afternoon . . ."

He told them the story, being careful however not to identify the Soldier or the Great Man, nor to give any inkling of the subject of his conversation with the latter. But he told the rest in full, and there was a long pause at the end of the recital.

" Crikey ! " suddenly ejaculated Longworth, and buried his face in his beer. When he could speak again : " Oh Crikey ! what-ho ! Lor lov a duck and drake. *Irma !* Oh, crikey ! "

" I gather," smiled Drummond, " you are not displeased ? "

" What, when the ravisher turns up practically in person again ? I should say I am not displeased, with nobs on ! "

" When do we start, Hugh ? " asked Darrell quietly.

" Well . . . do we start ? At all, I mean . . . ? "

Both Darrell and Longworth abruptly sat bolt upright.

" I beg your pardon ? " said the astonished Darrell.

" Don't beg his pardon," said Longworth. " Crack him over his nut, that may bring him to his senses. Of all the daft questions he has ever asked, that's miles the daftest. Great heavens and Scot, what have we all been doing in the past five years but praying for something like this to prise us out of our vegetable dotage ? Irma's a public benefactor, that's what that girl is, turning up out of the red, white, and blue to give us a meaning to life again. My gosh ! " he looked at Drummond almost angrily, " and you ask do we do anything about it ! My sainted aunt—Emily, the one that left me a thousand and her bonnet—that dope must be still circulating in your system. Here, have some more beer ! "

He seized Drummond's tankard and refilled it. Darrell smiled.

"I should like to place on record," he said quietly, "that I associate myself with every word that our friend has just uttered."

"There you are !" exclaimed Longworth. "You see? You're goofy . . ."

"Half a minute, chaps," Drummond took the tankard back from Longworth, and smiled a thanks, but he was speaking very seriously.

"Times have changed from . . . how long was it ago ?"

"Too long," interjected Longworth with decision.

"That's as may be. But this may be a far, far bigger thing, as somebody once nearly said. It isn't only Irma, of unsanctimonious memory. You may have gathered there's something behind all this. Personally, I'm going in . . . if they want me. Even if they don't, I am privately going after Irma—that girl's been loose too long. Of course, if you two would like to be in on it, who am I to say no." He laughed at the sigh of relief which escaped from both of them. "But if you do, you've got to come in with your eyes wide open. Either way, it won't be fun—wars both private and public have become unpleasantly total since our day. If you come in with me, you must understand that nothing is barred, including inhumanity, that it's all in with no sort of reservations. I mean what I say, and I've never been more serious in my life. Don't think I'm trying to put you off—there's nothing I should like more than to have the pair of you with me. But fair's fair, and you must be warned."

"We have been warned," replied Darrell quietly.

"When do we start ?" asked Longworth.

Hugh Drummond grinned : there was a lot that had no need to be put into words between these three. Drummond, in any case, would have found it difficult to phrase his thoughts, at that moment, without appearing sentimental. He was deeply touched, and felt years younger; that number of years, in fact, since such a scene had been enacted between the three before. Their supreme faith in him, their obvious unwillingness to allow him to take any risks without sharing them, their youthful enthusiasm for a spot of adventure . . . all acted as a tonic to him, particularly after his humiliating experience of that afternoon . . .

Drummond laughed happily.

" We've got to wait until we know whether it's to be a private or part of the public war. A few hours, maybe a day or two. In the meantime, we must contain ourselves in silence."

" Mums the word," agreed Darrell. " Hear that, Algy ? "

" When I wish," announced Longworth, " no clam nor even oyster can be more reticent, retiring, or non-committal. Strangers' words bounce off me : it's an art."

Drummond got up.

" I'm going to throw you fellows out," he said. " To be quite frank, that dope still lingers . . . "

" Incidentally, Hugh," asked Darrell, " how did you explain yourself to the admiring throng at the station . . . when you found yourself there ? "

" I was a bit self-conscious, and very angry," smiled Drummond. " And even I knew that I was reeking . . ."

He looked at Longworth : that worthy grinned.

" Dentist ? "

" It was the only thing to say . . ."

.   .   .   .

The two reports came in one immediately after the other.

" *He seems a very charming fellow,*" said the first. " *I am sure we will become great friends.*"

" *Not only has he risen,*" said the second, " *but he is well and truly hooked.*"

The fair lady smiled with satisfaction : things were going well.

VIII

THE BLONDE IS CRITICISED

IT was certainly a luxurious headquarters, even for one situated in a great city. The office in which the two men stood was magnificently furnished : it looked as if the furniture was composed of museum pieces. This was, in fact, true : the Gestapo has always known how to look after its own interests, and has always possessed among its travellers one or two men with an artistic eye and the knowledge of what would go well with the pieces already collected and sent home . . .

One of the men wore a superb, if sombre, uniform : the other was less resplendent but still smartly dressed in plain clothes. Both were serious as they chatted together in their guttural native tongue, and neither seemed completely at ease with the other : the trade which they practised was not conducive to too much mutual trust. They had one thing in common, these two otherwise contrasting men : they shared the thin lips which can, on occasion, betoken an unexpected cruelty of character.

At this moment however, they seemed to be reminiscing in a reasonably friendly manner.

" It is a great pity," said one.

" So," said the other.

" Unquestionably, had our great armies been loosed upon that ridiculous little island, we should have lost a large number of very good men."

" What better end than to die—gloriously, in battle—for the Fatherland."

" Obviously nothing better. Specially since those cursed British would not have been able to stand up to us. We should have been the conquerors of the world by now . . ."

" Yes." But the man in plain clothes seemed a trifle worried : he glanced anxiously at the door, and seemed relieved to find that it had not opened by itself during the conversation. "All the same, mein Herr, I do not think that we should talk like this. Of course, between you and me . . ." he laughed rather sheepishly, "But still, what we have said might sound to an outsider just a little like criticism . . . do you agree with me?"

The officer grunted.

"You are right," he said slowly, "but nevertheless it is a great pity, after you and I had laid our plans so carefully. Our delightful colleague, the splendid Irma, would have enjoyed herself, imposing our will on the nation she so greatly hates, persuading people to tell her things they so greatly wished to keep secret. A wonderful woman, that!" He sighed at the recollection of such wasted talent. "She was fascinated when I explained to her some of our methods, absolutely fascinated! And such a quick learner! Did I ever tell you that she actually suggested some improvements? We are using them now all over the place, and specially in Paris."

"Nevertheless she is curiously inactive now."

"Eh?" There was just a suggestion of a challenge in his voice.

"Well, mein Herr," continued the other, disregarding the warning, "when it was clear that she could not head our London headquarters, we gave her—if you remember—a special mission . . ."

"She was to insinuate herself into London society, and tell us all that she could discover from her contacts."

"Precisely. It is true that she started off well enough, but very little of any use has come through in the last year."

The officer grunted again: it was evident that he was not altogether pleased.

"You are aware, no doubt, that the English have worked hard on a campaign against careless talk?" he suggested.

"I am. But we employ people with figures and faces, such as the glamorous Irma possesses, for the very purpose of defeating such a propaganda campaign. And with the British habit of gallantly trusting their mistresses anywhere with anything, written if requested, her task should be one of the easiest . . ."

There was a pause.

" I have found it necessary," continued the man in plain clothes stiffly, " to send one or two messages lately . . . quite sharp messages. I felt it necessary to state that we expect more than we have been receiving, both in quantity and in quality."

The officer grunted again : the conversation was taking an unpleasant turn : he had distinctly pleasant memories of the Adlon and the beautiful Irma in the year before the war. He decided to change the conversation.

" What time is it ? "

The other looked at his watch.

" Ten minutes before we need go in to the meeting."

" What is on the agenda ? "

" France."

The officer said nothing : France was a difficult subject, and promised a lively discussion. Why wouldn't those fools of Frenchmen realise they were a beaten nation, and accept their rôle as vassals of the Nazi world-power ? Why would they persist in giving trouble at every opportunity, like derailing German troop trains, blowing up head-quarters, and even—he shuddered—making it unsafe for men like him to roam the streets at will ? They even waged open warfare in the mountains, against . . . that really was disgraceful ! . . . the urgent orders of the sensible Pétain ! And in lesser ways, too, they made themselves unpleasant : he remembered vividly when last in Paris noticing how very smart and attractive the girls all were—how they did it, with the lack of everything, goodness only knows ! But would they look at a German, a nice, healthy, well-fed Aryan youth ? Not they, not one in a thousand ! Why they bothered to dress themselves up, he couldn't understand . . . unless it was merely to annoy !

And these Résistance groups—they really were becoming a menace. What was their latest impertinence ? oh, yes, to announce from within France—actually from within German occupied France !—that they had formed a council of resistance ! What cheek ! what infernal cheek. He decided to bring that up at the meeting, to suggest that a drive, a very special drive, should be directed against these hooligans. No pity to be shown at all. Shoot on sight and question—his eyes lit up : yes, ' question '—all the female members of the dead men's families to find out who else was in the game. He decided to offer to lead such a drive himself, in person : he would soon find a way of making those traitors talk, of breaking up this self-styled council of resistance . . .

He looked up to find his companion staring at him questioningly :

" Thinking of France," he said gruffly.

" Oh, I see." The other smiled. " I really was quite frightened ! You were scowling as if you were on the point of attacking someone."

" I'm not at all sure that I'm not."

" You said, mein herr ? "

" I said that I was not at all sure that I was not going to attack someone. Many people, in fact. I am thinking of going to France, and wiping out this ridiculous council of resistance."

" Ridiculous but elusive," said the other quietly.

" It's an impertinence ! "

" It is more than that," said the man in plain clothes soberly, " it is an outrage, but a thorny outrage. I have put some of our best men on to it already, but as I said . . . it is elusive, and . . . rather dangerous. One of our fellows, a man we can ill spare, was washed up from the Seine yesterday morning. He had not been drowned : he had been knifed before he reached the river."

" All the more reason to wipe the thing out ! "

" Quite."

" You have taken hostages, of course ? "

" Of course."

" And they will be shot ? "

" Some of them, no doubt : we can scarcely expect a confession. But with these senseless French, that doesn't seem to do much good."

The officer drew himself up to his full height, and puffed out his chest.

"I shall suggest that I should go to Paris myself," he said with decision.

"I think," said the other, going towards the door, "that they will now be ready for us. Shall we go to the conference room? After you, my friend . . ."

The officer passed out of the room. The man in the smartly cut civilian clothes paused for a moment, and looked at his desk and then round the room : no, there was nothing lying about which should not be lying about. Gently he closed the door behind him.

IX

HUGH DRUMMOND MEETS AN AMERICAN

Eisenhower Platz, or to give it its official title, Grosvenor Square, was rejoicing in a snatch of November sun. The American uniform and accent were everywhere prevailing, and everyone seemed to be reacting to the unexpected warmth. Complete strangers smiled to each other, salutes were exchanged with a carefree and spontaneous abandon very foreign to the tardy reluctance with which a strict and nuisance order is normally obeyed, and a naval rating actually saluted a very junior second-lieutenant indeed. Good humour and bonhomie was in the air : even the cats refrained from spitting at the dogs.

Inside one of the great houses which surround the Square, a meeting was being held. It was an Allied meeting : American and British uniforms sat at the same long table with American and British civilian suits, differing accents questioned and answered each other. It was very evident that the pleasant and polite mood of the Square outside had permeated into the room, for the degree of agreement was remarkable. The pale November sun, watching apprehensively the dirty weather coming up from the east, was at least doing its best in its hour or two of cloudless freedom.

A decision had been arrived at, and apparently without too much difficulty.

" Who's going to brief them ? " suddenly asked someone from Boston, Mass.

" Drummond," replied an Oxford accent, " has already been briefed."

" I'll be responsible for Mat," volunteered a New York voice.

" Can you make it to-day ? " asked the original speaker.

" Sure, if he's in London . . ."

It was decided that Mat probably was in London, it was confirmed over the telephone and a luncheon date was made for that very day.

" How soon can they meet ? "

" I can get Drummond up from the country by this evening," stated the Oxford accent.

" How about you, Jim, getting them together ? "

" If Mat's agreeable, I'll give them both a drink to-night, and leave them to get acquainted," suggested the man from New York.

" Where shall I tell Drummond to be, and what time ? "

" Tell him to come to my apartment, at six-thirty . . . okay ? "

" O . . ." said the Oxford accent, ". . . kay."

. . . . .

" Mat Harlow," said the man from New York, " Captain Hugh Drummond."

" Glad to meet you, Captain . . ."

They shook hands. Drummond looked with interest and a certain amount of curiosity at the American to whom he had just been introduced, the Great Man had been very complimentary about this Matthew Harlow . . .

He saw before him a man of medium height and medium build, but somehow or other there was an impression of strength and suppleness of muscle. Drummond wondered for a moment if this were because he already knew that

Harlow had quite recently been playing baseball up to professional standard, but rapidly decided that it was not; the proportions of the man looked athletic. He had a good firm handshake—none of those fishy touches which always, to Drummond when meeting a stranger, put him off. He was clean-shaven, not precisely good-looking but with pleasant features, and his smile was genuine. Round his eyes, little lines ran away towards his temples, and Drummond decided that he had laughed a good deal in his life. His voice was possessed of that peculiar and attractive quality which enabled him to speak quietly and yet make every syllable, without apparent effort, very easily heard.

" I've been told a lot about you . . ."

" So have I about you," replied Drummond with a grin, " isn't it embarrassing ! "

Matthew Harlow laughed gaily.

" I can't say you look particularly embarrassed," he said, " and I don't particularly feel it. But I'm certainly glad to meet in the flesh the man we've all heard about . . ."

Drummond, for once, really did feel a touch of embarrassment, but Harlow had spoken so genuinely that he could not help but feel pleased.

" Now, listen," broke in the New Yorker, who had been watching their first reactions to each other and felt satisfied. " I've warned Mat here, but I've got to break it to you, Captain, I'm afraid I've got an engagement which I can't duck, and I've got to go straight away. But you two have got plenty to talk about, and you're very welcome in this apartment for as long as you care to stay. It's a nice quiet place where there's nobody to overhear you . . ."

The small man was puzzled, and for several minutes felt frustrated and rather hurt : what on earth did Hugh Drummond mean by coming to such a place where, once he had traversed the front door, he could not be followed ? For a moment the small man flirted with the idea that Drummond was paying a sentimental visit, nothing to do with business, for this house was obviously split up into flats—the door-bells clearly indicated that. But on second thoughts he rejected the idea ; it was too foreign to everything he had been told about Drummond. He looked closely at the door-bells, as if for inspiration, but found no help from this examination, he had been too far away to see which one of the four Drummond had pressed ; but he made a mental note of the address.

It was not the small man's way to give up easily. He could very well wait, he knew, for Drummond to emerge from the house and then continue to shadow him. But it was on a greater reputation than mere ability in shadowing that the fair lady had decided to employ him, and the small man made up his mind to have a quick look round. There was an alley way one door down that might lead to the back of the house.

The small man found himself in a mews, and he realised that he was indeed at the back of the row of houses. It took him a minute only to place the house into which Drummond had disappeared.

He approached it silently and carefully ; he tried the back door, it was locked. He looked about him, and at once noticed something which gladdened his heart.

Either the black-out was perfect in the top three flats, or else there was nobody in them. But the ground floor was less well darkened, and was plainly occupied ; and the reason for his certainty about this particular floor pleased him enormously. He could just see a thin crack of light, and that only occasionally from the particular angle at which he was standing ; it was caused by the wind playing with the imperfectly drawn curtains of an open window.

The small man went up to this window very cautiously, very soundlessly, he drew back the curtain just sufficiently to enable him to look into the room. It was a bedroom lighted by a forgotten bedside lamp only, and it was empty.

The small man was accustomed to make quick decisions. One minute he was outside in the mews, the next he was standing in the bedroom. He made a quick note of the placing of the furniture, and then extinguished the light. He moved as silently as ever to the door.

He put his eye to the keyhole, the sitting-room beyond was plainly occupied, although he could see no one. He put his ear to the keyhole, he heard Drummond's voice . . .

The small man smiled with satisfaction, and settled down to listen.

" . . . nobody to overhear you," repeated the New-Yorker. " There's a bottle of Scotch and a bottle of gin on that table—help yourselves, and keep on helping yourselves—that's all right with me. Mat, perhaps you'll come and talk to me in the morning . . .? "

He said good-bye, and left them alone. A moment later he was back.

" I don't believe I put the light out in my bedroom," he said apologetically. He opened the door and looked in. " Oh! must have! " He closed the door again. " Don't forget, help yourselves . . ."

He was gone.

Drummond went to the table.

" Gin ? " he asked.

" Scotch, thanks . . ."

" Soda ? "

" A drop of water, please . . ."

" For myself," said Drummond, " it shall be gin."

" And what ? " asked Harlow.

" It looks to me," Drummond smiled, " as if it was going to be just plain gin."

" No need," said Harlow, moving to a cupboard. " There are a lot of worse things than plain gin, but there are a lot of better." He turned with a bottle which he had extracted from the cupboard. " Gin and French, for instance . . ."

" Not real French vermouth! " said Drummond, startled.

The other laughed.

" No, I'm afraid not. But a passable substitute ; I tasted it last week . . ."

They settled themselves, and eyed each other. Their eyes met. They both smiled.

" I feel," said Harlow, " just like I did when I was up for my first job. I was very nervous and I wanted the job badly. The man who could give it to me made me sit down. I nearly missed the edge of the chair, and held on by the nap of the cloth of my new trousers. The man was trying to be nice to me, and asked me some questions—simple questions. I was delighted that I knew the answers, but horrified to find I couldn't speak. At last a croak came out, which nearly frightened me off the chair, and then I found that I couldn't stop speaking. I listened to myself with a growing certainty that I was talking myself out of the job, but nothing that I could think of doing would shut me up. I wouldn't let him get a word in edgeways. About the following spring I stopped as suddenly as I'd begun. He said I could have the job. I jumped what I felt certain was a clear seventeen inches—without doubt the record for the sitting high jump—and the chair fell over with a noise like the Empire State Building collapsing. I picked it up and fled. It was only when I was outside the door, and breathing the pure, scented air of his secretary's parlour that I realised I still had that chair with me. She was a nice girl, she took it away from me quite gently."

Drummond had listened to the recital with a growing approval ; here was a man with a pretty sense of the ridiculous, something that always appealed to him.

" At the moment," went on Harlow, " I am not particularly nervous, but I want the job just as much as if I was. It is having the curious effect of making my Scotch and water taste exactly as if it was a Scotch and soda."

Drummond looked quickly at the table, and then back to the American.

" I'm awfully sorry," he said, " here, let me . . ."

" I wouldn't dream of it," Harlow was laughing. " It's a great relief to know that these bubbles are real and not some manifestation of the nervous system. To continue, I am not at all certain that I am not talking myself out of this job. The curious thing is that I can be as silent as the grave when a cemetery seems indicated, but I don't expect you to take my word for it, of course. Perhaps I'd come to a period, and might manage to break off there, if I started up in French . . ."

" How are you in French ? " interjected Drummond.

" Okay," replied Harlow, " as a matter of fact, pretty good."

" Bi-lingual ? "

" That word," said Harlow, " is much too loosely used nowadays—but I suppose I've got as good a claim to it as anybody else."

" You should know that I can only speak a very few words very badly."

Drummond was watching him closely, but Harlow never hesitated.

" That's okay with me."

" It might add to the dangers of visiting France at the moment."

" And it might not. Too great a confidence in your superb accent might be an even greater danger."

Drummond smiled.

" And," concluded Harlow, " you can always be dumb, or something. Or just keep in the background ; after all, it's not the streets we're going to visit, if I'm coming with you, that is : it's the big boys who have reason to keep pretty much to themselves as it is . . ."

" Do you know all about the Gestapo ? "

Harlow looked at him sharply.

" I know plenty."

" They've got a new one now, I believe," went on Drummond quietly, " for people they want to make talk— and they'd certainly want to make you and me talk if they had half a chance. They say it's much more efficacious than merely burning your flesh or flogging you to death, although it doesn't sound quite so frightful. They put you into an icy cold bath and hold you under until you pass out; then they bring you round and if you won't talk they repeat the charming process . . . three or four times, if necessary. If you still won't talk, they get a bit rough just for good measure, put you into a cell made for one which you share with two or three others—and which you're all lived in *without even being allowed to leave, even momentarily,* for a week at the very least—and repeat the process the next day at the same time—something to look forward to. What I'm saying is not imagination, it's the solemn truth; many gallant Frenchmen are undergoing that treatment to-day—Frenchmen and Frenchwomen —and are still not talking."

" Yes," said Harlow quietly, " I know that you're speaking the truth."

" Still keen on the job ? "

" Very."

There was a short pause.

" Why ? " asked Drummond abruptly.

Harlow did not immediately reply. When he did, he spoke gently and it was very clear that he was chosing his words with particular care.

" If I told you that all the penalties of failure left me cold, I'd be a liar. I'm just as scared of the sort of thing you've been talking about as anyone else. But if I told you that, in my opinion, the gamble was worth taking, I think that would be just about expressing what I really feel. I'd never been to England before six months ago, and I've seen enough in that time to make me like the place and the people. They're queer at times—quite often in fact !—but I daresay you think we're just as queer . . . and the behaviour of some of our fellows is no great advertisement until you remember that they're at least three thousand miles away from home and expecting . . . well, perhaps not exactly expecting to get killed, but knowing that they've got a damn good chance of never seeing their homes and families again . . . that makes them do things they'd never do at home in a year of first Fridays in April. I've seen enough, though, to recognise something which seems to me of far more importance than my life or yours, and I mean this : if war can be stopped—peace for our children, and that sort of thing—then a combination of America and Britain is about the only thing powerful enough to stop it. So anything a man can do to bring our two countries closer together is a job worth doing. Luckily, when we've had to work together—in North Africa, shall we say, which I saw for myself this summer—Americans and British have found it easy to walk the same road. I don't mean to say that there haven't been the usual perfectly healthy jealousies, of course there have. You wouldn't think much of an American, would you, who thought that an Englishman was better than he was ; and neither would I of a Britisher who thought that way of an American. When things go wrong it's human nature to blame the other fellow . . . and both of us have made mistakes. It's the men of both countries who have seen the thing clearly enough, and helped to explain it to those who didn't, that have really done a swell job . . ."

He paused, and finished his drink. Drummond watched him silently, he knew that this was a declaration of faith, a solemn statement, and he respected it as such. And he knew that it was not quite finished.

"This job," concluded the American suddenly, " seems to be my chance of doing that very thing. I know what the top boys are thinking about France at home, and I know that it's not quite what you boys are thinking over here. That's bad ; that we should think differently about what may be a major point. If I can do anything—and you can do anything on your side—to convince our Mister Bigs to think the right way—whatever we may be able, on the spot, to convince ourselves the right way may be—if we can make them think together, then the risks on the way simply do not count."

He suddenly, unexpectedly laughed.

"There you are, Captain," he said simply. "Am I hired ? "

"Only, Mat, if you'll remember that my name is Hugh." Harlow leapt to his feet.

"Oh, boy!" he laughed. "When do we start?" He suddenly remembered something, "when do we start, Hugh?"

"They tell me," said Drummond, "that the earliest will be in about a fortnight . . ."

"Two weeks?"

"Yes."

"Just the pair of us?"

Hugh Drummond smiled a trifle ruefully.

"I had hoped to be able to take a couple of other fellows with us. However, apparently it can't be done. It may be all for the best, all the same: if you don't mind, they'll be part of our team, only with rear echelon duties which, maybe, will keep them fully occupied. Nice couple; you'll like 'em . . ."

"Sure I will."

"Thirsty types . . ."

"Brothers in affliction. Shall I get you one while I'm filling up my own?"

"Thanks."

A few moments later:

"Bung-ho!" said Drummond.

"Here," said Harlow solemnly, "is to the skin off your nose, if that is necessary, but certainly to nothing worse!"

Drummond grinned.

"Thanks." He thought for a moment. "You know I'm not quite sure that you're completely up-to-date."

Harlow looked at him, surprised.

"How so?"

"Ever heard of a woman called Irma Peterson?"

"No, I don't believe I have . . ." replied the American, but a little doubtfully, "although the name does seem to ring some very faint bell. Pretty name, isn't it?"

"Well . . . I hadn't thought about it that way!" Drummond laughed, a trifle drily. "But she is certainly a very beautiful woman."

"Do we meet her?" asked Harlow hopefully.

"I should say, almost certainly."

" Good."

Hugh Drummond laughed.

" Let's go and get a bite of food," he suggested. " We'll meet Peter Darrell at my club—he's one of the two I talked about. The other—one Algy Longworth—is down in the country still, keeping an eye on Phyllis."

" Who's Phyllis ? "

" I'm so sorry, of course you don't know ! Phyllis is my wife."

Drummond smiled : Harlow returned the smile.

" Peter Darrell," said Drummond, rising to his feet, " will tell you all about the glamorous Irma between mouthfuls—he is always charmed to talk about Irma."

" Good."

" What I like about you Mat," said Drummond, as they went out into the street, " is that you don't ask too many questions."

" What I like about you, Hugh," said Harlow, as he switched on his torch, " is that it wouldn't be any good if I did . . . "

The little man missed this proof of Allied understanding and unity. He was hurrying along the mews in the opposite direction. What he had to say to the fair lady simply could not wait . . .

X

MAT HARLOW BECOMES AN HONORARY MEMBER

In the next few days, Mat Harlow practically became an honorary member of Hugh Drummond's club. They met there every morning at eleven—Drummond, Harlow, Darrell, and Longworth who had been summoned up from the country—ostensibly for matitudinal refreshment. In fact, it was at these meetings that Drummond explained his plans, went over them in every detail, received and decided on suggestions for improvement, and satisfied himself that his three followers were word perfect in the parts they were destined to play. Up to that time Hugh Drummond had normally worked on impulses and hunches, dictated on the spur of the moment by circumstances: and in this sense it was a new experience for Darrell and Longworth to have so much time available for careful, painstaking preparation. It was also a revelation even to them who knew the man so well, to find that Drummond— certainly a proved leader of unchallenged ability in action in the field—was also capable of the staff duty of detailed planning on which the success of an operation so often finally depends.

As for Mat Harlow, he was supremely happy. All his life, in America, he had thought of an Englishman as a dull stick, bound by a tradition which he could not shake off to a life within the strict boundaries of what other Englishmen thought was and was not done ; a confirmed and frequently affected prig, and a man seldom troubled by a sense of humour except with regard to a totally incomprehensible delight in horse stories. Horse, to him whenever he had thought of an England which up to then he had never seen, was really the operative word : stories, clothes, outlook, and even women . . .

It was true that since he had been in England, this theory had suffered several rude shocks. In fact—except for the ill-concealed sense of superiority which it was so irritating to come up against, and which unfortunately was so frequently manifest in all walks of life—it was extremely difficult to substantiate anywhere. A glimpse at certain of his own compatriots far from their homes, together with the discovery that ' horse ' was not by any means the operative word, particularly in the case of girls, had brought home to him the undoubted fact that to judge a nation by those who travel far from its shores is a highly inaccurate and misleading basis. However, he had noticed a tendency not to deviate from the railway lines of so-called good conduct, not to steer for oneself . . .

But now he had found, at one fell swoop, three delightfully mad Englishmen. Six months ago he would never have thought such a thing possible : anyone like Drummond, like Darrell and perhaps particularly Longworth, would in England—or so he would have thought—have long since been incarcerated in an asylum. Three months ago he was beginning to realise that the British could laugh quite heartily and really fairly frequently if often unexpectedly. But now he had the living proof that an Englishman could be quite as pleasantly mad, if not considerably madder, than anything America could produce : and combine it, as in America, with sound common sense and plenty of ability. There was not so much difference in the two nations after all . . . plenty on the surface, perhaps, but nothing very much once you scratched the veneer . . .

He thoroughly enjoyed the morning conferences. In the first place, it was very pleasant to find that your respect and friendship for the man with whom you were about to start on . . . well, on what could only be described as a perilous adventure . . . was increasing daily by leaps and bounds ; and secondly the meetings were frequently really very funny indeed. It was nice to have plenty to laugh at when any other attitude might have increased a nervous tension which, inevitably, was daily making itself surreptitiously felt more and more . . .

There was one drawback of course : bitter beer. Harlow had first accepted the morning pint as a gesture, finding that the other three never even thought of any other liquid at that hour. Lifeless and warm, it had not appealed to his palate, trained on iced drinks. But after a week of the treatment, he was rather reluctantly compelled to admit that the stuff grew on you, and slipping down the throat quite easily, did provide a certain satisfaction. In fact, he was almost ready, now, to join in the morning discussion on the quality of the day's barrel. Another day or two, and he felt he would be in it up to the neck . . .

It was a few minutes after eleven when, on that particular morning, Mat Harlow made his appearance at the club. The hall porter, quite an old friend now, smiled a welcome.

" The gentlemen have already arrived, sir. You'll find them in the smoking-room."

" Thanks, Williams . . . "

What a difference, thought Harlow, not without satisfaction, as he divested himself of his hat and coat, from the first few days when he had been formally and almost suspiciously escorted until he could be handed over to the member whom he had come to visit. He joined the others in the smoking-room.

They always used one corner of the large room for these conferences. His pint, Harlow noticed, had already been ordered and was awaiting him. He smiled to his new friends, and took his place.

" You're late ! " said Longworth. " No excuse will be accepted, so don't make one. Just sit silently until you're spoken to, when you may take it you've been forgiven . . . "

Drummond laughed.

" Morning, Mat. Algy's only beaten you by thirty seconds, so he should talk ! "

" How's the beer this morning ? " asked Harlow.

His three mentors beamed.

" You tell us ! "

Harlow tasted it.

" H'm," he said, " A certain absence of hops. An over-application of H two O. However, satisfactorily clear . . . how am I doing ? "

" In another week," said the delighted Longworth, " you'll be able to tell the make with your eyes shut."

" That used to be an easy thing to do back home with Scotch," said Harlow. " You just closed the eyes, took a mouthful and swallowed it quick, and then waited to see how long it took for the top of your head to come back to you. Every brand had a different interval."

" I've heard," said Darrell, " that sometimes you never opened your eyes again . . . ? "

Mat Harlow laughed.

"That," he said, "was one of the minor inconveniences of prohibition!"

"Gentlemen!" announced Drummond. "The meeting is called to order . . ."

"That means 'stop your prattle,'" explained Longworth. "The great man is about to lay an egg . . ."

They looked at Drummond expectantly. But for once, Hugh Drummond did not immediately announce the subject for discussion. Instead, after a moment of hesitation, he looked up at them and smiled.

"Sorry, chaps!" he said. "Fact is, what I've got on my mind is a spot difficult to explain. Frankly, I'm a trifle worried . . ."

He paused again and they did not prompt him. Darrell and Longworth knew far better, of course, than to attempt to extract anything from Hugh Drummond before he was ready to volunteer the information. And Mat Harlow, being a quick learner as well as a shrewd judge of character, had noticed that one did not hurry Drummond : in any case, there was very seldom any need.

"It's Irma," said Drummond abruptly.

"What's the matter with Irma?" asked Darrell, greatly daring.

"I don't know," Drummond smiled, "and I don't like not knowing. She's in this somehow—not a shadow of doubt about that. She knew about the offer that was going to be made to me before I did myself, remember? For some reason best known to herself, she tried to put me off it : odd, I should have thought she might have welcomed another tilt. In fact, for a couple of days, she did me the compliment of paying me particular attention—concentrating on me you might almost say. Since then—when I've done the very thing she apparently didn't want me to do—complete silence. I am ignored. No nicely phrased message. Not even a telephone call. There is no doubt about it, I am hurt!"

"Somebody told me there was a lot of 'flu about . . ." suggested Longworth.

"Irma," said Drummond, "could run a temperature of

a hundred and four and still make her presence felt. It's a great pity that she seems to have lost interest, because it makes all the harder . . . your job."

He was looking at Darrell and Longworth as he spoke. Neither answered him, nor asked the question which was obviously on their lips. Drummond went on speaking quietly.

"As you know, Mat and I are the lucky ones, and you two have to form the rear headquarters here in England. But, while we are away, there is plenty for you to do. The principal thing is to find Irma, of course : but remember I shall never forgive either of you if you deal with her before I get back : Irma is my personal and private cup of tea. The only possible excuse for you to act at all violently with her would be if there was any prospect of her getting away . . . "

"Don't worry, Hugh," Darrell spoke quietly, "we know how you feel . . . "

"I wouldn't touch a hair of her head," said Longworth, "with an asbestos poker seven yards long . . ."

Harlow laughed.

"Popular lady ! " he hazarded.

"But," went on Darrell, "I must say I would like to know why you are so darned certain she is connected with the bigger thing."

"Simple ! " Drummond smiled, as if humouring a small boy. "In the first place, she knew that the General was coming down to the country to see me about something, and that he was going to ask me to come up to London. If you like, you can say that ringing me up, when he was actually there, was a fluke, but she knew about it. Secondly, she knew that I had come to London on the following day, and she tried to frighten me off keeping my luncheon engagement. Thirdly, after I had kept my luncheon engagement, she proceeded to teach me a short, sharp lesson : that, as always before in our long acquaintance, it was dangerous to ignore her advice unless one kept one's eyes skinned and one's senses very much on the alert. In the course of this lesson, she had conveyed to me one of her delightful personal notes, informing me that the next time I disobeyed her wishes, the lesson would be far more serious. Getting it ? "

" Yes."

" And what happens ? " asked Drummond of the three impartially, " I proceed to disobey her in every possible way, to throw her wishes back into her pretty teeth, to challenge her power . . . and what happens ? Absolutely, completely, and indisputably nothing. It's over a week, and as far as I can see, she hasn't moved a muscle . . . odd, most odd . . . completely out of character."

" This Irma," said Harlow slowly, " must have a reason for not wanting you in this . . . "

He paused. Longworth laughed.

" She's got a darned good reason ! " he said emphatically. " She's come off a poor second best whenever she's tried conclusions with Hugh : fact is, she's been unduly unlucky not to have found herself a patient for the official hangman ! "

" Sorry," said Harlow. " I'm expressing myself badly. What I mean to say is this : if she doesn't want Hugh in this little effort—and of course she's got plenty of reason for not wanting him, as she's never got away with it yet when up against him—she must be on the other side . . ."

Drummond, sitting back and smoking lazily, did not appear to be paying particular attention. But in fact he was watching the American closely.

" On the other side ? " asked Darrell.

" Yes."

" What other side ? " asked Longworth.

" Don't you see ? If she doesn't want Hugh, it's because Hugh is the man who can bring off the job, and therefore she doesn't want the job brought off. And if she doesn't want the job brought off . . ."

He stopped, rather alarmed at the conclusion to which his own argument was bringing him. He looked up at Darrell and Longworth : they were staring at him. He glanced at Drummond, to find him smiling.

" Finish it ! " encouraged Drummond.

"If she doesn't want the job brought off, she's . . . she's an enemy."

"Precisely." Drummond grinned. "She's that particularly dangerous and unpleasant thing, a German . . . or at least German-employed . . . loose in this country, and apparently extremely well informed."

There was a long silence. Longworth broke it.

"This morning," he said with decision, "we shall indulge in a second pint. And, since miracles have not yet ceased, I shall volunteer to pay for it."

"Thanks," said Darrell automatically.

"So," said Drummond quietly, "you can see why I'm a little troubled about it, losing touch I mean. Because we've got absolutely nothing to go on, to find her: McIver has given up trying to trace those telephone calls: it was a very long shot, anyway. Our only chance is for her to make a mistake, and lead us to her: a long shot too, but the only possibility . . . and it becomes an impossibility if she simply won't make a move . . ."

Longworth turned to Darrell.

"Jolly good job we've got!"

"Yes. Almost too easy . . ."

"There's a bit more . . ." said Harlow hesitatingly.

"Go on," encouraged Drummond.

"Just a moment . . ." warned Darrell.

The waiter had approached their secluded corner in answer to Longworth's ring. The order was given, and he went away.

"Yes?"

"Oughtn't we to tell someone about Irma?" Harlow seemed troubled. "It seems to me that her knowledge indicates a very serious leakage somewhere pretty high up . . ."

"I've thought about that," said Drummond. "If we were certain she knew all the facts—about the expedition—then the only possible answer would be yes. But I don't want to drag in the official sleuths too early: they're a smart lot, bet she'd be a match for them, I feel. That sounds conceited, Mat: it isn't really if you look at it this way. Irma is no ordinary person—very far from it. If she's working for the Nazis, you can bet she would only accept a very big job. In that case, she's certainly got most of the official boys taped : must give her the credit for that, she's no fool. That being so, they might get her with a lot of luck, but they wouldn't get the whole gang, and the danger would continue. We have much more chance, by giving her a bit of rope, of wiping out the whole gang, with the official boys called in later to do the rounding up . . . "

" I see."

" I must admit," went on Drummond, " that I prefer backing greyhounds to backing horses. You can do everything to a dog that you can do to a horse, but he hasn't got a jockey just to add to the uncertainty . . ."

Harlow looked up quickly, startled ; but the reason for Drummond's sudden change of subject was approaching their table carrying four foaming tankards. The waiter withdrew with the empties.

" I must admit," said Drummond with a smile, " that I am prejudiced about Irma : I want to be in on the battle which finally disposes of that lady. I've almost come to feel that her fate is my fate : it's her or me. I might cry my eyes out if somebody else had the privilege of dotting her the final one. However, the point is extremely important : what do you boys think ? "

" You're sure she's got a gang ? " asked Harlow.

" Yes," said both Darrell and Longworth at once.

" There's no doubt of that," said Drummond. " I am informed that a leopard does not change its spots, and the lovely Irma has never changed her fundamental methods. Perhaps she feels sentimental about it : no doubt our late friend Carl Peterson taught her all she knows. She's always had a gang, Mat : usually composed of as pretty a collection of thugs as you're likely to meet in a lifetime . . ."

" Personally," said Darrell quietly, " I think Hugh is right. The official boys are magnificently worthy, but they're a bit heavy handed, and they don't know the odds.

We do. No point in them blundering in and warning her . . . Irma warned is a nasty prospect . . ."

" I'm voting the same way," said Longworth. " The only chance, it seems to me, is for the chaps with local experience—that means us—to undertake the preliminary work—then the others can come in and help in the cleaning up."

They all looked at Harlow.

" This is your country . . . and your woman ! " he laughed. " No doubt you know best."

Drummond looked at him doubtfully.

" I'd like this really unanimous if possible. I'm not convinced that you really agree, Mat . . ."

For a few moments the American hesitated.

" Look here ! " he suggested, " why don't we have a time-limit ? We say nothing to anybody until we are certain that we haven't a chance ourselves. After that we've got to tell what we know: how's that with you ? "

" It suits," said Drummond.

" When's the limit ? " asked Darrell.

" One week after we come back," said Drummond, " just in case she decides to congratulate me . . . she was rash enough to do that once, and it nearly cost her her liberty. Okay, Mat ? "

" You bet."

" And if we should get concrete evidence that she knows the details of the—of our operation, Mat, then of course we've got to inform the authorities at once."

" You're sure she doesn't ? "

" No. But I'm equally uncertain that she does. As a matter of fact, it rather looks as if she doesn't, because if she did, I have a feeling she would have mentioned it—or at any rate dropped a pretty good hint—when she was communicating with me. That would be running true to form, and that's our justification, old chap."

" Good enough."

" Then that's all settled," smiled Drummond, raising his tankard. " This morning's session is at an end. Here's to the *plume de ma tante*."

" *Santé, mon capitaine* . . ."

" Even to my inexpert ear," said Longworth solemnly, " your accent, Hugh, is of the excruciating variety. I should forget all about the plume of your tante if I were you. I should stick to the meaningless, cleft-palatelike noises at which you stand by yourself after the sixth pint . . ."

" Not as soon as that," corrected Darrell, " unless there have been several gins with or without French before the pints."

Drummond smiled at Harlow, who answered the smile.

" That's all fixed," he said, " but the fewer who know about it, the better." He looked at his watch. " I must be off, boys : I've promised to feed a fairy, and then take her to some charity do at the theatre . . ."

" What ! " laughed Darrell. " Five guineas for upper circle standing room only ? "

" It'll only cost me the lunch. The old girl has bought the seats . . ."

" In one breath," complained Longworth, " you refer to her as a fairy, thus raising my hopes, and in the next you call her the old girl thus dashing them to the ground almost before they are born. Make up your mind : which is it ? "

Hugh Drummond laughed.

" Somewhere in between the two : an aunt of Phyllis's . . ."

" Good health to her," said Longworth, " and to you. I shall not ask for an introduction. I am well supplied with my own aunts. How are you off for aunts, Mat ? "

" Not too badly."

" That's a pity," Longworth smiled. " So generous is my nature that I was about to offer you a couple. How about a nice pair of cousins instead ? "

" Blonde ? "

" As you will : I stock them all colours. To-night at the Savoy at eight ? "

" I'd like to . . ."

" Do you trip a measure ? "

"Dance?"

"Yes."

Harlow laughed.

"It depends on the girl . . ." he said, "sometimes she won't trip with me . . ."

"Which seems," said Drummond, leaving them, "neatly to describe the present unco-operative mood of our friend Irma . . ."

XI

PHYLLIS'S AUNT CECILY ENJOYS HERSELF

THEY reached the theatre early : trust Phyllis's aunt Cecily for that ! So early that Drummond was prevented from expending the exorbitant sum demanded by all public places for a glass of red but otherwise unrecognisable port. Arrived there, Drummond was surprised to find that Phyllis's Aunt Cecily had done the charity proud : they had two seats in a box, and not unexpectedly were the first arrivals of what—to judge by the chairs provided —was to be a party of four. Drummond glanced at the programme ; apparently he was not going to suffer the boredom which he usually experienced at such functions, for a sort of variety show had been arranged, and there were one or two well-known comedians on the bill. Drummond suddenly became aware that Phyllis's aunt Cecily was talking to him.

". . . I'm certain you'll love her, Hugh ! " Aunt Cecily leant forward, and suddenly began to talk in that tone of voice which she imagined to be attractively kittenish, but which always reminded Drummond of a rogue elephant. "In fact, I quite hesitated about introducing you to her . . . for Phyllis's sake, I mean ! "

Aunt Cecily laughed, to her own ears, a silvery laugh. Drummond started.

"I'm afraid, Aunt Cecily, I didn't catch the name?"

"The Countess Lilli . . ."

"Lily ? "

"Yes, Lilli."

"The Countess Lily what ? "

"Eh ? " said Aunt Cecily.

"Lily what ? "

Aunt Cecily laughed gaily, her humouring laugh.

"Ha, ha, ha ! " And then suddenly : " What ? "

Hugh Drummond looked at her sharply : surely that half-bottle of claret could not possibly have produced any bemusing result . . . ?

"I said Lily what ? "

"Why ? " asked Aunt Cecily.

Drummond sighed to himself.

"Let's start again," he suggested.

Aunt Cecily found herself laughing gaily once more : it seemed the only thing to do in this extraordinary conversation. She had always felt vaguely ill at ease with this slightly insane relative by marriage, but he seemed to be growing worse with the passage of years. However, if he wanted to play a game . . .

"Ha, ha, ha. Do let's ! " she said gushingly.

"What's her name, Aunt Cecily ? "

"The Countess Lilli."

"Lily ? "

"Yes, dear . . ."

"The Countess . . ." said Drummond slowly and distinctly. "Lily what ? "

"I give it up," said Aunt Cecily generously. "You tell me . . . What ? "

"But I don't know ! " Drummond could not prevent a note of exasperation creeping into his voice. "Lily is a Christian name . . . her last name is . . . what ? "

"Watt ? "

"Eh ? "

"Well, I've never heard of it, if it s," said Aunt Cecily with decision. "All I've ever heard her called is Lilli . . . capital L—i—double l—i . . . like that. And I really ought to know . . . she's been a friend of mine for—let me see—two years at least. Now that I come to think of it, I sent her the cheque for these seats in that name, and addressed the envelope in the same way, and it reached her . . . so that must be right. What on earth made you think her name was Watt ? "

Hugh Drummond felt a strong desire to rush from the box, tearing his hair and biting programme sellers on the way. It seemed the only fitting conclusion to the conversation ; but he resisted the temptation, and smiled at Phyllis's Aunt Cecily.

" I'm so sorry, auntie . . . entirely my mistake. Lilli, you said ? "

" We aren't starting all over again, are we ? " asked Aunt Cecily suspiciously.

" Oh, no ! " Drummond grinned : then he added, mischievously, " Enemy alien ? "

" Oh, my dear boy, no ! " Aunt Cecily seemed shocked. " I know her story, she confided in me once, shortly after we first met. When she was very young, she married an Irishman—of Spanish extraction of course, you can tell that from the name, one of the families that got stranded in Ireland, or something, and made the best of it with the local girls . . ." She paused a moment, a startled look in her eyes : she went on quickly "—married in a church naturally !—Well, her husband was descended from that union, and it was, she assured me, a very good family indeed . . . must have been, because after all, he was a Count. So sad ! he was killed, shortly after the last war, in the hunting field . . . a terrible blow to her, poor girl, as they were very much in love. She's still in love with his memory, obviously . . . because a woman as attractive as she is must have had lots of tempting offers of marriage, and she has remained single . . . I mean a widow. When this war started, she was one of those splendid Irish who did not believe de Valera was doing the right thing and determined that they, at least, wouldn't be dictated to by him. So she came over here and devoted her life to helping the war charities, and she really is wonderful at it ! They say she's collected thousands, literally thousands . . . and, you know, there's a whisper that her name will be in the next honours list ! "

" Wonderful ! " said Drummond.

" Yes, it is. That's just the word . . . wonderful ! But," said Aunt Cecily, with a return of her roguishness, " when you see her, don't forget Phyllis ! Or," she wagged her finger warningly, " I shall have to tell on you ! Family's thicker than romance, you know ! "

Aunt Cecily beamed. She was very pleased with her little joke. Hugh Drummond contrived a smile : he was beginning to wish that Phyllis had not made him promise to look up Aunt Cecily while he was in London. Still, the comedians might make it worth it . . .

The theatre was filling up rapidly : already only a few seats were still vacant.

" Is this one of her shows ? " he asked.

" It is. And you can see what a lot of money it's going to bring in . . ."

Aunt Cecily looked over the edge of the box with a satisfied smile : it was clear that she took almost a possessive interest in the occasion.

Hugh Drummond looked at his watch.

" If she doesn't hurry up," he said, " she's going to be late for her own show . . ."

" She's a dreadfully busy person . . ." began Aunt Cecily, but she never finished her sentence. The orchestra struck up, and it struck up with a vim and an abandon which made Aunt Cecily immediately realise, champion conversationalist though she might be, that she had met her Waterloo. No sentence, no matter how much bellowed, could possibly challenge the brass and the drums. Aunt Cecily set a smile on her face : she was going to enjoy the show in spite of anything that might happen on the stage, and everyone who looked at her was going to know it.

The orchestra stopped as abruptly as it had begun. In the stunned silence which followed, the principal drummer very gently began to roll, the sound increasing in violence until it bid fair to challenge the preceding combined efforts of the orchestra. The curtains swept aside, and a tall and graceful blonde stepped down the stage towards the footlights.

"Oooh!" said Aunt Cecily. "There she is!"

Aunt Cecily started to clap with an energy which was remarkable. Others took it up until it was quite a sizeable round of applause. The blonde on the stage looked up and smiled at Aunt Cecily, who redoubled her efforts, and only reluctantly subsided when she found that she was alone. The blonde began to speak, and the moment she did so, the inevitable coughs and rustlings ceased as if by magic: here, thought Drummond, is undoubtedly a woman with personality.

"I won't keep you a moment," she said in a low voice which nevertheless could perfectly be heard even in the upper circle, "before you enjoy the splendid artists who have so generously given their services to-day in aid of our good cause . . ."

"Hullo!" said Drummond to himself. "I've seen this woman before, somewhere . . ."

". . . but I felt I must thank you all, every one of you," she glanced up at the gallery, "on behalf of my committee and myself, for supporting us so generously. If you want to meet the clever people who are entertaining you, you will find them during the interval, some in the foyer, some in the bar, and . . ." she laughed, a pretty sound "they will willingly autograph your programmes in exchange for a further contribution! Thank you all, thank you very much indeed for coming and helping us to-day!"

The curtain concealed her again, as the audience applauded. The orchestra struck up the signature tune of a well-known comedienne, and the show started.

"Isn't she lovely!"

"Yes," said Drummond. Where on earth had he seen her before?

"I expect she'll be here any minute now!" loudly whispered Aunt Cecily.

"Good."

Hugh Drummond meant it. Quite apart from the

natural pleasure a man takes in the proximity of a lovely lady, a closer inspection might assist his memory . . .

He was not disappointed. She stood for just a second framed in the doorway of the box, certainly a very beautiful figure. And as she stood there, with the light from the passage-way outside playing on her very fair hair, Drummond's thoughts flew back a few days to the lounge of the fashionable hotel where he had committed the blunder of offering Inspector McIver of Scotland Yard a cup of tea. As if to confirm his memory beyond any shadow of doubt, the rotund full Colonel followed her into the box.

Hushed introductions were made by Aunt Cecily. Hugh Drummond made way for the Countess Lilli, and found himself next to the red-tabbed officer. That gentleman took a cigar from his crocodile case and lighted it : he then leant forward, and began puffing into Aunt Cecily's neck.

Drummond decided that the back seats of a theatre box were not the best places to occupy if you wanted to enjoy a show. He could hear all right, but he could see very little : and the comedienne who was so convulsing the audience evidently depended more on her actions and her expressions than on her patter. He made a half-hearted attempt to elongate and twist his neck into an appropriate left bend, but the Colonel's great bulk had established a monopoly on second-row vision. He leant back, lit a cigarette, and idly examined the charitable Countess . . .

Aunt Cecily had been correct in all she said : this woman was extremely attractive if not actually beautiful. Drummond wondered how old she was : she must have been married really very young for—allowing for her fairly free use of cosmetics—her face was still youthful. It was odd that she should have such very dark eyes, but they only added to her beauty. A trifle soft and gentle, perhaps, to be his type, decided Drummond ; but somebody whom the sentimental Algy would have fallen for with a resounding thump. Drummond grinned to himself: how annoyed Algy would be when he heard what he had missed . . .

She certainly knew how to dress: and she certainly was gifted with a natural grace of which she made the most. She was leaning back in her chair—not merely, decided Drummond, to escape the fumes of the Colonel's cigar, but also because in that attitude she obviously would appear particularly decorative to anyone looking up from the stalls. Suddenly she turned towards him.

"Can you see, Captain Drummond?" she whispered.

"Imperfectly!" smiled Drummond.

"Pull your chair up closer . . ."

He did so, and contrived a view of half the stage without becoming too familiar. He became conscious, as well, of a faint but most intriguing perfume: she had it on her hair, no doubt. The comedienne was undoubtedly funny if you could see her . . .

What the devil was that perfume? Something that Phyllis used? No, it was too heavy, too exotic. Yet he knew it, surely? Some woman whom he had known, and been interested in enough to notice it, had certainly used that scent: he couldn't have made a mistake, for normally he was not aware of such things . . . a long time ago, perhaps? Drummond found himself running through a mind's-eye gallery of pre-Phyllis ladies . . .

The comedienne was succeeded by a singer, and then a conjurer who achieved the impossible with impertinent ease.

"I've always heard you were a fast worker, Captain Drummond," very faintly whispered a low voice. "But *really* ! . . ."

Drummond jumped. He realised abruptly that his nose had actually been touching her hair. He looked at her, and saw with relief that she was still, apparently, absorbed in the magician's skill: but he noticed that a little smile was playing about her lips. Well, a little flirtation might enliven the afternoon: he could not offer an apology which could only sound ridiculous.

"What scent do you use?"

He spoke as softly as she had; he saw her smile again.

"*Vol de Nuit.*"

"Guerlain's from Paris?"

"You're very well informed."

"I remember the name. I've been in there buying scent for my wife."

"Don't make excuses."

There was a pause, while the conjurer gave way to another singer. Who on earth had made a habit of using Vol de Nuit . . . ?

"You couldn't get me some, I suppose?" said the soft voice. "Naturally my stock is pre-war and very nearly exhausted . . ."

It took all Drummond's self-control not to jump again: he almost prayed that he had given no sign of his sudden shock. Drummond felt inclined to give himself a stern lecture: such innocent remarks must not disturb him as this one had done. Of course, the Countess could have no idea that she was asking something which in fact might prove perfectly possible within the next few weeks: the bottle she had bought before the war, or more likely that some admirer had presented her with, was nearly done: it was the perfume that long since she had decided really suited her, and if some friend could find another hidden away in some dark drawer, and get it for her . . . well, she would be delighted. Hugh, said Drummond to himself, you've got to be very careful indeed, my boy: none of these nervous—almost guilty— reactions, see!

"I'm afraid it would prove a useless search."

She turned and looked at him for the first time. That rather challenging smile was still in evidence. Drat it, thought Drummond, if you meant to make someone get mad about you, there are very few men who could stand up to it . . . I'm feeling a trifle odd meself!

"Glad you like it, anyway . . ." she said unexpectedly, and turned back towards the stage.

The interval arrived.

"Countess," said Hugh Drummond suddenly. "You know all these artists, I suppose?"

She turned to him and smiled.

" Of course."

" Would you like to come and see how well they are collecting in the foyer ? " He grinned. " As a matter of fact, Aunt Cecily paid for my ticket, so I feel I ought to meet one of them at least—and get my programme signed . . ."

" Certainly, I'll come with you . . . "

She rose. So did the Colonel, hurriedly.

" I'll think I'll . . ." he started.

But Hugh Drummond was ready for him.

" Nice of you to stay and entertain Aunt Cecily," he cut in. " We shan't be long."

The Colonel opened his mouth, and then shut it again without saying what was undoubtedly in his mind. But he gave himself the pleasure of giving Drummond a look calculated to kill instantly.

" Be good ! " chirrupped Aunt Cecily. " Come and sit here, Colonel . . ."

There was nothing he could do about it: the Colonel sat.

It was the conjurer to whom the Countess introduced Drummond. While apparently using both hands to autograph the programme, he achieved a greater result, for he handed back the programme and then Drummond's wallet.

" How much of this may I keep for the cause ? " he asked.

Laughing with the admiring throng, Drummond looked into the wallet. It was empty.

" I'd hate to meet you on a dark night ? " he remarked.

" You'd be much safer. I couldn't see to work ! " the conjurer handed back a few notes. " I've fined you a quid for not keeping your eyes open ! "

Drummond made way for another victim.

" Clever, isn't he ! " suggested the Countess.

" He's a marvel . . . but it's lucky he's honest . . ."

" There's one drawback to that sort of skill," she went on, " he daren't play cards, of course . . . not even with his friends . . ."

"If he won, they'd think he was cheating?"

"Naturally. They just wouldn't be able to help it. How cruel and unfair, when you come to think of it, human nature is . . ."

Hugh Drummond laughed.

"Not merely in human relationships, I'm afraid . . ."

"No, I suppose not." ·

She sighed: the thought seemed really to sadden her. Drummond found himself drawn towards this woman who, so obviously intelligent as well as blessed with beauty, had given up her life to make her contribution towards alleviating the sufferings of the fighting man.

"You do a lot of this work?"

She gave him a little smile.

"I do all that I can. It's so little in the big scheme of things, but I apparently can do it well . . ."

"That's obvious."

"Thank you." She suddenly laughed. "Rich men like . . . well, like your friend the Colonel . . . seem quite to like giving me their money for the boys . . ."

"I'm not in the least surprised . . ."

She gave him another little smile.

"Thank you again."

They were heading back towards the box. Hugh Drummond suddenly made up his mind.

"Countess," he said. "I'm not a rich man, and I'm afraid I'm useless to you, therefore, from the work point of view! But if you'd like to take a holiday for a few hours . . . why not dine with me?"

For a moment she did not reply: in fact she made no sign of having heard him. She was walking just in front of him, and he could not see her face. Perhaps it was because of the fact that she permitted herself the luxury of a silent triumphant little laugh: her lips, just for a flash, bared her lovely white teeth . . .

"I should like to very much. But I'm afraid I have a great many engagements . . . work, of course!"

"Break one . . ."

"Well . . . when would you like me to come?"

" To-night . . . ? "

" To-night ! " she laughed outright. " Captain Drummond, there is no doubt that you really are a fast worker ! I couldn't possibly . . . I'm dining with the Colonel . . ."

They had reached the closed door of the box : Drummond made no move to open it for her.

" D'you mean to say," he said softly, " that you can stand that old dodderer for nearly a whole day ? "

She shrugged her shoulders expressively.

" My charities benefit . . ."

" You're overworking," said Drummond seriously. " You'll have a nervous breakdown if you go on at this pace ! Then where would the charities be ? Even Field-Marshals take a day off once a week . . ."

She smiled to him.

" What can I say ? " she asked.

" Literally anything ! " grinned Drummond. " The strain of this show has given you a racking headache . . . your brother has turned up unexpectedly from the Far East . . . your old mother has developed whooping cough at Woking, and you've got to go and see her . . ."

" Why must it be to-night ? "

" Well," said Drummond. " I may not be in London for long . . . I only come up occasionally . . . as a matter of fact, very occasionally . . ."

" You're leaving London soon ? "

" I may be," said Drummond awkwardly. " I can't be sure. Shall I fetch you at eight ? "

She laughed.

" No. I'll meet you . . . where ? "

For a moment Drummond hesitated. Then he thought of Algy Longworth, and a mischievous light came into his eyes.

" The Savoy ? At eight o'clock . . . no, at eight-fifteen ? "

She nodded. Drummond opened the door for her.

She dressed herself with a great deal of care. She was ready in plenty of time. She put in a telephone call before leaving the hotel.

"Is that Alaric? Good," she spoke softly. "I am dining with *him*, at the Savoy to-night. Never mind how. No, of course it's not foolhardy, but you can take the usual precautions . . . now listen very carefully, Alaric . . . we may be leaving within a week. Understand? Yes, I'll do my best to find out more definitely to-night . . ."

She hung the receiver on its hook. She moved to the mirror: what she saw satisfied her.

As she left the hotel she was smiling.

XII

ALGY LONGWOTRH BECOMES JEALOUS

MAT HARLOW decided that, even allowing for war-time, Algy Longworth's taste in blonde cousins left absolutely nothing to be desired. The pair he had produced were young ladies of quite exceptional charm, full of gaiety and neither at all averse, apparently, to tripping a measure with him. What was more, they both tripped very well indeed, and in effortless unison with his own movements, giving him the impression that he was quite a performer on the ballroom floor. This Harlow knew to be flattery, but it was pleasant enough all the same: and he decided that he was enjoying his evening very much indeed.

Longworth had ordered an admirable meal, and they were drinking champagne. Longworth had ordered it with an abandon which had delighted the heart of the wine waiter, who ever since had been hovering round like a hen looking after its brood. Wondering rather vaguely what the size of his check—no, he was in England now, the bill—was likely to be, and thankful that he was not to have many more evenings so delightfully ruinous in

Longworth's extravagant company, Harlow looked round the crowded room rather curiously noting how many others had gone to the supreme but splendid folly of a magnum of the Widow . . .

There was, he was surprised to find, quite a few tables sporting the ice-bucket and the wired top of champagne, many more than he would have expected. They were tables at which the host was not normally in uniform : evidently business was brisk even in war-time. Harlow had never before visited Carol Gibbon's kingdom, but he had been told about it : and he found himself wondering whether or not it had looked much better when everyone had been in formal evening dress. The women suffered, of course, in these nearly day-time costumes and specially in service dress, but there was something rather attractive about the many varied male uniforms. At any rate, it was a pleasantly gay and carefree scene . . . .

Harlow, who had been lounging in his chair, sat up with a jerk. Could it be . . . ? It indisputably was, and with as attractive a lady as he had set eyes upon in many months . . .

" Algy ! "

" Eh ? " said Longworth, surprised. He was in the middle of telling rather a long and complicated horse story to one of the apparently enraptured blondes.

" Friend of ours over there . . ."

" Really ? " Longworth turned back to the blonde.
" Well, as I was saying . . ."

" With something rather special. Is it Phyllis ? "

Longworth started.

" Phyllis ? "

" Yes. Is it ? "

" Where ? "

Longworth, who was sitting with his back to the space reserved for dancing, wheeled round and stared at the slowly gyrating throng.

" Not dancing at the moment. At that table for two in the far corner . . ."

Longworth looked in the direction indicated. He

stared motionless for so long that Harlow began to wonder if to break the spell it would be necessary to give him a push, like one sometimes did to a setter frozen into a point.

But just before he decided to do so Longworth spoke.

" The . . . the . . . the . . ." he said, selecting a word " the snake ! "

Harlow could not help laughing.

" I gather it isn't Phyllis ? "

" It is not."

" Anyone you know ? "

" It is someone I am going to know," said Longworth with decision, " and pretty soon at that ! "

" Who on earth are you talking about ? " inquired one of the cousins suspiciously.

" You're too young to know," said Longworth promptly. " Sheer bravado, bringing her here . . ."

" Who ? Me ? " asked the other cousin, in a scandalised voice.

" Not you, ducky," Longworth spoke without hesitation.

" I'm always thinking of you, but not so always as all that. Let's dance and make faces at him ? "

" Who ? "

" That large man over there with a face like the back of a good-humoured rock. No wonder he's looking good-humoured . . ."

He rose, and the girl followed him on to the already crowded dance-floor. They inserted themselves into the couples, and disappeared.

" Shall we dance and make faces at him too ? " asked the other cousin, as if it was the most natural thing to do in all the world.

" Yes," said Harlow rising.

" You'll have to point the target out to me," she informed him, and added : " As a matter of fact, I can make the most awful faces . . ."

" I don't believe it ! " said Harlow gallantly.

" Just you wait and see ! "

Harlow steered her with great difficulty, and at the

cost of several black looks and one or two other minor collisions, diagonally across the room until he had caught up with Longworth and his partner. He took up a tactical position, following just behind them : he was not quite certain of the form, and did not want actually to start anything although he was game to follow anywhere . . . besides he was a trifle alarmed at his partner's enthusiasm at the prospect of contorting her pretty features . . .

To the observer, Hugh Drummond was behaving like the perfect swain. His eyes scarcely ever left his fair companion's face, he leant towards her as he engaged her in chatty conversation, and he was solicitous to a degree that she should have everything her lightest fancy indicated. The Countess, for her part, seemed flatteringly interested in him : she admitted to having heard a good deal about his exploits, but she wanted to know much more at first hand. And what had he been doing during the war ? Something very secret, she supposed, that no one would ever know about . . . but if he could give her a little hint, she would not tell a living soul. Vegetating in the Home Guard ? Now, really, he must not think her as simple as all that ! A man like he was, and with his record . . . Never mind, she quite understood : one had to be so careful about what one said, nowadays, and—archly—after all, they did not know each other very well yet, anyway . . .

Why did he come to London so seldom then ? Was that really true ? They seemed to have received him here to-night as if he were an old friend . . . Oh, the credit of a misspent youth ! Well, well . . . useful at times, eh ? she had heard a table at short notice was almost an impossibility, and this was a very good table. When was he coming up again ? She would so like him to meet some of her friends . . . he really didn't know ? Oh, come . . . surely he had some sort of idea ? She'd be so pleased to arrange a little cocktail party . . .

Perhaps in a few weeks ? Would he promise to let her know . . . ? Splendid, she'd look forward to that. Oh, by the way, she had a cocktail party fixed for Thursday week, ten days from now—a very big charity party, and she was very short of help . . . could he possibly manage to assist her . . . he did not expect to be in London ? What a shame !

Now, tell her more about his adventures . . . there'd been a woman rather prominently concerned, wasn't she right ? Someone who had made a miraculous escape from the police. Of course she was interested, she really wanted to know . . . No, a dance later on would be lovely, but wouldn't he tell her about the woman first ? She really was enthralled . . . it was so seldom that one could talk over the sort of thing one read about, with the man who himself had lived through the thrills . . .

Hugh Drummond suddenly decided to let himself go. He told the story extremely well, and he did not spare his great opponent Irma Peterson. Never before had he recited any of the adventures which he had experienced : it was not his way. But something made him do it that night, and do it with a zest which surprised even himself. He told of the fierce feline cunning and cruelty displayed by this woman who outwardly was so very attractive, of her passionate and absolutely unscrupulous search after money, of her despicable lust for power. With her brains and her beauty, concluded Drummond, she might perhaps have been a very great lady and done a very great deal of good in the world : but she had deliberately chosen selfishly to pillage all about her, regardless of whose property that which she coveted might be, determined only that she herself should want for nothing, determined to satisfy her dreadful pleasure in imposing pain on others . . .

When he had finished, there was a long silence. Drummond looked at his fair companion with interest : he was astonished to see that she was looking straight in front of her, apparently absorbed in memories : her eyes were fixed on the orchestra, but it was obvious that she was looking far beyond them, lost in a brown study.

It was scarcely the sort of reception which he had expected; she had asked for the story, but it seemed to have had an odd effect on her. Rather abashed, and mildly annoyed that his powers as a story-teller had held her so little, Drummond lighted a cigarette. But he determined also that he would finish what he had to say: dash it, she had asked for it: she was going to get it to the bitter end . . .

There was only one possible explanation, said Drummond, for the horribly warped mind of this caricature of a woman. When he had first met her, she had passed as the daughter of one Carl Peterson, truly a fiend incarnate if ever there was one. He did not believe she was the daughter of this man: far more likely to have been his mistress, possibly his wife. But two things were certain: she had been both utterly under his domination, and devoted to him. There could be no doubt about that whatsoever, and there could be no doubt either that she had been grossly influenced by him. He, Hugh Drummond, was happy to be able to say that he had been responsible for the obliteration of this devil . . .

Drummond imperceptibly started: he could not believe the evidence of his own eyes. He stared down at the table, at her slender right hand: and looked away abruptly as soon as he realised what he was doing. But she had noticed nothing: he glanced at her face, and saw that apparently she was still absorbed in her brown study . . .

Yes, said Drummond firmly, watching her very closely as he spoke, he, Hugh Drummond, could claim and was delighted to claim that he was responsible for hunting Carl Peterson until he had got him where he had wanted him, caught like a rat in a trap! He, Hugh Drummond, could claim that he had rid the world of one of the greatest pests with which it had ever been infested! He, Hugh Drummond, was entirely responsible for the death of . . .

She broke in abruptly: her voice was as gentle as ever.

"Captain Drummond," she said, "something very odd

is happening. Two couples on the dance floor seem to have gone quite mad ! "

It was not she who had been compelled to pull herself together : it was far more Drummond, who had worked himself up to a pitch of excitement which seemed excessive merely at the recollection of a master criminal. All the time that he had been speaking, however, he had been surreptitiously watching the fingers of that right hand . . . He managed to control the turmoil of his feelings, however, without apparent effort. He looked in the direction in which she was looking : and he found himself starting at the contorted and rapidly changing faces of Algy Longworth and a normally pretty little blonde. What their expressions were intended to convey he had no idea, but they were giving a very fair imitation of loopy rubber-featured Red Indians in the middle of the most hectic spasm of a war-dance.

Just behind came Mat Harlow with another blonde, both doing their best to out spasm Longworth and his partner. The crowd on the dance floor moved them on. Drummond laughed, and looked back towards the fair lady. She had a puzzled expression on her face, and was watching him enquiringly.

" It's a crazy friend of mine aptly called Algy, and another pal whom I didn't know was quite so mad . . . I can only think that they are only attempting to register strong disapproval."

" Disapproval ? Why ? "

" Because I've brought such an attractive and charming person here all on my own, and not shared her with them." She smiled.

" Thank you . . . very prettily put."

" Come on, let's dance . . . ! " suggested Drummond.

He was watching her closely, and he could have sworn that he saw her shudder.

" No . . ."

She seemed to be searching for some excuse . . .

" Don't you like dancing ? "

" I . . . oh, yes, I do, normally . . . but I'm afraid,

Captain Drummond you were prophetic when you were suggesting excuses to be used on the Colonel . . ."

" I don't quite understand . . . ? "

She smiled, a trifle wanly.

" I've got that headache you thought of . . ."

" Oh, I'm so sorry." It's palpably an excuse, said Drummond to himself. He leant forward towards her : was it his imagination, or did she recoil . . . ?

" Can I do anything ? "

" I'm afraid not." She seemed to make up her mind. " Would you think it dreadfully rude of me if I asked you to take me home ? You see, when I get one of these headaches, I know from experience there is only one thing to do.

" Which is . . . ? "

" Go to bed and sleep it off."

" I'll get the bill at once . . ." said Drummond.

He paid. He followed her out. As they went, they passed the table where Longworth and his party were sitting. Hugh Drummond apparently paid no attention to them : he followed her out of the restaurant . . .

· · · · ·

" Hullo ! " said Longworth, " I do believe we've driven them out. Serves the old boy darned well right, trying to keep a Thing like that to himself ! Suppose she thought we were too vulgar for words . . . ! "

They watched Hugh Drummond approach in the wake of his fair lady : they watched him pass . . .

" Odd ! " said Harlow to the blonde on his right. " Do they keep birds here for local colour ? I could have sworn I heard the hoot of an owl ! "

" The hoot of an owl ! " echoed the cousin. " You're crazy ! "

" It was very soft, but . . ." Harlow happened to glance at Longworth as he was speaking : his voice died away in astonishment. That worthy was staring after Drummond with his mouth open, but with a curiously intense expression in his eyes : his body was rigid, his hands were on the table, apparently ready at a moment's notice to push it away.

"What on earth . . ." he began, but he got no further.

Algy Longworth was on his feet.

"Sorry, girls," he said quietly, a strange, new authority in his voice which Harlow would never have expected. "It's make your own way home to-night . . ."

"What ! "

"You heard. Millions of apologies and all that, and we'll make it up to you some other time . . ."

"Really ! " duetted two scandalised voices.

"You can finish the bubbly . . . we won't be back. Don't worry, I'll pay on the way out . . . So long . . ."

He was already starting to move.

"Come on, Mat ! " he said. "We're busy . . ."

Bewildered and speechless, Harlow followed him rapidly out of the restaurant.

XIII

A COUNTESS IS COUNTED OUT

As they left the restaurant, Harlow saw that Hugh Drummond was coming back towards them. He handed Harlow his cloakroom ticket.

"Quick, Mat, please : get my hat and coat while I have a word with Algy . . ."

It never occurred to Mat Harlow to hesitate even for a second. While he was impatiently waiting for the leisurely and distinguished individual to exchange Drummond's garments for the ticket, he had time to note this fact not altogether without surprise. Harlow would never have described himself as a born fetcher and carrier : he was by nature and practice far more likely to have somebody else to do the fetching and carrying for him. Harlow smiled to himself : he certainly had to hand it to this fellow Hugh Drummond for personality, and he found himself glad that he was so much a member of the team, and clearly accepted as such, that he was given orders by the leader which he obeyed instantly and without question.

Mat Harlow was grinning as he returned with the hat and coat, his mood was not only one of pleasurable excitement, but he had just remembered the expressions on the faces of the cousins . . .

He found Drummond alone.

"Thanks a lot, Mat," said Drummond, taking his belongings. "You'll find Algy telephoning . . . it's up the stairs and sharp round to the left—then on your right. Scoot will you!" Drummond was smiling. "I don't want her to get a glimpse of you, because you're committed as a pal of mine . . . and she'll be out any moment now . . ."

Once again Mat Harlow obeyed orders unhesitatingly: he found the experience exhilarating. There was something about the way he did it that made a man glad to do just as Drummond told him, and which gave a lot of confidence. Harlow began to understand the complete unquestioning trust which both Darrell and Longworth so willingly accorded to Hugh Drummond.

He discovered Longworth busily telephoning in a glass box. Waiting for him, he found that he was in a good position to observe, without himself being observed, the stairs by which Drummond and his fair companion must leave the hotel. There they went . . . a particularly good looking couple, thought Harlow. Drummond with his broad shoulders but still slimmish figure, the woman graceful and beautifully clothed. What could there be about this woman that had caused all this sudden and totally unexpected fuss? She was not known to Longworth: he had said so himself, rather ruefully! So what on earth could it all be about . . .?

He watched Drummond and the mysterious lady disappear through the revolving doors of the lounge. As he stood, he suddenly found Longworth beside him.

"What now?"

"Well," said Longworth, "we've got a conference on

at Peter's flat : I've just warned him. As a matter of fact, we've probably got time to go and weave a beautiful fairy story to the blondes, but, honestly Mat, I don't think I dare ! I'll make our excuses to-morrow, when time the great healer has had an opportunity to get to work. Let's walk to the flat . . . we probably wouldn't be able to get a taxi, anyhow, without waiting for ages . . ."

" Okay."

They collected their coats, not without a certain apprehension about meeting the blonde cousins : but these two were evidently still in the restaurant.

" Following my suggestion about the wine, no doubt ! " laughed Longworth, " and vituperating like bingo, I shouldn't wonder ! "

They walked most of the way in silence. Towards the end, Longworth suddenly spoke.

" Congratulations, Mat ! You're learning very quickly : matter of fact, you might be said to have learnt ! "

" What d'you mean, Algy ? "

" We," said Longworth slowly, embarking on about the only completely serious speech that Harlow was destined ever to hear from him, " who have been in things with Hugh, quite a lot of occasionally thoroughly unpleasant things, obey him instantaneously—it's the only safe way. You did to-night : well done, not so easy at first time of asking ! "

" I was a bit surprised myself ! "

Longworth laughed shortly.

" And secondly, we don't ask questions . . . what he says goes in a big way with us. You didn't ask any questions in spite of the wildest provocation. Point number two in your favour."

" Thanks," said Harlow. " I admit I was tempted . . ."

" Of course. As soon as we get inside, ask away to your heart's content until Hugh comes : then it's the old boy who will do the talking . . ."

" I understand."

They found the house in which Darrell possesed a flat. They mounted to the second floor, and knocked on his door. Peter Darrell, in pyjamas, immediately opened it to them.

"What's up?" he asked, as he made way for them to enter.

It was quite a relief to Harlow to find someone else who had not the faintest idea of what was happening, but Longworth did not answer until the door was closed behind them.

"Scene : Savoy Restaurant. At one table, yours truly and Mat with a couple of twoosies. At another Hugh with a Queen twoosy, a blonde to end all blondes, but a magnificently divine one for all that. Yours very sincerely is undoubtedly touched by the green and knobbly hand of jealousy, and makes up his mind to rag the stand-offish Drummond. Faces are made at him from the ball-room floor. Very shortly afterwards Hugh and his goddess depart. They pass our table on their way out. Hugh, out of the corner of his mouth and without batting one eyelid, gives the owl signal . . ."

"What!" Darrell sat up with a jerk as the word escaped him.

"It was even as I have said. Yours faithfully leaps to his feet, seizes Mat, leaves the two twoosies goggling, gaping and gasping for breath and wildly searching for a few pungent words, and follows Hugh from the room . . ."

"Go on . . ." said Darrell.

"I can't," replied Longworth. "We had a brief moment with Hugh alone. He told Mat and me to meet him here, and to warn you. He said he'd be along as soon as he could make it and we weren't to drink ourselves silly before he arrived. Then he vanished into the black-out with the twoosie-woosie."

"Who was she?"

"Peter!" said Longworth, shocked. "D'you think I'd tell you even if I knew?"

Darrell turned to Harlow with a smile that seemed to say, look what I've got to put up with! But Mat Harlow had one or two questions he wanted to put on his own account.

"Touching on this owl signal . . ." he began.

They both looked at him with a grin.

"Yes?" said Longworth. "Touching it . . . incidentally an extremely difficult thing to do . . ."

"Shut up, Algy!" Darrell turned to Harlow. "I gather you know nothing about the . . . the hoot of an owl?"

Harlow shook his head.

"Well," said Darrell, seriously. "The hoot of an owl means the hell of a lot to Algy and me . . . and it has done for years wherever Hugh Drummond is about. You see, long ago—just after the last war, to be exact—when Drummond first got on to the track of the Petersons, and we had a fairly lively time one way and another for a spell, it became necessary for us to have some sort of rallying call. Probably because Hugh is by no means a first class animal mimic, and the hoot of an owl was the only sound he could imitate tolerably well, that signal was adopted. Since then it has, on very many occasions, proved extremely useful. What you've got to remember now, as one of us—is that wherever and whenever you hear it, you drop whatever you may be doing instantaneously, and you trot off in the direction from which you heard it—using a certain circumspection, of course—to poke your nose into whatever's going on. In short, it means you're wanted, quick. Got it?"

"Yes," said Harlow. "Thanks."

"Not at all," said Longworth. "Any other time, just ask me. I'll keep you informed in half the verbiage . . ."

A well aimed cushion propelled by Darrell put a full stop to his sentence. At exactly the same moment they heard a knock on the door. Darrell opened it, to admit Hugh Drummond.

"Evening, boys . . ."

Longworth examined him closely.

"What?" he said, apparently slightly pained. "No powder on the lapels? Not even one blonde hair caressing the collar?"

"Sorry to disappoint you, Algy!" Drummond smiled.

" Nothing like that at all. Gather round, me hearties . . . ! "

They obeyed him at once. Drummond came to rest in a big armchair, the others grouped themselves around him. They waited for him to speak. He did not do so until he had lit a cigarette.

" D'you remember," he started thoughtfully, " in the club this morning, when I was bemoaning the disappearance of our dear Irma ? " He did not wait for an answer. " Well . . . I'm happy to say the lady has turned up again, alive and kicking ! "

" No ! " said Longworth ecstatically.

" Yes ! " laughed Drummond. " As large as life, although under a new colour. Rather a decorative colour, as a matter of fact . . ."

" Your . . . blonde ? " asked Harlow.

" Don't be ridiculous ! " said Algy. " Our sweet Irma isn't at all like that ! She's . . ."

" Mat is right, Algy ! " interrupted Drummond. " At least, I'm practically certain he is . . ."

" But . . . but," expostulated Longworth. " Irma is as dark as sin . . ."

" Don't be silly, Algy," said Darrell a trifle irritably " black into white is only a matter of an hour or two with any woman . . ."

" Yes, but . . . you haven't seen her ! " Longworth was comical in his amazement. " Damn it, this girl's got a straight nose . . . a beautiful straight nose. Irma's was lovely too, but it had a definite suspicion of old Rome . . ."

" I'm not surprised at your astonishment, Algy ! " broke in Drummond. " As a matter of fact Peter, the Countess Lilli . . ."

" Who ? "

" That's the name she's using now. The Countess Lilli is about as unlike Irma Peterson as you can well imagine : figure, natural grace, and lovely clothes, yes . . . everything else entirely different. As for this nose question, Algy, you're right, of course—but just as black to white is only a matter of an hour or two, so Roman to straight is only a matter of a week or two in the hands of a clever plastic surgeon. So you can't stand on that . . ."

"Well, I'll be dashed!" said Longworth, obviously already considerably dashed. "I simply can't believe it!" He thought for a moment. "But Hugh . . . what about her voice? She couldn't have fooled you over that!"

"D'you remember," Drummond asked him, "some years ago a certain missionary was visiting London, with his delightful daughter?"

"Peterson and Irma," said Darrell promptly.

"That's who they turned out to be. Peterson gave himself away to me that evening, but Irma could have got away with it forever!"

"Ye-es . . ." said Longworth doubtfully.

"That girl," Drummond spoke with decision, "is a consummate actress. Her voice, when Irma is Irma, is low, attractive, but with an undercurrent of determination and—and something less pleasant . . . which sometimes nearly frightens one. To-day, the voice of the Countess Lilli is almost too soft and gentle—all sweetness and honey. The change is well within our Irma's histrionic powers . . ."

"There's something more concrete which has made you make up your mind, no doubt?" said Harlow.

Hugh Drummond grinned.

"Thanks, pal. Yes, there is . . ."

He paused for a moment, deep in thought. When he spoke it was slowly and as if he were relishing the recollection.

"I picked her up," he said, "at the charity show Phyllis's Aunt Cecily took me to this afternoon. She was running it, this Countess Lilli : she's apparently extremely prominent in charity organisations, so much so that her name was a good bet for the next honours list . . ."

"Was?" It was Darrell who spoke.

"If I'm right, was is the correct word. Something made me start a mild flirtation with her, probably that chemical affinity which makes one sometimes do such extraordinary things . . . if you remember, I've always had a weakness for Irma . . ."

"Which," said Darrell with mock severity, "she's frequently used to her own advantage."

"However that may be," continued Drummond, "I persuaded her to dine with me : it seemed flatteringly easy, but now I realise what huge fun it must have been to her, feeling secure in her Countess impersonation. I took her to the Savoy, because I knew Algy was there, and I thought I would tease him a trifle . . ."

"You certainly succeeded ! " laughed Harlow.

"For quite a time," went on Drummond, "we talked pleasantly of this and that. Then, suddenly, I got suspicious for the first time : not in any way suspicious of what I now believe to be the truth, but just vaguely suspicious. I got the impression I was being pumped ; that my fair companion was much too interested in how long I expected to remain in London . . ."

Harlow sat up a little in his chair.

"She got off the subject, rather reluctantly I thought, when I think she saw I was getting a little uncomfortable. And then she started something which must have been sheer, unadulterated joy to her : she got *me* talking of *our* previous tussles. She led me along like a child : she professed great interest in the woman she said she had read about." Drummond laughed, a gay sound. "Well, chaps, something made me pitch it hot and strong, something to which I shall always be grateful. Something inside me made me tear up Irma properly, in really most ungallant terms, and . . . *and she didn't like it !* I don't know what she expected me to say, but what I did say did something to her, and she couldn't take it. And still I didn't guess the truth ! Anyone got a light ? "

Drummond lit another cigarette from Harlow's lighter.

"Then I started in on old Carl Peterson. She was looking at the orchestra, but really out beyond them into the blue. I happened to glance at the table as I was speaking, and I saw her hand resting on it . . ."

He stopped.

"Carl's trick ? " It was Longworth who had spoken, almost involuntarily in a hoarse whisper.

Drummond nodded.

"That benevolent old missionary all over again. The middle finger tapping a tattoo on the table cloth. A mannerism, no doubt, picked up from him, which was his weakness, in moments of stress he just couldn't help himself. I am quite certain she had no idea that she was doing it."

"Oh!" said Longworth. "Go on . . .?"

"Frankly," said Drummond, "it shook me. I nearly gave away the whole thing by stopping in the middle of a sentence. But I just managed to make myself go on talking normally. Only . . . other little things—little things she had said—flashed back into my mind and assumed a new importance."

Extravagantly, he crushed out his half-smoked cigarette.

"In the theatre, I had noticed the perfume she was using. A very lovely scent. Vol de Nuit from Guerlains of Paris : it suited her to perfection. When I remarked on it, she said it was the end of her pre-war stock : could I, by any chance, get her any more? An innocent enough request, probably, but just possibly a challenge? At any rate, it mildly alarmed me, but I put it down to my own sensitiveness about any mention of France at the moment. But, if by any chance she did know, then her interest in the date of my departure from London became something of major importance. And taken altogether with the undoubted fact that Irma knew of the offer which was to be made to me, and had apparently done her best to prevent me accepting it . . . well, the circumstantial evidence was piling up in support of that tapping finger ! "

"Oh, boy !" said Longworth, still in his hoarse whisper. "Yes? What happened then ? "

"I decided to apply another test," continued Drummond with a smile. "Whatever one may say about Irma—and one can say plenty—you can't take away from her an astonishing devotion to Carl Peterson, and a tremendous faithfulness to his memory . . . Irma must have loved him much more than most women love men. So I began to boast . . . horribly. I told her that I alone was responsible for Peterson's death, that I took a very great pride in that fact, that I was delighted to be able to think that it was I who had rid the world of such an unsavoury character. The finger went on beating that sinister little tattoo. Then, having laid it on as thick as I could—I owe you two boys an apology for having pinched all the credit! —I leant towards her and suggested a dance . . . "

" Good Lord! Why? " asked Longworth.

" Well," said Drummond guiltily, " was it likely that—if this was really Irma and feeling as she does—she would be prepared to tolerate the physical proximity as a dancing partner of the man who gloried in the destruction of her idol? She reacted just as I expected she would. She made an excuse—headache or something—and asked to be taken home. It was more than she had bargained for: the evening which was to have been such a triumph for her—leading old Hugh up the garden path right to the gate—had turned the wrong way: she just couldn't take it! "

" Then," said Harlow, " you summoned us! "

" Yes. The sooner you were all up to date the better."

" What did you do with her? "

" Took her home to her hotel."

" In a taxi? " asked Longworth.

" Yes."

" Any further tests? " persisted Longworth, " As to proximity, I mean?"

" I can assure you," said Drummond, " they were quite unnecessary. She sat as far wedged into her corner as possible . . ."

" You left her there . . . in the hotel? "

" Yes."

Mat Harlow cleared his throat awkwardly.

" Of course," he said, " you people know best. You've had experience of this woman—if she is the woman—and I haven't. But was it wise—allowing that the Countess is really your Irma—to leave her alone in the hotel? I mean oughtn't we to have her arrested on suspicion, or something? "

"Sorry, Mat," Drummond was smiling apologetically. "I've been a trifle inaccurate, I left her there, but not until I had communicated with Inspector McIver of Scotland Yard, and was satisfied that his minions had her under observation. As a matter of fact, he'll be coming round any moment now to bring final proof."

"Proof?" asked Darrell. "Whether she's really Irma or not?"

"Yes."

"And how," asked Longworth, "is our worthy but somewhat thick-skulled friend going to settle that burning question for us?"

"Don't be rude about Mac!" said Drummond, "he's frequently done us proud!"

"Yes, but fairly slowly . . ."

"Anyway, this time it's pretty mechanical—just a technical job."

"What do you mean?"

"When we reached the hotel," said Drummond, "the Countess, in getting out of the taxi, most unfortunately dropped her handbag. I helped her again to pick it up . . ."

"Again?"

It was Darrell who asked the question.

"Yes. You see, I'm afraid I had also assisted her in dropping it—just a tiny sharp push, which might have been caused by anything, in the darkness. She thanked me prettily when I had collected the strewn contents with the aid of my torch. Then she said good night and went up to her suite. I rang up old Mac immediately and when he arrived I gave him the little mirror I had so carelessly omitted to return to her. It struck me as the best thing I could collect which would be bound to have her finger prints, because it had a shiny back . . ."

"Well done, Hugh!" said Darrell quietly.

"Mac," said Drummond, "should be round any minute now, with the result of the comparison—the Countess's and those in the official collection which we know belong to Irma."

" There's just one thing," said Harlow, " I seem to have read somewhere that even finger-prints can be changed now . . . by those plastic experts you referred to . . . ? "

" No," said Drummond. " You can obliterate the print from the end of the fingers . . . but that leaves rather a mess from which the Countess's fingers do not suffer. You can't change the actual print."

" That's good to know," smiled Harlow.

They had to wait longer than Drummond had expected, however, before Inspector McIver showed up at the flat. In fact, they were nearly at the end of their patience when at last a car drove up outside, and a cheerful whistling as he mounted the stairs heralded the Inspector's entry. Darrell let him in and Harlow was introduced.

" You can speak freely," Drummond told him, " Mat Harlow is our new boy . . . he's one of us . . . "

" I'm not at all sure I can speak freely in front of any of you . . ." announced the Inspector, but he had a twinkle in his eye.

" Why not ? "

Inspector McIver laughed.

" The military have taken a hand," he said. " I just mentioned the matter to them—said you, Captain, had been in touch with me about it—it's a matter of form, these days, we work very closely together as you may know, and anything at all unusual, well, they like to be in the picture, see—they've taken a big interest in this one . . ."

" Was I right, Inspector ? " asked Drummond.

" In the past," grinned McIver, " I've said yes too often, for my personal pride, to that question, sir. But the answer is ' yes ' again."

" It's the same woman ? "

" Without a shadow of doubt."

" Oh, Irma ! " said Drummond under his breath. " How you must have enjoyed yourself this afternoon ! and when you set out this evening . . . but am I going to laugh last . . . ? "

" Known as Irma Peterson, wanted for every sort of high-sounding felony, and also for . . . murder ! "

The word murder sounded magnificent as McIver pronounced it.

"However," he concluded regretfully, "they won't let me arrest her!"

"Why ever not?" asked Darrell.

"Well, Mr. Darrell . . ." the Inspector spoke slowly: his eye was on Algy Longworth who was busy with a bottle by the sideboard.

"Have a spot, Mac?"

"That's very kind of you, Mr. Longworth." The Inspector accepted gratefully. "Don't mind if I do . . . cold night outside . . ."

"Why won't they let you arrest her, Mac?" asked Drummond quietly.

"They say where she is there are others. And they seem to be interested in her pals—apparently she's been going about a lot with service men—very senior service men in some cases . . . apparently they've had their eye on her for some little time, and now they know who she is it's quite excited them."

"Not such fools as they look, eh, Mac?"

"I never said they were fools!" the Inspector defended himself stoutly. "Not even that they looked fools. Don't go and put words into my mouth, Captain!"

Drummond laughed gaily: baiting the ever rising Inspector was a weakness with him.

"I'm sorry you're disappointed, Mac!" he said, "but personally I'm delighted you're not to be allowed to wreak your fell designs upon her . . . not to-night, at any rate.'

Harlow had been watching him speak.

"Why?" he asked.

Hugh Drummond looked at him and smiled.

"Because," he said slowly, "she's coming to see me—for a tête-à-tête—in this very flat, to-morrow afternoon. You see, she wants to fix the actual date—perhaps even the hour—of our departure. As for me, I should very much like to know what she's really up to . . . I'm looking forward to it: it really should be great fun . . .

But that was all they got out of him that night.

XIV

HUGH DRUMMOND FENCES WITH A LADY

To the man observing from a window on the far side of the street, all that happened at the hour appointed was that a taxi drew up outside the house. From it stepped a particularly glamorous lady, she went straight in by the door. The only slightly unusual feature was that she addressed no word to the driver, who automatically stopped his engine, lit a pipe, pulled out a paper and started to peruse it. Either he was accustomed to driving this lady, and knew her habits : or he had been warned that he would have to wait.

The glamorous lady mounted to the second floor, as she had been informed she would have to do, and knocked on the door. Hugh Drummond himself opened it for her.

" Countess ! I scarcely dared hope you would be so punctual ! "

She smiled as she entered.

" A male weakness of mine ! "

" An unusual and delightful one ! "

He helped her to take off her magnificent mink coat.

" There's not much choice, but where would you like to sit ? "

Drummond noticed that she chose the chair with her back to the light from the window. He laughed to himself : she was welcome to that advantage, if she wished it.

" I do hope you're feeling better ? "

" Much, thanks . . ."

" Headache quite gone ? "

" Absolutely," she smiled to him. " I was very sorry, Captain Drummond, to spoil such a pleasant evening . . . but I really couldn't help myself."

" My dear lady ! " Drummond smiled to her in return. " I understand perfectly. Of course I was sorry, but it just couldn't be helped ! "

"It's nice of you to take it that way . . ."

There was a pause. He offered her a cigarette, and lit it for her: he lighted one himself. In spite of himself, Hugh Drummond was compelled to admit that this woman, no matter how much evil he knew about her, was confoundedly attractive.

"It's nice of you to come to-day. I know how busy you must be . . ."

"I'm afraid," she said, "I can't stay very long. It really was rather difficult to fit this visit into my afternoon . . ." She smiled at him again, a smile which—said Drummond to himself—would have given the impressionable Algy a rush of blood to the head. "But you were so insistent on wanting to see me, that I felt I really couldn't refuse, specially after the way I behaved last night."

"I hope that wasn't the only reason . . .?"

She did not answer him: but she glanced at him shyly and left him to interpret the glance just as he wished. It was a skilful piece of acting.

Hugh Drummond was enjoying himself hugely. So must she be, he thought to himself, secure in her certainty that he had not the slightest idea of her true identity. But how he would laugh when he would be able to tell her that all along he knew that the Countess Lilli was no other than his old friend Irma ! Well, not quite all along . . . she had most successfully fooled him for several hours : but that was not an unconscionable time when up against an opponent of her calibre. No doubt she was laughing now, up that pretty sleeve of hers, thoroughly enjoying making such a complete ass of Hugh Drummond . . .

"What did you want to see me about ? "

She brought him back to earth with a bump. He looked at her, and saw that she was watching him closely. There was a slightly questioning look in her dark eyes, as if she were trying to read his thoughts. Darned lucky, said Drummond to himself, that she can't know what's in my mind . . .

"I was anxious, of course, to see you again as soon as possible . . ."

She smiled.

" Was that so important that you insist I should come on the very next day ? "

" Without question. But there was a more definite reason."

" Which is ? "

Hugh Drummond sat down, facing her.

" You can help me, Countess, if you will," he said seriously. " D'you remember last night, talking of a certain woman—one Irma Peterson ? "

" Of course, I do ! " she laughed. " You were most gallant about her, if I remember rightly . . ."

So it rankled . . . ! Excellent . . .

" Well, I'm doing rather a ticklish job at the moment . . ."

" Home Guarding ? "

" You were right about that ! " said Drummond confidentially, " but of course I rely on you not to tell a soul . . ."

" Of course ! I quite understand . . . How can I help ? "

" By your obvious knowledge of human nature," continued Drummond impressively, " and in particular female human nature . . ."

She laughed.

" Is there so much difference ? "

" I'm inclined to think there is. Anyway, you have another asset, if you'll forgive me for putting it that way . . ."

" What is that ? "

" You know everybody who is anybody in London."

" What has all this," she asked, " to do with Irma Peterson ? "

" Just this." Drummond spoke in a low voice, as if he were imparting a very secret piece of knowledge. " That woman is about, loose in London somewhere. And I am disturbed to think that she knows something about . . . well, about my plans for the future."

" Your ticklish job ? "

" Yes."

" How on earth could she know that ? "

" I can't answer that," said Drummond slowly.

" You won't or you can't ? "

" I can't ! " said Drummond truthfully. " I wish to goodness I could ! But I've got proof that she does know : you see, she was aware—before I was—that the job would be offered to me, and she did her level best to prevent me taking it on . . ."

" Goodness ! Why ? "

" Well . . ."

" I'm sorry ! " She spoke quickly. " I shouldn't have asked you that ! Of course she didn't want the job well done, and you were the ideal person to do it . . . isn't that it ? "

" Grossly exaggerated, but something of the sort, I suppose . . ."

" You're very modest, Captain Drummond, for a man of your achievements." Then she added lightly : " I like modest men . . ."

Oh, lord : said Drummond to himself, I must never leave Algy alone with her for a fraction of a minute . . .

Aloud he continued :

" Then she tried a spot of mild violence . . ."

" What ! "

" Oh, very mild . . . for her. I told you she was a dangerous animal. All she did was to try to teach me a lesson, but it didn't come off. As a matter of fact, what with my peculiar nature, it only made up my mind for me . . . the wrong way, from her point of view ! "

He laughed : she laughed very heartily with him. She seemed to find the thought very amusing : well, he had to admit she accepted what must be rather a bitter pill extremely well . . .

" And then . . ? "

" Nothing. That's what's worrying me. She's disappeared off the face of the earth No manifestations whatsoever . . ."

" How disappointing ! "

"It's worse than that!" went on Drummond. "Frankly, it's got a bit on my nerves. You see, she, she warned me that things would happen to me—very unpleasant things—if I persisted in this business. But . . . nothing at all has happened. No sign of her hand anywhere. It's rather disturbing."

"It's very nice of you to tell me all this," said the fair lady suddenly, "and I appreciate your confidence. But I don't see how I can help you, much as I should like to . . .?"

"You can help me in two ways." Drummond spoke very earnestly. "From your knowledge of female human nature, you can tell me why you think she's done this disappearing act: that's the first way. Secondly, you can keep your eyes open for Irma, or someone who might be her, wherever you go. You see, she's a person who is particularly adept at disguising herself, and she is very fond of turning up as some great lady—she's done that before, so you might easily run across her in the circles in which you move. If you do strike someone who doesn't seem quite genuine, I wish you'd let me know . . ."

"But of course I will!" She took out her cigarette case. "No, really, Captain Drummond, it's very kind of you, but I'd prefer to smoke one of my own . . . why don't you try one? They're specially made for me, and they're one of the few things I can still get . . . not like Vol de Nuit!"

She smiled. He took one, and lit them both.

"Taking your two requests in the order in which you made them," she said, "I should think her disappearance is because she has done all she can: she tried to prevent you taking on the job, and she failed . . ."

"But you'd think," objected Drummond, "that having failed to prevent me taking on the job, she'd make quite certain that I couldn't carry it out . . . arrange a nasty accident, or something!"

"My heavens, what a woman!"

"She'd stop at nothing."

"I'm afraid," she said, "that my experience has not

stretched quite so far as a woman who would do that sort of thing, so I can't help there. But, of course, I'll keep my eyes open for the lady. What does she look like ? "

Hugh Drummond enjoyed the next few minutes to the full. He let himself go, describing Irma as he had seen her when looking her best. He fancied he noticed a tendency to preen herself on the part of his visitor.

When he had finished, she spoke softly.

" She must be very beautiful . . ."

" She is . . ."

" You speak almost as if you were fond of her ! "

" In a peculiar sort of way," said Drummond perfectly seriously, " I am."

" How soon," asked the glamorous lady, " do you want to know . . . if I meet her, I mean ? Is there any time limit . . .? "

Drummond was immediately on his guard.

" Well," he said easily, " just as soon as possible."

" I ask you that," said his fair visitor, " because, if you remember you said last night that you were going away very soon . . ."

" I see . . ."

" . . . and it would be a pity if I found her too late."

" Yes."

" You're going away on the job, I suppose . . .? "

There could be no harm in answering that : she knew all about it, anyway.

" Yes."

" Can't you tell me even about when ? "

" Well . . . shortly." He tried to laugh . naturally. " I'm not absolutely sure exactly when . . ."

" You know," she said, a trifle coldly. " I think you are being a little inconsiderate. So like a man ! You trust me practically the whole way, but you draw back about a detail which is very important to me if I'm really going to help. You see, if time is really very short indeed, I shall have to change my normal plans and really get down to the finding of this woman . . ."

" Yes," replied Drummond thoughtfully : he was

conscious of a slight buzzing in the ears, a vague mistiness in front of his eyes. As he looked at her, Drummond found that she . . . and the window . . . seemed to have receded in some peculiar manner, seemed actually to be in the process of going away from him, slowly but surely . . . He made a great effort to concentrate, and found to his relief that she was back again at a reasonable distance. " I can't tell you," he said simply, " You must understand that it isn't my secret. I can't tell you . . . I simply can't tell you . . ."

How odd his voice sounded : high pitched at the end of a sentence, altogether strange. Rather funny really : Drummond laughed. But he stopped laughing abruptly : the sound of his mirth was most extraordinary and seemed to do something to his ears.

He was aware that she suddenly leant forward in her chair : her face seemed to rush towards him : surely she wasn't going to kiss him ? Forward hussy ! Her face seemed to stop its wild rush within an inch or two of his : how large it was ! Where was the window ? Odd, no window at all : surely he had noticed a window just behind her head ? Pity it wasn't there any more : he would rather have liked to have opened it, and got a little air . . .

Irma Peterson got up from her chair. There was a gleam in her eyes which Hugh Drummond completely failed to notice. She went up to him and bent down over him.

" Not so clever as you think you are, my Hugh ! " She spoke very softly, but there was a hard, harsh undercurrent to her usually melodious voice which entirely altered it. Now, had Drummond really been able to hear, he would have recognised the voice which, in the past had sometimes haunted his thoughts. As she went on, a note of triumph crept into her words. " Not nearly so clever ! This is the second time you have accepted one of my cigarettes . . . true, the first was a long time ago, but you pride yourself on your memory. I've told you before . . . you're slipping, my Hugh . . . you're slipping . . ."

Hugh Drummond felt a sudden urge to wipe her face away : it really wasn't done to shove your face into somebody's face and keep it there indefinitely : for a few moments, yes, if you really wanted to, but not indefinitely. Definitely not indefinitely . . .

He tried to move his hand to push it away. Funny, it wouldn't work. That's odd, one's arm should work if you want it to. Oh, well, no use forcing the thing. It either would work or it wouldn't, and this was evidently one of the bad days . . . perhaps she'd remember her manners and take away her face of her own accord . . .

" Tckk," said Drummond.

That was explicit enough. No room for doubt there. He was sorry to be rude, but really one had to draw the line somewhere.

She had no right to withdraw her head abruptly and then rush it back again into his : why couldn't she stay in one place for more than a second at a time . . .

She raised her voice, spoke firmly.

" When do you go to France . . .? "

" Tckk."

She slapped his face.

" When do you go to France ? "

" Eh ? "

" That's better, my Hugh." She spoke almost caressingly, but still with the harsh caress of a cat. " Tell me, Hugh my dear . . . when do you go to France ? "

Drummond made one last supreme effort : she was asking him something, and perhaps if he answered she would take that horrid face away. How on earth he could ever have thought she was pretty, he now had no idea. The thing didn't make sense : for one thing she had distorted features, something which he had never admired. And moving features : her nose spread right across her face, and then thinned to a sharp line which was most unbecoming.

" When . . ." he said, " when . . ."

That ought to satisfy her : perhaps now she'd go away. He was confoundedly sleepy : it was rude to fall asleep in front of a lady, but really he doubted if he could help it ! Anyway, she wasn't a lady : no lady could possibly own that face . . .

Irma Peterson took her gloves in her right hand, and hit Drummond with them as hard as she was able. He opened his eyes, with a surprised look. She did it again, unhesitatingly : slashed at his cheek with all her power. She knew that she had to work fast, the drug would over-power him completely, probably in less than a minute.

" Hugh Drummond, when do you go to France ? "

" To . . . France ? "

" Yes, tell me. *When do you go to France ?* "

" In . . . in the summer, usually. To . . . to Cannes, yes. There's a cas . . . a casino there. Charming ! "

Drummond unexpectedly grinned. Vaguely he won-dered what this intense, lovely woman was doing bending over him. She seemed a trifle angry, but fancy asking him when he was going to France ! The idea of it ! Much as he would like to tell her, that wasn't his secret. Oh, no . . . others were concerned. A nice American bloke, for instance. What was his name ? Anyway, when was he going to France . . .? He'd very much like to know himself . . .

Hullo, the beautiful but angry lady was fading away. Why ? He liked looking at her . . . oh, lord, here was that awful face again ! He did wish it would keep its nose quiet. Never heard of such a thing, a nose which kept on enlarging and decreasing just for the fun of it . . .

He laughed. He slept.

The woman wasted no more time on trying to make him speak. With deft fingers she went through his pockets, and examined everything which she found. But apparently with unsatisfactory results, for her frown deepened. She then turned her attention to the room : there was a desk in the corner. She moved to it quickly, but as she started to look at the contents of the pigeon-holes an unladylike exclamation of annoyance escaped her. Rapidly pulling open a drawer, her suspicion was confirmed.

" Darrell's flat ! " she said aloud.

But she was in no mood to leave any stone unturned. With a professional speed she examined every paper that she found : evidently none were of the smallest interest.

She went to the window, and looked out carefully from behind one of the curtains. Her taxi-driver was still reading his paper and smoking his pipe. She looked down the street : a high-powered car was standing outside a big house, and the chauffeur was lounging unostentatiously by its side. She smiled a superior, condescending smile.

She turned back into the room and put on her mink coat. As she did so, she looked at the large figure of Drummond, sprawling in his chair. She went close to him, and stood before him.

" I would like," she said, and although she spoke softly, there was a bitter intensity in her voice, " I would like to kill you *now*, Hugh Drummond. But you can still be of use to me, you are going to lead me to the others. So, for the moment, you are safe. But when you fall into the hands of my friends of the Gestapo, then I shall come and watch your agonies, and revel in them . . . for it was you who killed my beloved Carl, and it is you who glories in that deed . . ."

She paused. She drew herself up to her full height. Her eyes blazed as she looked at the recumbent figure of this man she loathed with all her being.

" I never knew how much I hated you until last night. You did yourself no good, Hugh Drummond, when you spoke of Carl . . . in the way that you seemed to enjoy speaking of Carl . . ."

She turned abruptly and went to the door. But before leaving the room, she spoke once more.

" And to think, you fool, that I would not miss my mirror and realise what that meant ! Or, after all these years, fail to know when I'm followed . . ."

She laughed : it was a mirthless sound.

The Countess Lilli made her final exit.

XV

INSPECTOR MCIVER COMPLAINS

THE office of Inspector McIver in the rather grim building which is Scotland Yard is not at all what the small advertisements would describe as 'furnished in luxurious style'. It is larger than most—but then, Inspector McIver is a very senior officer—and it has a table as well as his desk. One or two very hard chairs are dotted round the walls and a slightly less hard one, with arms, is stationed by the table. The Inspector's own chair is magnificent in comparison : the leather, although worn thin in places, is still recognisably red.

Scarcely an hour after the Countess Lilli had so dramatically walked out of his life, Hugh Drummond was sitting in the slightly less hard chair with arms. Inspector McIver was in his own chair behind his desk. Silently watching the two principals in the scene, Longworth and Harlow sat in the remaining chairs, while Darrell was standing leaning up against the wall.

" If only," mused McIver aloud, " they had let me arrest her last night ! "

Hugh Drummond laughed, although a little shakily.

" Well, there's no real harm done ! " he said, as cheerfully as possible. " She might have slit my throat or anything, but she didn't . . ."

" What did she do, Hugh ? "

Drummond looked at Darrell.

" Frankly, I am not at all certain, Peter, old cock ! Ransacked your room all right, that was obvious . . ."

" It jolly well was ! " put in Longworth. " When Mat and I found you, Hugh, after the taxi had driven off, you never saw such a state as the place was in ! Everything out of the desk just thrown anywhere . . ."

" And everything out of my pockets all mixed up ! " Drummond laughed a trifle grimly. " But she took nothing—not from me, at any rate." He paused a moment : then spoke irritably. " All my own flaming fault too . . . I really would have thought I was old enough by now not to smoke, one of Irma's own cigarettes . . . and she told me they were specially made for her ! "

" Never mind that, Captain." Inspector McIver spoke pompously. " We all make mistakes sometimes. We wouldn't be human if we didn't. I do wish they'd let me arrest her last night ! "

" You keep harping a bit, Mac." Drummond was smiling again. " I appreciate that we are old pals, but I have a feeling I'd flatter myself if I put it all down on my account. Why are you so sorry you didn't lock her up yesterday ? "

Inspector McIver seemed reluctant to put his thoughts into words. Finally he allowed himself to be persuaded.

" Well, it's like this, gentlemen. We could have got her with no trouble in the first hour after you tipped me off last night, with no fuss whatsover . . ."

" Why only in the first hour ? " asked Longworth.

" She went out, then. Went to a night-club, and none too respectable a one at that . . ."

Drummond was interested.

" Did you recognise any of her friends there ? "

" She didn't seem to have any friends there. The man who was watching her saw her speak to no one . . . "

" Odd ! "

" Well . . . if you ask me, she knew about that place . . . we've had difficulties there before. There are four exits : not too easy a place in which to effect an arrest unless you mobilised a pretty big force, and you couldn't do that easily in that neighbourhood without her being warned—if she'd laid it on."

" Oh ! "

" She left there at five in the morning. She went to a little all-night restaurant and dawdled over breakfast."

" All in the dress she dined in with me at the Savoy ? "

" Oh, no. She'd changed before going out. But she

was asking for a lot of trouble in a big mink coat . . . round about that part of the world ! "

" And she got none ? "

" No."

" Some people have all the luck ! " smiled Drummond.

" Or are known in shady places," said McIver, with a slight return of his pompous manner. " Then she did a quick-change journey."

" And what," asked Longworth, " might that be ? "

" It's something someone does," explained the Inspector " when they want to find out if they are being followed . . . tube, bus, tram, walk, bus, underground . . . that sort of thing." He chuckled. " But my fellows know their work. She was evidently satisfied, because then she went back to her hotel."

" I wonder," said Drummond thoughtfully, " why she thought she might be under suspicion ? "

" Probably just taking no chances," suggested Darrell. " She's got enough on her conscience to make her careful . . . and she'd just been out with Hugh."

" Quite possible," conceded the Inspector.

" All that," said Drummond, " leaves my question unanswered : why are you so sorry you didn't arrest her last night ? "

" Because all that," said McIver simply, " coming on top of her performance with you this afternoon, now makes me think she had smelt a rat. You see, it's this way : she's burnt her boats now. We've got to arrest her, we've got no choice after what the Captain has told us. She's forced it on us. Why ? Because she knows the game's up, anyway ? "

" Seems silly to commit suicide like that ! " said Harlow. " Why not just have tried to do a bunk ? "

" Exactly, sir."

" Don't forget," said Drummond, " that she wanted to . . . er, to find out how long I was likely to remain in London."

" Why ? " asked McIver.

Harlow looked at Drummond, wondering what he would

say. But Hugh Drummond answered without any hesitation.

"I had hinted, even stated," he said easily, "that I was not staying in London long. What more natural than that she should want to settle with me—the cause of the Countess's sad demise—before leaving?"

"And did she?"

"Well . . . not exactly. She was obviously after something which I apparently possess, and didn't find."

"Not very satisfactory."

"No, it isn't Mac, but what else can you suggest? D'you think she thinks I've got something which I haven't? She did me the honour, at dinner, of implying that I was obviously employed by our Secret Service . . . by jove, that may well be it!"

He laughed uproariously: it cost him a big effort, for his head was throbbing pretty badly. Damn Irma! this was the second headache she had handed to him on a plate . . .

"I suppose you aren't?" asked the Inspector suspiciously.

"My dear Mac! Have I ever kept any secrets from you?"

"Plenty."

"Well, if I ever sign on with the hush-hush boys, they'll probably be the first to tell their old chum the Inspector . . ."

"Which brings me back to my point," grumbled McIver.

"Eh?"

"I wish I'd gone on my own and arrested her last night. They stopped me—the hush-hush boys. I can see why, of course, but when you've got as slippery and experienced a customer as Irma Peterson you oughtn't to take any chances . . . not even a half-chance more than you can help."

"You seem to think, Inspector, she's going to get away . . ." remarked Harlow.

"Yes, sir, I do. She's through with her hotel, with the Countess business: that's obvious from what she did to the Captain here, in broad daylight, openly in the character of the Countess. Therefore she was perfectly confident about the getaway—and when a woman like that woman is certain of herself, she's usually got a right to be. Of course, I don't say she'll disappear for long, but I'm ready to take a bet that she'll give us the hell of a lot of trouble now, all of which could have been avoided if . . ."

". . . if you hadn't been stopped arresting her last night ! "

"Thank you, Mr. Longworth. Just as you say."

A uniformed policeman entered the room and handed a typewritten sheet to the Inspector. McIver read it.

"All right, Baxter. You can go."

The policeman left the room.

"This, gentlemen, may interest you." The Inspector spoke seriously, but he could not prevent a note of self-satisfaction creeping into his voice. "I'll read it to you: it's a report from the men who were shadowing her . . . were shadowing her. It says : "Got into her taxi : drove off. Turned into Piccadilly. Down St. James's Street. Up Lower Regent Street. Up Regent Street. Left down Oxford Street. Left down Park Lane. Left through Grosvenor Street and Grosvenor Square into Bond Street. Bond Street to Piccadilly, and left to Circus. Red light against taxi entering Circus : crowd of pedestrians crossing. Door of cab opened, and someone in mink coat got out. Vanished down to tube station. Followed as closely as possible, half-way down found small crowd staring at discarded mink coat on stairs. Continued and questioned civilians and officials. No one answering description had been seen. Apparently no blonde noticed anywhere. Returned to cab. Traffic hold up as driver had disappeared. Ladies' garments found inside cab, obviously those she had been wearing. Cab number checked, and found to be that of cab stolen from Ealing midday to-day. Full report follows."

Inspector McIver looked up at his startled audience. "Would you call that neat ? " he inquired. "I would."

He refrained from adding no neater than he had expected.

"She can move, that girl!" remarked Longworth, with a touch of unwilling admiration.

"The really unsatisfactory part of it," said McIver ponderously, "is that she didn't slit Captain Drummond's throat, or otherwise do him in."

"Mac! What did you say?"

"It's all right, Captain. I was speaking from the purely professional point of view." McIver vouchsafed one of his rare laughs. "You see, she can only hang once, and she's already booked. Another murder or two won't make any difference to what happens to her when we finally get hold of her, and she knows that. She doesn't like you: why didn't she get rid of you when she could?"

"I've been asking myself that for the last hour."

"Nothing happened, when you were speaking to her, which might explain it?"

"Nothing. I tried to find out what she was up to, and she tried to find out when I was leaving London. Both of us failed: it was sort of stalemate. Then I suppose the cigarette got to work, because all I remember is wanting fresh air, looking for and not seeing any window, and then not being able to move. I don't remember anything else at all until I saw Algy and Mat here pouring water all over my head, except that I've got a vague recollection of something to do with a face . . . unpleasant, I think it was . . . probably a dream."

"That doesn't help us much."

"Not at all, I'm afraid."

"Well, gentlemen." Inspector McIver rose: it was obviously the signal of dismissal. "There we are! Nowhere at all. I do wish . . . oh, well." He suddenly giggled: Longworth, startled, looked sharply at him. "It'll be rich if the hotel ring me up and ask me to look for the missing Countess! Keep in touch with me, gentlemen: and don't lose heart. She'll turn up again—they always do. But if I were you, I'd be very careful indeed for a bit. Next time, she may be more serious . . . and next time you may not know who she is . . ."

" I'll be very careful, Mac ! "

" I wouldn't like to lose you," said the Inspector gruffly. " Good day, gents . . ."

.   .   .   .

That evening, a slip of paper in his hand, Drummond stood by the fireplace of Darrell's flat, his three friends around him.

" So there it is," he said quietly. " Mat and I leave the day after to-morrow. Peter, you and Algy have got to find Irma if you possibly can. Keep her nice and ripe for me when I get back. Remember, she may be mixed up in what we're going to do . . . if you do get in touch with her, and there's anything you think we should know, pay old Dick a call at the War Office. In the meantime, do your damndest to find her . . . it'll be like looking for a needle in a haystack, but a needle has been known to be found in a haystack before now . . ."

He laughed, that infectious sound which made his words almost optimistic.

" How are you feeling, Mat ? "

" Thrilled ! "

" So am I. It's the waiting that's the bother, isn't it ! Thank heaven that part's over . . . Boys, lunch is on me to-morrow ! I shall spare no expense ! Where shall it be ? "

XVI

NOTHING IS GIVEN AWAY

Author's Note :

Shortly after the last war, a book was written which enjoyed a very wide circulation. It concerned the personal experiences of the writer in a certain aspect of warfare. I, and many thousands of others, enjoyed it enormously.

I doubt whether I should have done so, had I realised that some twenty years later the information in that book might be used against us in another world war. Had such a result appeared possible, the author—a very gallant gentleman—would never have written it.

In common with millions of others, I am hoping that this war will end wars, and that a lasting peace will result from it. But I am not quite certain, and I am determined that on no account shall Bulldog Drummond even unintentionally ever assist any enemy.

It is a very well-known fact, that in time of war every country inserts its agents into territory occupied by its enemies. I believe there are various methods of so doing, and it certainly would not be difficult to invent one. But it has been impressed upon me that an intelligent guess is one of the worst forms of careless writing, and it is possible that in describing the insertion into France of Hugh Drummond and Mat Harlow, my imagination might get too near to the truth. That is why there will be no Chapter XVI to this story. I am not prepared—and I am quite sure my readers would not have it otherwise—to risk making an unfortunately intelligent guess. I am sorry, because the subject rather lends itself to a chapter I should have enjoyed writing : I can almost hear Drummond saying, at some point or other : " I do wish I was insured ! "

It is possible that the authorities, in their wisdom, may at some later date divulge how the thing is done. If they do, then perhaps in some later edition, this story can be made complete. But for the present, I am sure those who are reading this will agree with me that there can be no Chapter XVI.

G.F. 1945.

XVII

DRUMMOND AND HARLOW LEARN FARMING

THE farm house to which they were taken by the man known as Pierre was extremely comfortable. Hugh Drummond was glad to notice that Mat Harlow had, if anything, been too modest about his familiarity with the French language. Of course, Drummond was not competent to judge about the accent, but Harlow babbled away never apparently at a loss for a word, and never having to repeat a sentence to a mystified listener. The sounds that he was making struck Drummond as comfortingly French, and they were accompanied by restrained yet typical actions. Drummond could follow the general meaning of the flow, except where enthusiasm made Harlow's tongue gallop too fast . . .

It was quite evident that Harlow and Pierre were getting along famously.

Pierre could speak a little English, but it was on a par with Drummond's French. However, they could understand each other. Hugh Drummond found himself warming to Pierre : there was a quiet confidence about the man which, in the circumstances, was very pleasant. He took an early opportunity of informing Drummond that he had not lost a visitor yet, but he said it in no boastful manner. Hugh Drummond promptly touched wood, but was glad to have the information. Pierre continued to say that one or two, after they had been passed on, had unfortunately experienced a too close acquaintance with the Boche, but that was not his fault, Drummond found himself agreeing : undoubtedly Pierre could not be held to blame. The great thing to remember, said Pierre, was that those beasts of the Gestapo—because that was all they were, the *salots*—were often rather slow thinkers, not always of course, but often : and they could quite easily be bluffed by a good story. If they were uncertain, that was : provided they hadn't got anything much to go on. Drummond promised to remember. And they could not stand a little derision : they were terrified of looking fools : if only they could realise that they always did, the brutes ! Strutting about as if the world belonged to them when everybody knew that France was just waiting for her friends to come . . .

Could the gentlemen tell him about when that might be ? There was a good deal of disappointment that the Allies had not already come . . . the men of the maquis were not finding it an easy matter to hold on in places : oh, they knew the difficulties, but still . . . France could help a great deal at the moment, but with every day that passed more young Frenchmen—potential allied troops—were being deported to Germany ; more heroes of the maquis in the high lands were being killed in action or, far worse dying of starvation and exposure ; the less would be France's own contribution to her liberation . . .

" And that, *messieurs*," concluded Pierre with simple dignity, " is essential. France must hold up her head again : that is why I, and my family, and so many other families like mine all over the country, willingly take the risks that we do. It is so that France shall hold up her head again."

They did not know ? Well, let us hope it would be soon . . . a pity to lose so much French help . . .

Before they sat down to a meal, Drummond and Harlow were shown the barn. It had a false end wall : you got behind it by means of a ladder to the loft, and then through a concealed trap door. At first warning, in the unlikely event of a warning, that was where they had to go . . .

They sat down to a meal. And what a magnificent meal it was, to those two accustomed for too long to the restrictions of British rationing. First of all an omelette cooked as only a Frenchwoman knows how to cook an omelette, and obviously Madame Pierre was no exception. Then a succulent piece of steak : real, honest-to-goodness thick steak ! After that, separately, a vegetable dish which by virtue of its freshness was magnificent : and apples made into a sweet by a genius. Pierre insisted on producing a bottle of red wine, which he unearthed from a hiding place in the garden : you could not be too careful with your wine, grumbled Pierre, the Boche was a thirsty brute, and the worst of it was that he drank for the pleasure of drinking, not for the taste of the wine . . .

" I thought," murmured Harlow to Drummond, " that the French were starving . . ."

Pierre, quick of ear, overheard him. " You must understand, gentlemen," he said, " that out in the country it was different to inside the towns. The food was grown, was reared, out in the country districts, and although the thieves of Germans did their best to steal it all for their own purposes, their Vichy lackeys were not always the traitors they might seem to be. The local overseer, for instance, employed by Vichy on behalf of the Germans, was a good Frenchman : he had to allot a certain proportion of the produce of the fields to the Germans, but it was a small amount compared to the real capacity of those fields. The rest went in many ways to help in the general effort : some of it went to the needy in the towns, some of it went to the maquis, and some, of course, went to the black market. It was, you see, patriotic to have a flourishing black market in France to-day : it made the Germans spend their money, and that money could be used in a variety of ways to inconvenience them . . ."

Hugh Drummond pushed his plate away.

" I don't know whether it's because my tummy has lost the habit, or what it is," he said ruefully, " but I just can't eat any more. This is truly a wonderful day ! "

They retired to their sleep in the hay of the barn very soon after feeding. They were informed that on the following morning their papers would be brought to them, false identity papers which would establish that they had a perfect right to stay there and work in the fields, until instructions were received for their ultimate disposal. This would probably take two or three days, maybe a little longer. Until then, Pierre and his wife wanted them to realise that they were more than welcome.

Drummond and Harlow said little to each other before falling asleep. They had been through a great deal in the last few hours, both physically and mentally, and they were glad to rest. But they both were astounded at the ease with which they had been inserted into France, and the warmness of their welcome . . .

The following morning, secure in their new identities, they were out in the fields early . . .

.   .   .   .   .   .

In his magnificent offices situated in the most fashionable

hotel of Paris, the distinguished, if heavy-jowled officer waited impatiently for the arrival of his visitor. He had been given to understand direct from Berlin that his visitor was not only important, but might be able to help him considerably. Although he disliked acknowledging it even to himself, he could do with a little help just at that moment . . .

He had now been in Paris for some time, with the task of cleaning up this Council of Resistance which the impertinent French had apparently formed with the intention of making things as difficult as possible for the occupying Power. Practically its first act had been to declare its recognition of General de Gaulle, that thorn in the flesh of the admirably senile Marshal Pétain, as the leader of fighting France. Fighting France ! How dare they use such a term, unless they were referring to Doriot's excellent men—nearly worthy to be called good Ayran Germans—who had volunteered for the plentiful pay offered to those who would fight against those cursed Russians. To apply the term to the few who were fighting against Germany, that was absurd ! Everybody knew that there was no such thing as Fighting France nowadays : France had been crushed by the military might of the Fuehrer, and France had got to realise that her best interests—indeed her only hope of survival—lay in willingly accepting her rôle as a vassal of Germany. She was being troublesome about it, of course, trust the obstinate pigs of Frenchmen not to see what was good for them ! She was even being rebellious towards her properly set up government which Germany had been so careful to control through the medium of the admirable Laval, but she would soon come to her senses when a few more thousand men and women hostages were shot, and when the hot-heads of this infamous council were rounded up, made to disgorge the names of their accomplices, and then disposed of summarily . . .

However, since arriving in Paris he had not got on very fast. These scoundrels were elusive, there could be no question of that : and it looked as if they were being assisted to evade authority by the general public, the silly idiots ! He would have to teach them a severe lesson very soon, if no progress was made. Take a few hundred off the streets, and shoot them in the Bois de Boulogne. He was averse, of course, to wholesale butchery, but this could not by any stretch of a warped imagination be described as that : this would be a necessary step to teach the fools that you cannot oppose the master will of Germany.

There was another reason why he might have to give the order soon. Berlin was not very pleased with him. Berlin was seldom pleased with those who were slow in producing results. And he had to admit he had achieved very little since his arrival. Berlin was actually threatening to replace him by another, who seemed anxious to come. That was why he was so very much looking forward to this visitor, this visitor from whom so much was expected. Where the devil was she ? She was late . . .

He came to a halt in front of a long mirror : he examined himself in the glass. Yes, he was looking very smart indeed. It was really a most becoming uniform. There was no question about it, she ought to be impressed . . .

She was ushered into the room. He turned to receive her.

" Good morning, mein herr . . ."

" Good morning, Fräulein. Pray be seated . . ."

She took the chair he offered her. He was not disappointed : he had been told this woman was lovely, and lovely she most certainly was. It would have been better, of course, if she had been of true Ayran blondeness, but still . . . although dark, there was plainly no Jewish blood in her veins. There could not be : because before being employed she must obviously have been vetted . . .

" I am sorry for being a little late . . ."

" Nearly five minutes . . ."

She raised her eyebrows slightly : evidently she was not accustomed even to the mildest discipline. Well, it was just as well to start the way you proposed to go along. He was the big man here, and the sooner she realised and accepted that fact, the better it would be for both of them.

" I am a very busy man, fräulein, and my time is valuable.

When I make an appointment I am always punctual. I expect my visitors to be just as punctual. Do I make myself clear ? "

" Painfully."

" Eh ? "

" I am sorry for being a little late," his visitor spoke softly, " and it will not occur again."

That was better : for a moment he had feared she was about to be impertinent.

" Forget it. I have been looking forward to seeing you . . ."

He smiled ingratiatingly : after the little lesson, then it was good to make friends as soon as possible.

" That is kind of you. I, also, have been looking forward to seeing you. I have heard a great deal about you, mein herr, a great deal to your credit."

This woman was really charming : he offered her a cigarette.

" You have come from England ? "

" Yes."

" It was not too troublesome a journey ? "

" Not after reaching Ireland."

" A kindly country," smiled the officer, " but a little simple . . . I wonder what the Irish expect from us after we have won ? "

His visitor smiled. The officer took a cigar from a box on his desk and lighted it.

" To business, Fräulein Peterson."

" Certainly."

" You have come to help in this Council of Resistance nuisance ? "

" I hope to help . . ."

" You have found someone who will lead us to these scoundrels ? "

" Suppose I tell you the story ? " suggested Irma Peterson.

He looked at her sharply : had there been a touch of unbecoming asperity in her voice ? But she gave him no chance to inquire into the matter, for she took it for granted that she was given leave to speak. And after her first few words he forgot about the incident and listened attentively.

" There is a man who is called Hugh Drummond. He is an Englishman of undoubted courage and ability, and blessed with more than his fair share of luck. He is also extremely fond of adventure, and he has found plenty of it. He is a dangerous opponent because he is physically extraordinarily powerful, because he is very quick-witted, and because although he will always stick his head into a noose, he has the most astonishing capacity for withdrawing it again just in time."

" An interesting gentleman . . ."

" Very. This man, up to a short time ago, was not being employed by the British. Suddenly, however, he was approached. I came to discover this fact."

The officer smiled contentedly.

" Clever of you ! "

She gave him a little smile.

" At first I had no idea why, or how, he was to be employed. Now I know. He is to come here, to France, to make contact with the Resistance Groups."

" Very interesting ! "

" He has undoubtedly been furnished with the very best introductions."

" Yes ? "

" Well," said the woman, " it occurred to me that, if you do not already know the identities of the members of this Council, all you have to do is to follow him to them. I'm sure they will be on his visiting list ! "

The officer said nothing for a few moments : he half closed his eyes and gave himself up to the sheer joy of anticipation. What a splendidly simple scheme ! It would solve all, or most of, his difficulties : because even if this foolish fellow Drummond did not lead him to more than a few, once he had those in his clutches he would soon tear out of them the names of the rest ! The more he thought of it, the more he liked the idea : it was so beautifully simple that practically nothing could go wrong . . .!

" You know this man ? "

" Yes."

" You know him well ? "

She smiled again.

" Very well."

There was something in the way she said the two words that made him glance at her quickly.   She was not looking at him, but over his shoulder into space.   Hardened though he was, he almost shuddered : he told himself that he had never seen such bitter hate in any woman's face . .

" Good."

She looked back at him.

" I beg your pardon ? "

" Nothing."   He picked up a large card, looked at it. He looked up at her and smiled.   " I see that you are well qualified to keep your eye on him . . ."

" That is why I came."

" And the job which you will enjoy ? " he hazarded.

" Yes."

" Then it is all settled.   Call on me for any help that you will need.   When does this man arrive ? "

" Maybe to-day, maybe any day now."

He frowned.

" You can't be more definite ? "

" I'm afraid not.   He may even have arrived yesterday, although he could not have arrived before that . . ."

" A pity.   The exact date would have been useful . . ."

" I know."

She remained silent.

" People have a habit of disappearing as soon as they arrive.   That is why it is just as well to be forewarned."

" I know that.   I did my best . . ."

" You would know this man anywhere ? "

Irma Peterson hesitated : she was an expert at disguise herself, but she had on more than one occasion been forced to admit that Drummond was little if any less expert than herself.   However, there was no point in disturbing this pompous officer more than she need.

" Yes."

" Then it is just a question of finding him for you ? "

" Exactly."

" Not so easy, but we must not fail. You may not know that we are particularly well placed for that sort of thing just at the moment." He rose. " Will you lunch with me, Fräulein ? I should like you to meet the officer who will be your principal assistant . . ."

" You are very kind . . ."

Characteristically, he led the way from the room.

.   .   .   .

Hugh Drummond and Mat Harlow spent three happy days working on the farm. It was just what they needed to tune them up physically after their stay in London. But on the afternoon of the third day they were warned that someone of importance was coming to take them away that night.

Neither was sorry. The farm had been very pleasant, but the job was waiting to be done.

XVIII

DRUMMOND STRIKES FIRST

HUGH DRUMMOND and Harlow returned early from the fields. Not that they had any packing to do : the very few belongings that they possessed were either in their pockets or went into the small canvas case which they shared. But they felt rather like someone who has a train to catch and is not happy until he is at the station in plenty of time with no possibility of a transport breakdown to make him miss it.

They found Madame Pierre in cheerful conversation with a young man of jolly appearance. He looked a typical son of the French soil, perhaps from the south since he was tall and dark. His face bore the healthy tan of life out of doors, but the most noticeable thing about him was that he seemed to be perpetually smiling. He rose as they entered, looked at them both, and laughed.

"I congratulate you, gentlemen." His voice was deep and soft. "You might never even have seen the inside of a big city! Your hands?" He looked at them. "I should advise a little more earth in the finger-nails. In fact, if I were your employer, I should be inclined to think you were rather lazy . . .!"

He laughed again.

"Presumably," he went on, "you are Captain Drummond? I thought so . . . I was warned you were rather big. And you are Mr. Harlow? Splendid. As for me, everyone calls me Jacques."

"You speak English quite uncommonly well!" remarked Drummond.

"Doesn't he!" agreed Harlow. "Like a native . . ."

"Yes, I do, don't I," smiled the man who was called Jacques. "In point of fact, I was at school in England, and I finished my education at Oxford."

"Oh, I see . . ."

"And I was born in Sussex . . ."

"Oh!"

"Of English parents. I wish I could speak French as well as my own language . . ."

Both Drummond and Harlow grinned.

"How long have you been here?" asked Drummond.

"Oh, for a little. But . . . let's get down to business, shall we?"

Drummond found himself admiring this young man; he was a leader all right, with plenty of personality. And although that vague statement which he had made implied that he had been living the life of the hunted for a considerable time, there was no sign of the strain in his demeanour. Plainly he was rather enjoying his strange and uncomfortable life . . .

"I was, of course, warned you were coming," stated the young man, "but I didn't actually know you had arrived until yesterday. I came over as soon as I could. I gather you want to get to Paris, and meet some of the boys . . .?"

"That's the idea . . ."

"Well, the whole thing has worked out not too badly.

As it happens, the weekly cart goes off to-night . . ."

" Weekly cart ? " queried Harlow.

" Yes. Have you got an English cigarette ? "

" I'm awfully sorry," said Drummond, " but we . . ."

" Good," said the surprising young man. " Do you smoke a pipe ? "

" No."

" Neither of you ? "

" Very seldom," said Harlow. " I haven't got one with me . . ."

" Splendid." The young man seemed pleased. " That excludes the possibility of a stray Dunhill being found on your person—you've no idea how suspicious the Hun gets about a stray Dunhill . . ."

" We've got nothing on us even remotely English," smiled Drummond.

" Or American ? "

Harlow laughed.

" Or American."

" What could be better. I didn't think you would have, but one can't be too careful. And the funny thing is that it's nearly always on smoking things that fellows let themselves down . . ."

" Touching this cart . . .? " suggested Harlow.

" I shouldn't ! " The young man grinned. " It's much too likely to explode."

" But . . ."

" The weekly cart," he said quietly, " is apparently a cart full of farm produce. It very frequently is only full of farm produce. But sometimes it has other things as well . . . people occasionally, or some of those nasty things that go bang which our French friends are always screaming for. They love them almost as much as the Boches don't. It leaves here in the middle of the night so as to reach the local market town in time for the very black market. It always gets through unmolested partly because some of the stuff goes to the local German Officers' mess, partly just out of force of habit : if a patrol stops it, they recognise it and I daresay the Mess President has given instructions about it. Anyway, all they ever do is to prod a bayonet in here and there in rather a half-hearted manner : only one man's been slightly pinked so far, and he managed to keep it to himself until later : after that he made rather an unnecessary fuss, really, for what it amounted to . . ."

" I'm sorry to hear that . . ." said Drummond gravely. " Do we . . . er . . . take this cart to-night ? "

" You do," continued the young man. " You're very lucky, not only because you've coincided nicely with the cart, but also because you may see some fun. There's a do fixed for the early hours of the morning . . ."

" A do ? "

" Yes. Our French pals are proposing to molest a small factory which has been rather overdoing it in turning out something which goes into an aeroplane engine : I can't remember what, exactly, but they argue that if it is important enough for the R.A.F. to raid, then it's important enough to put out of action . . ."

" The R.A.F. didn't quite do that ? "

" No. They're marvellous most of the time, but this was rather a boob. So the boys have decided to finish the job . . ."

He said it in such a matter of fact manner, as if it were quite the most ordinary thing to do, that Drummond glanced at Harlow. The American was listening intently, but he flashed a quick smile at Drummond.

" The reason why you're lucky," went on the young man in the same quiet voice, " is that rather a big pot from Paris is coming down to see the job done. He may take you back with him . . ."

" That," said Drummond, feeling all the time a sense of bewilderment, " would be splendid."

" Yes."

" Are you on . . . this job ? " asked Harlow.

" I'm afraid not," said the young man. " I can't leave these parts for the moment. All I can do is to put you on the cart . . . and give you my blessing, of course ! "

" Er . . . who drives the cart ? " asked Drummond.

" A perfectly sweet old boy ! " replied the young man

enthusiastically. "Name of Phillippe . . . you'll love him. Are you chaps ready? Because as soon as it's dark, we ought to move . . ."

That night, after a meal wholly as magnificent as their first in France, only this time cooked by the attractive silver-haired Madame Phillippe, washed down by a bottle of wine which the elderly Phillippe would not hear of their refusing, and after listening to the B.B.C. news in French which somehow gave Drummond a very slight touch of homesickness, they set off in the weekly cart.

"Let us pray," said Mat Harlow piously, "that we are not really in the cart."

"At least," murmured Drummond, "the horses have been put in front of us."

They were not exactly comfortable, and since silence had been ordered, they spoke no more to each other after that. It was a pity, for discomfort shared is much more bearable if the victims may grumble together. However, Phillippe had been very strict about it, and this was Phillippe's party: what he said went. They were huddled together, covered by a variety of sacks, each containing fresh vegetables of many descriptions. Fresh vegetables are excellent things, and normally their odour is quite pleasant. Too close a proximity however, can pall: and the scent can become tedious . . .

Drummond thought suddenly of Vol de Nuit, and almost laughed aloud: what wouldn't Irma give to know where he was now! He wondered if Algy Longworth or Peter Darrell had got on her trail again—scarcely likely to so soon. Still, they wouldn't let the grass grow under their feet, those two: what a pity it was that they could not be with him now: just the sort of thing that they would have enjoyed enormously, although Longworth would have found the enforced silence a trifle disconcerting!

Hugh Drummond began to ponder on what they had seen so far. An utter, a magnificent refusal to knuckle under to the Germans, a splendid contempt for their unwelcome presence. The risks these gentle country people took, with their eyes wide open to the drastic consequences of discovery, were astonishing but never seemed to worry them. In fact, they almost appeared to enjoy the clandestine side of their lives. How they hated! And, judging by a few tales that he had heard about what happened to those who were caught opposing the Hunnish will, how much right they had to hate these inhuman, overbearing conquerors. Of course, they had mixed only with those who were known to their hosts to be safe : no doubt there were only too many in the country who, for selfish individual advantage, had forgotten their country's shame and had sold themselves to the enemy. But the other workers in the fields : they must have felt a curiosity about the two new arrivals, and yet they had asked no questions. Not even evinced an unusal interest in their appearance. He and Mat Harlow had been treated in no other way than they had treated all their other companions, except to be given an encouraging smile occasionally, and once or twice an impromptu but much needed lesson in how a particular job of work should be done.

It was at just about this stage of his thoughts that Drummond experienced his first tinge of cramp.

Very carefully he moved : ah, that was better! The hard bottom of a farm cart is not the most comfortable bed on which to lie. And the wooden wheels made the most of the indifferent road. He wondered how Harlow was getting on : no better, presumably.

It was just as Drummond was about to move in order to relieve his fourth bout of cramp that the cart came to an abrupt halt in answer to a guttural command. Drummond froze into the position in which he found himself. This must be the patrol which they had been warned they would almost certainly meet. Drat it, thought Drummond, it might have come just a few minutes earlier or a few minutes later! But he could not restrain the sensation of a certain thrill : he was nearer to a German now than he had been since September thirty-nine . . .

A voice spoke in execrable French, apparently asking some question. Drummond heard the cheerful tones in which old Phillippe apparently always spoke raised in reply.

The guttural voice gave an order, and somebody climbed on to the cart : Drummond found himself gripping his small automatic : if anything unfortunate did happen, the instructions were to scatter, and Drummond promised himself that, on the way, some German would suffer . . .

He heard old Phillippe chide the man who was giving orders. Tell your fellow to be careful, Phillippe was saying : tell him not to crush the eggs, or your officers will not be best pleased . . .

The intruder on the cart did not stop long, but he stayed quite long enough for Drummond. The anticipation of being pricked by a bayonet, thought Drummond, is just as bad as waiting for the dentist to reach for that awful buzzing tool . . .

He heard the German say something gruff to Phillippe : he heard the old man reply, and call to his horses. With a silent sigh of relief, he felt again the bumping of the cart as they moved off.

Very carefully, Drummond eased his position : ah, that was much better now . . .

The temptation to say something to his friend lying so near was almost beyond bearing : anything would do, the most monumentally stupid remark would be a relief. But Drummond resisted the impulse : Phillippe had been most emphatic on the point, for obvious and admirable reasons. It was odd, thought Drummond, how comforting could be the sound of the human voice in certain circumstances : provided, of course, that it was in no way guttural . . .!

The rest of the journey was trying principally because it became so tedious. Drummond found himself almost feeling that he had spent a large part of his life in that cart, and longing for the journey's end. He became bored with his own thoughts, and might have fallen asleep had it not been for his cramped position. He was glad that he had not got to resist sleep : he knew from experience what a desperately difficult thing that is to do. And it would have been highly dangerous : if another patrol were met, and at the moment when the bayonet was being applied to the sacks, a resounding snore reverberated from beneath them, unpleasant things would happen much too quickly. When he thought of all the foolish mistakes mere thoughtlessness could cause, and provoke disaster, he wondered afresh at the quiet courage of such a man as old Phillippe, whose life was in the hands of his passengers just as much as their lives were in his. When you came to think of it, he and Mat had a grave responsibility towards those who were shepherding them . . .

They were moving over cobbles now : perhaps the journey was nearly over. He wished he could peep out and have a look, but this was an impossibility : they had been most carefully packed into their places. At last the cart stopped moving . . .

Drummond heard old Phillippe climb down from his seat. He heard him say something—endearing it sounded —to his horses. Then, almost with a shock, he heard Phillippe walk away over the cobble-stones.

There followed a period which only lasted a few minutes, but which seemed, both to Drummond and to Harlow, to last an age. At length they heard the approach of foot-steps, and the voice of old Phillippe, slightly subdued now but still as cheerful as ever . . .

Someone climbed on to the cart. Someone stepped carefully on the sacks towards Drummond's head. A pause. Then old Phillippe's voice, in a whisper.

" Get up. Follow me . . ."

As he spoke the elderly man pulled some of the sacks aside.

He smiled at Drummond and Harlow as they appeared : he lent them successively his strong arm to assist them as they clambered down from the cart. They needed his assistance : too long in a cramped position made move-ment difficult . . .

His feet on the ground again, and painfully coming to life, Hugh Drummond looked around him. He could see by the light of the moon that they were in some sort of a yard, with gaunt black shadows of the houses all around them. His quick eyes detected a vague human outline here and there, but only when these shadows moved. This was seldom : but there could be no question that other men were about that night in that yard . . .

" Come with me . . ." whispered Phillippe.

Drummond and Harlow followed the old man. They approached a door in a house. Phillippe made way, but just as Drummond reached the door it was abruptly opened from within.

" Gut morning, Herr captain . . ." said a guttural voice.

Hugh Drummond was just within range. He hit the speaker full in the face.

XIX

MAT HARLOW MOVES QUICKLY

To Mat Harlow the events which followed always remained a trifle confused. Things seemed to happen with a rapidity which made it an almost impossible task to recapitulate the correct sequence of events. Of one thing Harlow was certain, although this certainty was afterwards tinged with surprise ; the first shocking moment when everyone, with the notable exception of Hugh Drummond, seemed to be paralysed by the suddenness and total unexpectedness of the sound of that guttural voice, was not accompanied in his case by any sensation of fear. Mat Harlow felt himself struck dumb and motionless, but he was not afraid.

Hugh Drummond struck the first blow of a battle which was short, sharp, and very fierce. He alone had not hesitated, and his fist crashed into the face of the German officer who had opened the door. The next instant and this officer was flat on his back, with the light from the room which his standing form had hitherto partially obscured, shining out into the courtyard. His disappearance also disclosed the ugly spectacle of two uniformed Germans with tommy guns at the ready, looking startled but alarmingly light-fingered on the trigger.

What Hugh Drummond would have done next, had he been left to himself, is open to question; he was given no time to do it. There was a split second in which Mat Harlow recovered full power over his faculties, before the German soldiers. A neat shoulder charge put Drummond out of the stream of light, and incidentally the line of fire, and almost simultaneously Harlow's automatic barked twice; even as he fired, Harlow dived for the sheltering darkness of the wall of the house, but as he went he had the satisfaction of seeing one of the soldiers crumple up.

A stream of bullets flew out of the open door. Harlow saw old Phillippe, his mouth still wide open with astonishment, go down and stay motionless in the awkward attitude in which he fell, evidently riddled by the bullets. And then an odd thing happened; an answering hail of bullets seemed to come from the perimeter of the courtyard. Flashes could be seen in the moonlight, and one or two sharp cracks against the wall just over their heads advertised to Harlow the fact that his present position, so near to the open door, was by no means healthy.

A voice spoke in his ear.

"Covering fire!" said Drummond, "and they won't be able to keep it up for long. This is where we buzz off!"

Harlow saw the large shape of Drummond start away from the door. He followed automatically. And as he went, Drummond's quick appreciation of the situation began to be justified, for the ominous rat-tat-tat of heavy machine guns burst out from the windows of the house, horribly clear above the shindy of the automatic rifles, sounding almost like the bark of a great dog as opposed to the yapping of a pack of Pekinese. But, like the Pekinese, Harlow was thankful to notice, those automatic rifles, after a moment of stunned silence, quickly resumed their blistering and courageous defiance . . .

Harlow, much younger and athletic though he was,

found it difficult to keep up with the speed set by Drummond. They passed old Phillippe's farm wagon, which had somehow become wedged and was resisting the frantic efforts of the terrified horses to get clear away; they reached the corner of the gate which led into the courtyard. The whole journey could not have taken more than a minute. Here Harlow ran into Drummond, who had stopped abruptly.

"Steady, old chap!" Drummond's voice was distinct to him in the darkness. "We must tell our pals that we've got clear, and that they can make their getaway now . . . otherwise they'll just hang on until they're murdered. Got a torch?"

"Yes."

"Let's have it."

Harlow handed over his small torch.

"Thanks. Ready?"

"Yes."

"It's a risk, but we've got to face it. I shall probably dazzle myself, so go in front at a sharp walk and I'll hang on to your coat. Turn left down the street, and when I put the torch out, run. It depends what happens then, what we do next. All set?"

"Okay."

"Let's go."

Mat Harlow stepped out briskly. He felt a tug on his jacket, and realised that Drummond had taken hold. The next moment he saw a beam of light from his torch, and risked a glance over his shoulder. A hazy idea of what Drummond proposed to do had occurred to him, but the audacity of the man rather took his breath away; on the other hand, Drummond was dead right, they could not possibly clear out without informing the gallant men who had contributed so greatly to their escape.

Hugh Drummond had directed the beam of the torch so that it shone full on his face. It was rather an eerie sight, it looked like a ghostly head and shoulders walking rapidly out of the gate. One rifle bullet cracked somewhere unpleasantly near as they went, but only one; the audacious ruse evidently startled the enemy, if they had seen it, into a fatal moment of indecision ; it was probable, said Harlow to himself and hoping that he was not indulging in wishful thinking, that the solitary shot had come not from an enemy but from a jumpy friend, as a first reaction before he realised the import of the odd spectacle . . .

Mat Harlow suddenly heard Drummond's voice again. " Scram ! " it said.

Harlow did not wait for a second bidding, he went off down that street like the wind, just such a sprint as he had often made for first base. But he was conscious of the large bulk of Hugh Drummond close at his heels all the time.

They went for about a hundred and fifty yards. Then, as if by common consent, they pulled up. They stood motionless, listening. One thing was at once obvious ; although the machine guns were plainly still in full spate the replies of the automatic rifles were rapidly dying away.

" I hope to high heaven," whispered Drummond, " that means that they're disengaging . . ."

" Yes," said Harlow. It seemed a hopelessly inadequate comment, but he simply could not think of anything else to say. None the less than Hugh Drummond, he realised the alternative and ominous meaning which that gradual cessation of fire might imply . . .

" I wonder," whispered Drummond, " how we join up again . . .? "

That thought was also in Harlow's mind. Out of the frying pan into the fire seemed, for them, to be particularly and unpleasantly apt at that moment. This was the first rest in which they had enjoyed time to think, except at racing speed and spurred on by the necessity presented by abrupt and surprising events, since Drummond had so promptly punched the unexpected German in the nose. Drummond himself was gently rubbing the knuckles of his right hand in the palm of his left. The battle had not lasted very long—indeed in space of time all that had happened since the well-aimed blow had occupied barely a few minutes—but since then their whole position had undergone a complete change. Only those few minutes before, they had been in the comparatively safe keeping of the French resistance boys, and now they were alone and lost in what was presumably a hostile town, or at the very least a town over-run by hostile men in grey-green uniforms . . .

The sound of running feet came to Mat Harlow's ears. He looked at Drummond quickly, and saw that the big man was listening intently. Harlow also noticed, subconsciously and almost at the back of his mind, that the pale, cold light of dawn was just beginning to deprive them of practically their only advantage in their present rôle of fugitives.

" What about that side-street ? " snapped Harlow.

Drummond glanced in the direction which he indicated. " Yes."

They moved across the street rapidly, but silently. Harlow felt Drummond pull him gently towards the wall ; they crouched close together. Then Harlow heard Drummond whispering softly in his ear.

" It's odd, Mat ! " said Drummond's voice. " There's only one man coming . . . either a very brave German, because they know there are two of us and that we're armed, or . . . can it be a friend . . . ? "

Harlow listened. As the sound of the footsteps came nearer, he realised that Drummond was right ; there was only one person approaching, and that person, whoever he might be, was coming rapidly as if speed mattered more than caution. It did not, or so Harlow told himself, really fit in with the German character ; the Huns could be fast enough, no doubt, when the occasion demanded it, but only when the occasion was accompanied by superiority of numbers or armament . . . he fingered his little automatic, with a vision of that crumbling German soldier in front of his eyes . . .

Drummond could not have seen him, for the darkness was still too dense. But he must have divined something of the thought in Harlow's mind, for he spoke again softly :

"Careful, old man. Even if he isn't a friend, we don't want to draw attention to our whereabouts unless we can't help it . . ."

Harlow nodded. It was only long afterwards that he realised that Drummond was most unlikely to see this acknowledgement.

The footsteps came up to the end of the side street, and stopped. They heard the sound of heavy breathing, but they could only just make out the vague figure of a man. He did not appear to have any headgear, and it was impossible to recognise what sort of clothing he was wearing. Scarcely daring to breathe, they watched motionless, ready to act instantaneously on any unfriendly action, hoping that in their crouching attitude they would pass unobserved.

The tension seemed to last for several minutes, although in fact it could not have lasted for more than a few seconds. Then the dim shape moved on again down the main street, and was lost to view.

Mat Harlow could not restrain a sigh of relief. But even as he relaxed, he heard the subdued sound of Drummond's whisper:

"Stay exactly here. Shan't be long."

And with that, Drummond was gone. It was the first demonstration that Mat Harlow was given of Hugh Drummond's uncanny knack of moving absolutely silently in spite of his great size, and apparently of seeing like a cat in the dark. One minute Drummond was there, crouching beside him, and the next he was not; it seemed as simple as that. In any circumstances the demonstration would have been mildly alarming, but in this present game of hide and seek with the prize not simply freedom but life or death, Drummond's so casual disappearance was very nearly panic making.

The only thing that really saved Harlow, in that moment, from blind fear, was the sudden surge of violent anger—perhaps coming from fear—which overwhelmed him. He never doubted that Drummond would come back, as he had said he would, he was already in the habit of expecting faithfully that what Drummond said would happen, did happen. But it was such an absurdly dare-devil thing to do, this abrupt decision to approach and identify their pursuer—for he had no doubt that Drummond had set himself that mission. True—and Harlow was fair even in those hair-raising minutes when he was alone—true, if the man was a friend, then to know that fact would be useful. But it was a risk which, in their present circum-stances, was scarcely justifiable. After all, they had seen enough of the spirit of the French people to know that they would very likely strike a friend if they looked around a little ; and, having had the luck of making their escape literally out of the jaws of the enemy, they would require far less luck to find help in concealing themselves until they could once again make contact with those who were expecting them . . . Darn the man, it was most incon-siderate of Drummond to vanish into thin air at just that moment : Harlow promised himself a few very well chosen phrases which would crystallise his opinion to Drummond when he returned . . .

Mat Harlow was indulging in the composition of a particularly ripe phrase, when his subconscious mind began screaming for attention. With an abrupt jerk, with a shock, Harlow forced himself to consider not the future but the present. Something was different, something was happening—or rather, something had ceased to happen.

Harlow was suddenly aware that the firing had stopped. The automatic rifles were stilled, and the staccato sound of the machine guns no longer rent the air. Evidently the battle of the courtyard was over.

This new silence of the night was, or so it seemed to Harlow, even more menacing than had been the sound of the guns. It was an obvious fact that if the shooting was done with, the Germans—no longer engaged in dealing with the patriots, and with liberty of movement regained—would now concentrate on chasing and finding the quarry which had eluded them. And that quarry was no other than Captain Hugh Drummond and Mat Harlow himself, not a very soothing thought . . . where the devil was Hugh Drummond ?

Furthermore, provided he had escaped from the fusillade from the patriots' rifles, the officer who had been the recipient of Drummond's massive fist would be mad as anything, and certainly extremely keen on the capture of the fugitives . . .

Stay exactly here—those had been Drummond's words. And in one way, of course, perfectly sensible, since even a minor movement might result in their missing each other when Drummond returned. But if Drummond thought he was going to stay there in blind obedience until he had lost his own chance of getting away, then Drummond had about a score of guesses coming . . .

"Right, Mat! Come along . . ."

It seemed to Harlow that he rose vertically several feet into the air. The words, spoken softly into his ear apparently from nowhere, so startled him that convulsively he very nearly pressed the trigger of his automatic, still at the ready in his right hand. Just as he had gone, Drummond one minute was not there, and the next was standing beside him large as life. It was uncanny. Worse, it was alarming in the extreme . . .

But even as the sweat broke out on his forehead in spite of the chill of the early morning, he felt a magnificent sensation of relief. In that moment, Harlow fully realised the comfort of Drummond's presence, and the confidence which his proximity exuded. All the scathing phrases were forgotten in his feeling of welcome for his friend.

Harlow was already on his feet. He noticed for the first time the outline of another man standing just beside Drummond.

"Lead on, Macduff!" murmured Drummond, apparently to the stranger, "Nous follow vous. Get me?"

The stranger evidently got him. He moved off swiftly, with Drummond and Harlow in his wake. As they went, Drummond took Harlow by the arm, and pulled him close.

" He's the bloke who was after us. Caught him down the street. Gave him a bad moment, I'm afraid, because I wasn't sure . . . matter of fact, I'm not awfully sure now, but it's a chance we've got to take. He's supposed to be taking us to the bloke from Paris we heard about . . . remember ? But just in case he's not, keep your eyes skinned and your trigger-finger supple. And by the way, Mat, thanks awfully for that shoulder charge . . . I was helpless then, and you saved me from carrying a lot of unwelcome lead . . ."

" You're welcome . . ." said Harlow softly.

It was beginning to get much lighter now, uncomfortably light. No sound, no sign of movement came from the shuttered houses. Not surprising, said Harlow to himself as they hurried along ; the inhabitants of the little town could not have failed to be aroused by the sounds of the recent battle, short though it had been, but no doubt were tactfully showing no sign of life just because of those sounds. The Germans always imposed a curfew, and in the circumstances would be ready and eager to shoot first and inquire afterwards if any unusual curiosity were to be displayed.

Suddenly their guide dived out of the street into an alley. Quickly Drummond and Harlow followed him. They found him a few yards down, trying to flatten himself against a wall in the shadows. He held a finger to his lips, and the pair froze beside him. In silence, motionless, they waited . . .

The sound of heavy boots marching rapidly became audible. Harlow once again felt affectionately for the trigger of his automatic.

A German patrol passed along the street which they had just left. It was a strong patrol—two sections at least—and it was marching swiftly. It was moving in the direction whence the sound of the firing had come. It was then more than ever that Harlow realised in how brief a space of time the events through which he had just lived had taken place.

The men were evidently intent on their mission, whatever it was. None of them thought of glancing down the alley . . .

They waited until the sound of the marching feet had died away. It seemed an age, but their guide appeared to be made of stone. Then Harlow felt a touch on his shoulder, and knew the apparently interminable pause was over. Their guide moved off, not back to the street but down the alley, and Drummond and Harlow followed him.

He had evidently decided, or so they told themselves, that even the less important streets were no longer safe. But, fortunately, he appeared to have a remarkable knowledge of the local byways. They passed along mean little streets barely worthy of the name, but sometimes they were compelled to cross, and occasionally to use for a few yards, real streets. Those were anxious moments, but they saw no more of the enemy. It was, however, getting much too light for comfort now. Harlow found himself hoping that they had not very much further to go . . .

" Seems to be taking us out of the town . . ." murmured Drummond.

It was true. The houses were getting more scattered, small patches of garden were making their appearance : and Harlow noticed that every inch of these little gardens was being made to give some yield. No doubt this was very essential to their owners, and perhaps made the difference between practically starvation and just enough to keep together body and soul . . .

Harlow suddenly realised he was still holding his little automatic firmly gripped in his right hand. It was much too light to do that now, and rather guiltily he thrust his hand into his pocket. But he kept a firm hold on the butt all the same . . .

Their guide turned in at a gate. Quickly he went round to the back of a small, unpretentious house. He knocked gently on the door.

Harlow, remembering that other door, stood ready.

An abrupt, heavy thud burst on the unnatural stillness of the early morning. The panes in the windows of the small house rattled. Another thud seemed to hit Harlow's eardrums, almost to knock him towards the door . . . and at that moment it began slowly to open . . .

XX

DRUMMOND AND HARLOW MEET JEAN-MARIE

THE door was opened by a little man of middle age, grey hairs beginning to creep up his temples. He solemnly shook hands with the guide, whom Harlow noticed now for the first time to be a big young man with a small black moustache. But they did not complete the courtesy ; they stood there, clasping each other by the right hand, smiling at each other, a curious light—almost a light of triumph—in their eyes. Drummond and Harlow appeared to have been forgotten ; indeed, for them the world seemed to be standing still. It was, in a way, a very uncomfortable minute or two for the Englishman and the American ; not only were they naturally anxious to take cover just as soon as possible from any prying eyes, and the inside of that house offered the opportunity of doing so, but also they both experienced the odd feeling that they were witnesses of an almost sacred moment in the lives of these two Frenchmen.

"Thank God," said the little man, softly, in French, "for our Allies and their air forces ! But thank God also that we true Frenchmen can also contribute to the fight ! "

In a flash Harlow understood. What was it that the pleasant young Englishman had said, only yesterday— it seemed an age ago !—when they had been talking in Pierre's farm ? You are lucky because you may see some fun—there's a do fixed for the early hours of the morning. They had seen some fun all right, unrehearsed fun, to use that word as the Englishman had used it ; but those thuds must mean the success of that ' do ' ! No wonder there was a light of triumph in the eyes of those two patriots . . .

They came out of their ecstatic trance as abruptly as they had entered it. At once, their manner apologetic, they stood aside and gestured towards the door. Harlow grinned and entered, followed by Drummond. The door was closed behind them, leaving them in darkness. The little man pushed past them in the narrow passage, and Drummond lighted the way with the torch. They went down several steps to a cellar, cold and dark, but a real haven—or so it appeared to Harlow and Drummond—after the hazards of the open streets. The little man shoved a sack on an old wooden box, and indicated that they should sit down. Then the two Frenchmen, talking low but rapidly, left the cellar.

Harlow looked at Drummond, the latter grinned at him. " Well, well, well ! " said Drummond. " Something seems to tell me this isn't the fire ! "

The same thought had been in Harlow's mind ; that frying pan saying had been very much in the forefront of his mind during the perilous journey through the streets.

" The little man thinks we're a couple of airmen trying to make our getaway," Harlow told Drummond. " I heard him asking our guide about it as they were leaving."

" What did the guide say ? "

" He didn't correct the impression. Seems it's almost a usual thing, not the first time he's brought fellows who've bailed out around to this point. D'you think he knows who we are . . . the guide, I mean ? "

" He knows we're something special," said Drummond slowly, " because he was in at the shooting, and when they saw us leaving by the gate he was sent along to collect us and bring us here. At least, that's the story he told me in his very broken—practically bust—English, when I caught up with him."

" I hope it's true ! " remarked Harlow fervently.

" So do I," Drummond laughed. " Anyway, it looks all right up to now. Are you, by any chance, peckish ? "

" I believe," replied Harlow, " I could manage an ox ! "

" So could I. Nothing like a bit of exercise to jerk the appetite, is there ! "

Mat Harlow smiled, that statement was very typical of Hugh Drummond.

As if this conversation had been overheard, and their prayer miraculously granted, the two Frenchmen returned with a very tolerable breakfast. The little man, having deposited the tray, made a small speech and stood back smiling. To Drummond the rapid words were totally unintelligible, but Harlow replied and evidently, from the gratified expressions of the Frenchmen, very suitably.

" He says," translated Harlow for Drummond's benefit, " that he is very sorry indeed to have to offer us such an unappetising meal, but he sincerely hopes that after we have won the war, you and I will visit him again and give him the chance of proving what a splendid cook his wife really is ! "

" Accept the invitation on my behalf, and tell him . . . "

" I've done all that ! " smiled Harlow.

" Good."

" Plees, zair ! " remarked the younger man with the black moustache.

" Eh ? " said Drummond, his mouth full.

" I go now . . . to tell of you to my head."

" By all means," said Drummond easily. " Go and commune with your head. I suppose," he turned to Harlow, " he means he's got to report having found us and duly delivered us here ? "

Harlow held a short conversation in French. Then, with cheerful bows and a wave of the hand, the Frenchmen left them.

" He's off to report, as you guessed. Our instructions are to wait here, because his head, as he calls the local big boy, will be along to visit us presently."

" Did you, by any chance, glean any details of what went wrong this morning ? " Drummond asked.

" No. I tried to, but the whole thing seems to have been as big an ugly surprise to him as it was to us."

" Ugly surprise is right ! "

"I've been wondering if old Phillippe . . ."

Harlow left the sentence unfinished. Hugh Drummond looked up at him.

". . . was all that he was made out to be?" he suggested. "I've been wondering that too. It'll be difficult even to know for certain, because the old chap has plenty of holes through him now; as many as if he'd had to face a firing squad. But somehow it seems difficult to believe that the old chap wasn't on the level . . ."

"Very. All the same, appearances do deceive . . ."

"Lamentably. And only too often. Don't say Savoy blonde at me, because I know what you're thinking! I say, this stuff's pretty succulent, whatever it is!"

It was not a meal to be compared with those they had enjoyed at Pierre's or even with old Phillippe: but it was hot and they needed it very badly after the uncomfortable night and the exhilarating if hectic events of the morning. All the same, both felt a trifle ashamed of eating this food, in spite of their hunger. It was very clear that even in this small town conditions were very different, in the matter of sustenance, to what they were in the country : and the look of the tray gave the impression that the old man had skinned his larder in order to do his guests as well as possible. Still, there was nothing to be done about it, and it was quite unthinkable that any of the food should be wasted. By the time they had finished, none was: the end of the meal came with the emptiness of the tray, and not with any failure of appetite.

After that, they had rather a long wait. Just how long, neither would have been able accurately to tell, since they both fell asleep in spite of the discomfort of the damp cellar. The lack of sleep during the night, and the natural reaction to the strain of the small battle, was making itself felt.

They awoke simultaneously to find their little host gently shaking them by the shoulder, and a tall stranger standing by the door, watching the proceeding with a tolerant smile on his pleasant face. Drummond sat up with a jerk, and Harlow scrambled to his feet. The stranger advanced to them, and held out his hand.

"My name," he said quietly in excellent English, " is Jean-Marie. At least, that is what I am called. I come from Paris."

"Mat Harlow. Glad to meet you," said Harlow, taking his hand.

"Mine is Hugh Drummond," said Drummond in his turn.

"I have heard talk of you, Captain Drummond," went on the quiet Frenchman. "I know your country very well. As a matter of fact, I was there very recently . . ."

" Recently ? "

The Frenchman smiled.

"Some of us pay visits, you know. Anyway, welcome to France . . ."

"Thank you . . ."

"I have been told of your mission. You can best accomplish it in Paris, where you can see . . . certain people, and talk with them, and afterwards you will be given an opportunity to see for yourselves, if you desire it."

"That is kind of you. Mat and I are anxious to reach Paris and make the acquaintance of these gentlemen . . ."

"And," said Jean-Marie pleasantly, "believe me, we are anxious that you should see all that you wish, and return and tell people : forgive me, but we have an idea that in England and America, France at war is not fully appreciated. We are, gentlemen, the first to admit our guilt for the tragedy of nineteen-forty : but that was a great betrayal of our country, by certain of our own people, as well as a great military defeat. We are trying to make up for that betrayal, in spite of the fact that the traitors are still officially in power ; and for that defeat. We know that we shall be liberated by our great Allies and friends, but that liberation will be valueless unless we ourselves—Frenchmen—contribute in large measure towards the sacrifices which it will entail. A nation cannot live without its soul : the soul of a nation can only spring from patriotic endeavour and a pride in sacrifice and achievement. You have not been long in France, but you may have already noticed certain signs that the greatness of France is being born again. Every birth necessitates bloodshed. France will live again through the shedding of a great deal of French blood, but even more . . . much more . . . of German ! "

He had spoken very quietly, with only the occasional movement of a hand. But to Drummond and Harlow it was a most impressive speech, an act of faith, a cold statement of a country's determination. Jean-Marie himself, tall, a trifle angular, but with the distinguished face of a scholar, lent dignity to his words : his firm but gentle voice carried conviction.

Hugh Drummond was at a loss for words with which to reply : he felt that some answer was required, but realised that anything he could say must sound flat and cold after what Jean-Marie had said. He was about to say something, however, when the sudden noise of the rattle of machine guns came from somewhere not very far away.

Both Drummond and Harlow looked quickly and inquiringly at the Frenchman.

" France will live again through the shedding of a great deal of French blood." Jean-Marie spoke softly, his eyes half-closed, an unnatural pallor on his face. " That, gentlemen, is a German firing squad murdering French hostages in cold blood, men and women they have dragged haphazard from the streets because of what happened this morning." He paused, but then he went on so softly that they could scarcely hear him. " But it makes no difference—*France must live again* . . . and much more German than French blood will be the toll . . ."

XXI

PARIS IS REACHED

THE journey to Paris was made in the simplest, most normal way. It was accomplished under the noses of the German authorities and the Vichy spies. Drummond and Harlow merely took a train on the morning following their meeting with the man who was called Jean-Marie.

True, they did not look much like Captain Hugh Drummond and Matthew Harlow. In appearance, they were indistinguishable from the couple of small local merchants which they were impersonating, or from the actual small local merchant who accompanied them. In addition, the lower half of Drummond's face was swathed in bandages, so that only his eyes and forehead were clearly visible. This had a double advantage : in the first place, it effectively prevented any possibility of his being forced to speak ; and in the second it did much to conceal his features, now an important matter since the discovery that the German officer who had received his fist had known his name : what more likely than that, with its usual thoroughness, the Gestapo had got hold of a photograph and circulated it, since his presence in the country was known. No attempt had been made to conceal his great size, in fact the very reverse had been simulated in order to complete the disguise. On Drummond's suggestion, his figure had been rounded and fattened, with the result that this soft, flabby man bore no physical resemblance to the fit, muscular Hugh. Much sympathy was drawn from their fellow passengers by the story which Harlow and the real merchant told of the serious injuries suffered by their friend as a result of the recent R.A.F. raid, and Drummond did his best to acknowledge this sympathy by doing his best to make his eyes smile . . .

The journey was simple, but it was not without its bad moments. The first occurred right at its beginning, when the officials, among whom were Germans in and out of uniform, had to be passed at the gate to the railway station. The fact that there were armed men around them ready at any hint of discovery to expose their arms, and risk their lives, in an attempt to retain for them their freedom, did not make running that gauntlet any less anxious for Drummond and Harlow. Rather the reverse, in truth, since if Jean-Marie and his friends thought this bodyguard necessary, then the risk was recognised as great. But the papers with which they had been supplied proved adequate, and the trio moved through and took their places in the train. Watching out of the corner of his eye, Hugh Drummond saw Jean-Marie himself enter a carriage a little further up the train. The curiosity of fellow passengers, any one of whom might have been a German agent, about Drummond's injury was, after the entry, a simple hurdle with which to deal.

Nothing very much happened during the actual journey, which took several long hours. There was always, however, the possibility of a German inspection of the train hanging over their heads. Harlow had been told of this unpleasant trick, in which the enemy herded all who looked young enough and active enough to do forced labour in Germany into another train waiting in some wayside station, and despatched it with its human cargo of potential slaves into the interior of their own country. This was not, however, thought by the experts very likely to happen at the moment, because fairly recently a consignment of unwilling workers had been sent off to Germany by a more normal means : still, it remained an unpleasant possibility . . .

One of the passengers, an elderly woman of plainly nervous disposition, began to surmise on the likelihood of a Spitfire attack on the train itself. Drummond found it very difficult to follow the conversation, but gathered that British fighters, sometimes singly and sometimes in small groups, attacked rolling stock and particularly railway engines sufficiently frequently to make travelling in France rather a hazardous undertaking. She started to complain about it all, and Drummond was surprised and gratified to note how little sympathy she got. The consensus of opinion in the carriage seemed to be the more the merrier, and good luck to the flying boys . . . every engine the less meant one more unable to pull trainloads of Frenchmen to exile in Germany . . .

It was shortly after the nervous woman had been reduced to a glaring silence that Mat Harlow dropped off to sleep. If he talks in his sleep, said Drummond to himself, I shall murder him. But I must say I could do with forty winks meself . . .

When he woke up, Drummond realised that they were nearly at the end of their journey. His fellow passengers were collecting their baggage, and generally restive. Their friend, the merchant, smiled to him : was it a smile of encouragement? Drummond remembered that he had been warned that it was at the beginning and at the end of the journey where most danger lay . . .

But none was obvious. They left their seats, and headed their way along the platform. The real merchant solicitously took Drummond's arm, and gave the impression of helping him along. Harlow followed behind, carrying what little baggage they had between them. Drummond caught sight of the tall, distinguished figure of Jean-Marie some way in front of them.

Leaving the station was really ridiculously easy. They just walked through, and nobody raised any query or objection. As they reached the open street, however, Drummond sensed more than heard a sigh of relief escape the merchant by his side.

It was still fairly early afternoon, and they walked through Paris. The Metro, apparently, was unsafe : the Gestapo was too fond of making swoops and pulling all suspicious characters into their net for a lengthy examination. There were, of course, no taxis. It was, so they had been told, in every way preferable to walk, and Drummond certainly had no objection.

It was an odd experience, that walk through Paris. Nothing very much was changed, except for the all too frequent spectacle of the grey-green uniform and a multitude of cyclists. They, the cyclists, were the most striking to the mind thinking only of Paris before the war, the immense number of cyclists and the total absence of those high-pitched motor horns which nearly all Paris cars used to claim as a right, and use with the abandon of a vice. Everyone seemed to travel by cycle, and the necessity struck Drummond as having affected the fashions in female apparel, for most of the skirts were uncommonly short. How lucky, said Drummond to himself approvingly, that such a large proportion of French women possess such attractive and shapely legs . . .

It was very noticeable in the faces of the people that they were labouring under a heavy strain, but apparently —at least as far as could be judged from outward appearances—not particularly physically, or from any noticeable lack in clothing. The women of Paris looked much the same as the women of Paris have always taken pride in looking, as smart as good taste will allow. But all the same, there was an expression in all eyes which was new to him, something which Drummond diagnosed as a curious blend of defiance and yet fear . . .

They reached a house in the eighth *arrondissement*, that quarter of Paris which is largely given over to big homes. The merchant only had to touch the bell for the great double-door to be opened : evidently they were expected. They found themselves in a narrow courtyard : they were ushered through another door and up some stairs. They found themselves in a luxuriously furnished entrance hall.

Jean-Marie came forward to meet them with a broad smile.

" Welcome to Paris ! I want you to meet your host, but as he was educated at Oxford, Captain Drummond, you will no doubt want to speak to him ! Let us remove the bandages . . ."

" Ah ! " said Drummond, with relief, a moment later, " that's *much* better ! "

" Ever been silent for so long ? " asked Harlow mischievously.

"Pipe down!" grinned Drummond. "It's my turn now!"

Jean-Marie led them up a winding stairway, and took them into a small study. It was very comfortable, and bore traces of its owner's early life at Oxford: a sporting group here, a small silver cup there.

A pleasant-faced man came forward, hand outstretched.

"Captain Drummond? My name is Michel. I'm so pleased to meet you. And Mr. Harlow? Delighted. You must be wanting a drink very badly after your long journey . . ."

He bustled off towards a table, revealing two men who had been standing behind him.

"Allow me to introduce Emile," said Jean-Marie, "and this is a compatriot of yours, Captain . . . Mr. Darwin . . ."

The Frenchman Emile shook hands and stood aside. Then, without a flicker of recognition on his face, Algy Longworth came forward and shook hands with Hugh Drummond and Mat Harlow.

XXII

ALGY LONGWORTH TELLS A STORY

It was fairly late at night by the time that the little party retired to bed. A plan of campaign was sketched by Michel and Jean-Marie for the immediate future of Drummond and Harlow. It seemed that a meeting of the elusive Council of Resistance was very fortunately due to take place in Paris within the next few days, and members were even then congregating in the capital for the event. Whether the visitors would be allowed to attend the meeting was extremely doubtful, but at any rate opportunities would be created for them to meet and talk with the leading lights of Resistance from all over the country. In the meantime, it was considered wise that Drummond and Harlow should not leave Michel's house: in that building they were comparatively safe. It was, apparently, used as some sort of headquarters, and day and night was guarded against surprise. That meant that although a sudden evacuation was by no means out of the question at any moment, warning of the necessity would almost certainly be received in plenty of time for the evacuation sucessfully to be carried out. The means whereby the house would be rapidly emptied, and the occupants got clear of the dreaded Gestapo, were not revealed : but the confidence of Michel and Jean-Marie that the business would be simple, was most comforting to Drummond and Harlow.

The conversation was general in character, although it did keep them going until nearly midnight. A bottle of gin greatly helped : a bottle which had, apparently, been bought in London less than two weeks before, and been brought over by Jean-Marie himself. It was a strain on Drummond and Harlow to feign complete ignorance of the identity of ' Darwin ' as Algy Longworth, but he had given them their cue and there was nothing to be done about it until an opportunity for an explanation could be found. It was more than a strain : it was a constant anxiety. His presence there—totally unexpected, almost incredible—and in the guise of a stranger, could be nothing but ominous. Did it mean that they were not among friends after all ? Could it mean that they were bungling in the mesh of some deep-laid scheme of the Gestapo, and that but for Algy Longworth's miraculous appearance would have fallen easy victims to the enemy ? Whatever it meant, the explanation could only be unpleasant and probably disturbing ; and while waiting for that explanation Drummond and Harlow found it very difficult, not only to conceal their tenseness of spirit, but also to display an adequate interest in the general conversation. Hugh Drummond found himself glancing appraisingly and surreptitiously at the three Frenchmen : surely there could be no doubt about Jean-Marie at least ? They had heard from his own lips his confession of faith, his almost spiritual belief in the future of France through sacrifice in defiance of the strong and apparently victorious enemy. They had seen the expression on his face as he had softly spoken the words explaining that Faith. If he had but been acting, then the man was the most consummate actor in the world. And Michel, the man who had finished his education at Oxford, who professed apparently so sincerely to claim England as a second motherland after his own? And Emile, more silent than the others but perhaps only because he was less fluent in the English language, evidently considerably less high in the hierarchy of Resistance than the others, but a pleasant and honest looking fellow all the same . . . It was very difficult to believe that these men were not what they made themselves out to be . . .

And yet, Algy Longworth had sprung from the blue, was in their midst in Paris calling himself Darwin when he should have been in London, and was resolutely treating Drummond and Harlow as if he had never seen either of them before in the whole of his life!

Odd! Most odd, said Drummond to himself. I wish to goodness I could have a few words in private with that blighter Algy! I bet he's enjoying himself: he's looking horribly smug . . .

The gin gave out. Algy Longworth produced a flask. Half-heartedly, the company urged him to keep the contents against the possibility of a more urgent use, but Longworth insisted . . . With a start, Drummond thought he recognised his own best brandy . . .

Drummond was asked by Michel for his first impressions of Paris under the heel of the hated invader. He gave them: he said he was chiefly surprised at the healthy appearance and smart clothing of the women. In England —and Harlow confirmed in America also—it was the belief that Paris was half-starved and half-clothed . . .

Not so far from the truth, stated Michel. Appearances were deceptive. Yes, wondered Drummond to himself, just how deceptive is the appearance of you three? To take food first, went on Michel, there was food in plenty if you could afford to pay the fabulous black market prices, but if you were poor, then you did not get enough on which to live. Oh, he knew that the rationing should keep you alive : it would, if you ever were able to get all that your card said you were entitled to . . . but that never happened for the poor. How did they exist ? Miserably, cadging from friends who were lucky enough to live in the country, if they had such a friend : otherwise helped to keep a desperate and aching body barely alive by what little the Resistance organisations could do to help.

And as for clothes . . . the women of Paris were determined to keep up their morale, and the best way any woman knows of doing that is to feel that she is looking as attractive as she can make herself . . . the clothes you saw in the streets were very often the only decent suit its wearer possessed . . . some women went without meals in order to save enough to buy the wherewithal to look good, often only in order that some German should make advances, and thus give an opportunity to be snubbed . . .

" But they look well, physically . . ." mentioned Harlow.

Jean-Marie made a suggestion. Before the war, consumption was serious in France : now it was a real menace, threatening to exterminate the French people . . . and the Germans were not displeased. Some put it as high as one in every six of the population . . . if you were a consumptive, it was a well-known fact that you frequently looked in the very best of health, and gained in beauty . . . it did not explain everything, but it would account for a few . . .

Longworth's brandy came to an end. Michel suggested bed : apparently they were all staying in the house. As he led the way, Michel asked them to be as quiet as possible, because his old mother and his daughter were already asleep, and as they worked very hard and under considerable strain, he would not like them disturbed. Nothing more : but the nature of the work done by that old and young woman was easy to guess.

Drummond and Harlow were given a room to share : it was large, airy, and comfortable. Algy Longworth, Drummond noticed with satisfaction, was put next door.

In a short time the party had separated to their respective rooms, and all was quiet . . .

" Hugh . . ."

Harlow spoke softly : Drummond answered in the same tone.

" Yes . . . ? "

" There's a communicating door to Algy's room . . ."

" Good."

" What the devil is he doing here ? "

" And why the frozen mitt ? Let's get him to tell us . . ."

But as Drummond moved towards the door, it opened silently, and Algy Longworth, a broad grin on his face, entered the room and carefully closed the door behind him.

" Welcome to Paris, boys ! " he whispered.

Hugh Drummond restrained a strong desire to hit him.

" Was that my brandy ? " he asked.

" Of course it was ! " Longworth laughed quietly. " You don't think I'd buy any of my own, if I could help it ! Jolly good it is too ! "

" Gather round, Algy." Drummond sat down on his bed. " Mat and I are anxious to know to what we are indebted for this visit . . ."

" Gosh ! " remarked Longworth. " I've had a time ! "

" Describe it, Mr. Darwin . . ." suggested Harlow.

" Darwin ! " Longworth looked mournful. " Fancy having a name like that ! I'm constantly afraid of being offered a monkey nut."

" If you haven't started in precisely five seconds," said Drummond fiercely, " I'll crown you."

Algy Longworth grinned at him happily : then he resumed his mournful expression.

" Poor Peter ! "

" What's happened to him ? " asked Harlow quickly.

" Nothing, I don't think. I mean I do think nothing."

" Now look here, Algy . . ."

" Mr. Darrell is in London, presumably. Presumably lamenting the loss of his dear friend, Mr. Longworth."

" Doesn't Peter know you're here ? " asked Drummond.

" No. Haven't you noticed that the Germans do not

encourage telegraphic facilities between England and France ? "

" For heaven's sake ! " Harlow spoke as patiently as he was able. " But he knew when you started ? "

Algy Longworth looked at him pityingly.

" Of course not. How could he, poor chap ? "

" Supposing *you* tell *us !* " suggested Drummond.

" If you chaps would stop talking," said Longworth. " I will. Now, where was I ? "

" At the point," Drummond told him plainly and distinctly, " just before you begin."

" Of course." Longworth laughed. " Sorry boys, but I just couldn't help it ! By jove, I am relieved to see you both. Do you know that I've had to be desperately serious, not crack one single jest, and keep the grey matter fairly buzzing over, ever since I left London ! I've been living with the Germans, and I can tell you it's a strain ! Merely to live, I mean. At any moment I expected them to discover that I wasn't the real Mr. Darwin, and plug me as full of holes as a sieve. I didn't want them to do that : I didn't think it would suit me ! "

" Who is this guy Darwin ? " asked Harlow.

" Well, Mat," replied Longworth, apparently troubled. " I'm afraid that bit's not very clear . . ."

" Skip it, then ! " Harlow said hurriedly. " Forget it . . ."

" I should know, of course, because I'm supposed to be him," went on Longworth, " but I'm regrettably ill-informed. Not a very pleasant johnny, I'm forced to gather. Thinks nothing of doing people in, and that sort of thing. My reputation's terrific for ruthless killing : even my Gestapo pals quiver a bit when I describe my achievements . . ."

" You don't describe these things . . . ? "

" But of course I do, Hugh ! It's expected of me. The boys fairly hang on my lips, drooling, when I tell them about it. But that bit's not nearly so hard as discussing music . . ."

" Music ? "

" Yes, Mat. I was asked for my opinion of Beethoven's

Second Symphony yesterday. I said I thought he harped a bit on the major, and that went down very well. But if they'd asked me for details, I was sunk. Oh, a most talented fellow, old Darwin is . . . I mean, was . . ."

" Was ? "

" Yes, Hugh. I dotted him one, extremely hard, with his own blunt instrument—in the shape of his own poker—in his flat in London, and he didn't come up again. Sad, but necessary. At any rate, it saves him from being tried as a traitor, and then drawn and quartered, or whatever it is they do to that sort of swine nowadays."

" We appear to have missed a lot, don't we ? " said Drummond to Harlow.

" We certainly do ! " Harlow turned back to Longworth. " I suppose we couldn't start even a little more at the beginning ? I feel it would make it a little easier for my weak intellect . . ."

" Delighted. Anything to oblige, Mat. What year shall I start at ? I was weaned in eighteen ninety-eight . . ."

" Pay no attention to him, Mat ! "

Harlow smiled.

" On the contrary, Hugh, I'm fascinated by him ! Algy Darwin Longworth is my idea of the perfect reporter, concise, humorous, gives a clear picture of the event he is describing in half the number of words his bungling colleagues would be compelled to use . . ."

" Thank you very much indeed," said Longworth.

" . . . and is too good to live . . . one minute longer . . . if he goes on at this rate. Agreed ? "

" Agreed," smiled Drummond.

" Unfortunately," said Longworth, " I can't start until that sterling fellow Michel arrives. Promised I wouldn't, you know, and we Darwins are men of our word. After all, he did arrange for us to meet, and he is our host . . ."

" He's a good chap, Algy ? " Drummond asked the question quickly.

" One of the best."

" And Jean-Marie ? "

" Michel vouches for him. A tremendous fellow, apparently."

" And Emile ? "

" One of the worst. A French Darwin. He's the cause of all the bother, and why I couldn't recognise you. Michel is putting Jean-Marie wise to him now, and they are planning Emile's future for him, but I don't suppose Michel will be long . . ."

" You're quite sure," said Harlow slowly, " that you are right about these men ? I ask, because we have had one unfortunate experience . . ."

" I'm dead sure, Mat." Longworth spoke very seriously. " And I'm in an unparalleled position to know. You may absolutely trust Michel and Jean-Marie—they're the tops. But Emile is a louse. Anyway, I doubt whether you'll see much more of him . . ."

The door opened and Michel came in quietly. He smiled to the three friends, shut the door carefully, and joined the little group.

" Sorry to keep you waiting, but as . . . Darwin . . . has no doubt told you, I had a little business to attend to."

" We're panting for the story ! " smiled Drummond.

" Well, then . . . let's go ahead."

" I'll start," began Longworth, in quite a different manner, " from a day or two after you boys vanished from London. I had just had lunch with Peter, and frankly we were a trifle lonely and disconsolate. Not a sign of Irma, either as herself or playing the part of the Countess Lilli—by the way, there's going to be a beautiful scandal about that charity ramp of hers unless it's all hushed up— and even old McIver was getting irritable and quite a spot difficult. He's got a bone to pick with you, Hugh, for jumping the gun without telling him : his only consolation was that he thought you'd jumped the gun on Peter and myself as well. I left Peter to fall asleep in an armchair of the club, and I strolled down Piccadilly thinking of this and that, and that and this : I promise you, absolutely nothing was particularly on my mind. Suddenly, out of the blue, I heard myself accosted, and coming to earth I found myself face to face with a chap I'd seen down at the pub at home . . . you remember, Hugh, the military-looking johnny who stayed down there a night or two and arrived the night you were stinking . . ."

" What ! "

" No, no ! Don't let your guilty conscience jump to conclusions. I mean the night you'd . . . you'd been to your dentist, or something, and arrived back absolutely odiferous. Remember the johnny ? "

" Vaguely."

" He seemed gratifyingly pleased to see me, and I told him top of the afternoon and all that sort of rot, and was just about to moon on when he reminded me that I'd promised to have a short one or two with him should we ever meet in London. You know, as far as I was concerned a sort of shipboard acquaintance promise, only it was on dry land. Well, I had nothing particular to do, so I said I'd meet him that evening for a snorter. He gave me an address in Bayswater, and I thought no more about it until the time came. I toodled up to the sleepy country-side round Bayswater, discovered the address, oozed in, and found that he had invited another johnny to meet me . . . this fellow Darwin."

Algy Longworth paused, and licked his lips.

" Dry work, talking," he said.

" Serves you right for pinching my booze ! " said Drummond severely. " Go on . . ."

" I discovered that we were really in brother Darwin's flat pretty pronto—I mean, he acted the host, and all that—and then I discovered another thing : I was being pumped, there could be no question about that. Those two birds were much too interested in you and your movements, Hugh, for it to be healthy . . . or unintentional. I fenced a bit with the usual Longworth skill, and the longer it went on, the more certain I became that I had been deliberately asked up to the flat in order to be cross-examined about you. However, the short ones were of a very high quality, and we became excellent friends—I mean the Darwin bloke and myself. The original fellow rather faded out of the picture, entirely in fact after about an hour, when he made some sort of excuse and disappeared. I had been studying mine host, and I had come to a definite conclusion by that time: the fellow was callow as well as being sallow, obviously an adventurer as insincere as they make 'em. Then the idea occurred to me that I could have some fun . . ."

He paused. There was a thoughtful look in his eyes.

"It didn't turn out precisely fun," he continued quietly. "I started off by asking him directly why he was so interested in my friend Captain Hugh Drummond. He pretended to be surprised: wasn't it natural to wonder what a man with Drummond's record was up to in this war? I went directly on to describe a new blonde I said I had just met—if I ever meet anything half so ravishing as I described I'll have to marry her—and painted a dreadful picture of how appallingly expensive it was to take her out: if I ever meet and marry her, I'll have to go bankrupt or get a divorce. He fell for it hook, fly, line, float, reel and rod. He thought I was telling him in his own language that I might—that I could—be bought."

Longworth paused again.

"Go on!" encouraged Harlow.

"Anyone got a cigarette?"

Michel provided him with one. Longworth looked at it a little doubtfully, but lit it and, apparently satisfied, continued:

"I must say he was extremely delicate about it all. He did his best to spare my feelings. He commiserated with me about the extreme extravagance of the lady, but suggested that perhaps it was providential we had met: he might be able to help me. He told me that a friend of his—he put in a romantic touch of his own here, and explained that this friend was an alluring blonde herself— was most anxious to be up to date in your movements, Hugh—and anxious enough to pay well for the information.

"It couldn't be anyone else but Irma, of course. And that placed this beauty perfectly for me, and in a class even below her. He was a paid traitor, a hireling, an

Englishman ready and willing to sell his country. She, after all, is international : she can't be said to be selling any country, she's just available to dispose of the lot, if the money is big enough. After that there was only one thing I wanted to do, and that was to get out and get hold of McIver : obviously I had stumbled across a cog in the Irma machinery, and the hush-hush boys would undoubtedly be interested in the name and address. However, I couldn't just rush out, so after a few moments I allowed myself to be persuaded there couldn't be any real harm in the idea, and anyway I implied that I simply had to have the money, so we began to discuss terms. Over that, I really made myself extremely difficult : I enjoyed that bit ! "

Longworth stubbed out the end of his cigarette.

" Well, I suppose I wasn't as careful as I should have been, or something, but he got suspicious before I realised it. Did I tell you that I have since discovered that he had a reputation for being wildly ruthless ? I think he got it in a flash that he was being fooled, and it was too much for him : he started at me like an enraged bull. I don't like enraged bulls—they're dangerous. I saw him coming, and I picked up the first thing handy, his poker from the fireplace. Frankly, I hit as hard as I could. More by luck than good judgment, I got him fair and square. One glance was enough for me : I'd killed him . . ."

There was a pause. Michel broke it.

" Any man who destroys a traitor deserves a bottle of wine. Just a minute, and I'll get one . . ."

He left the room.

XXIII

ALGY LONGWORTH COMPLETES HIS TALE

" FROM that moment," resumed Algy Longworth, after Michel had returned with the wherewithal, and dispensed it to the company, " things fairly bustled one another to happen as quickly as possible. As far as I can remember, I stared at the body on the floor for a few minutes—it may have been seconds—in a dazed sort of way, conquering a panicky impulse to seize my hat and coat, and fly. Then it occurred to me that I ought to get hold of McIver at once, and bring him up to date. I went to the telephone, and just as I was about to lift the receiver, the bally thing rang and thereby nearly scared me out of my wits again. However, I answered the machine, and a voice asked if it was Darwin speaking. I hesitated, and then said yes. The voice then told me that the car would be round any minute—it had apparently already started—that the voice was sorry it was a trifle late, but that all was now arranged and the chauffeur would have the necessary and all instructions. I just said yes again. The voice concluded by saying—most indiscreetly I thought, over the telephone —to give the speaker's love to the Lady, and said this *in French* . . .

" I replaced the receiver automatically. The old grey matter was doing the jitterbugs all round my head : I have never thought so quickly in all my life. And I was thinking remarkably clearly. In a flash everything seemed to connect up—the curiosity about you, Hugh ; the fact that Darwin was something to do with Irma ; the fact that he was being sent to Irma ; the fact that you were already in France and that now I was prepared to bet that Irma was also in France. I admit it was only guess-work, but I was as certain about it as I was that I had disposed of Darwin for good. And that being so, any fool would have realised that he was on to something very big indeed.

" I'm afraid I didn't think of the risks until after I had made up my mind on my course of action : if I had, I don't suppose I would ever have done what I did. I mean, there was a good chance that somebody might know Darwin by sight : and, at the end of the journey, Irma certainly would . . . and in addition would know me. However, those pleasant thoughts only came to make me feel sick after I had embarked on the adventure . . .

" One thing struck me immediately : I must be protected from the London end. No finding of Darwin's body by his friends to prove that an imposter had stepped in. No finding that a murder had taken place—for it would look like that to them—at that address by the police, to reach the newspapers and warn the enemy just as surely. So I promptly rang up McIver, and thank God he was in !

" You know, old McIver has his points. He's very quick to grasp a situation, and if he knows you, he trusts you. I briefed him as quickly as I could, told him to hush the whole thing up and that I'd have a lot of interesting things to tell him when next we met. And, heavens above, *have I !* "

Algy Longworth took a drink.

" I found Darwin's suitcase, already packed, in his bedroom," Longworth went on. " Evidently he was expecting the telephone call, and was ready for the summons. I hadn't time to do anything more because the car arrived. I'm afraid I didn't touch Darwin : just left him where he was. I was sorry not to be able to warn Peter that I was off, but I hope McIver has since told him the little he knows, and perhaps Peter will put two and two together and make at least three.

" The chauffeur was most obsequious : I was evidently quite a big bug. The car was a big limousine of American make, and carried what looked like official American identification plates—to stop any too great interest by our police, I suppose. If you'll forgive me, I won't go into the details of the journey : that is not relevant here although it will greatly interest the boys at home. It's sufficient to say that I went to Ireland, and then to France. And nobody doubted, all the way, that I wasn't the real Darwin.

" By now I knew exactly what I was up against. Irma was evidently in Paris, and had sent for me—or rather one of her most trusted minions. But, although I knew the game would be up the instant she saw me, I couldn't back out now even if I had seen a way to escape. You boys had to be warned : it was obvious that Irma knew about your visit, although she plainly wasn't quite up to the minute about dates. So all I could do was just to trust to the old Longworth luck, and hope to high heaven it wouldn't fail me at this most alarming point in my career!

"The Gestapo Johnnies met me in France, and tried to be most charming all the way to Paris. They treated me as an enlightened British brother : I could have kicked the self-satisfied blighters ! There was one in particular who insisted that I should smoke his German cigarettes —I shan't forget that one in a hurry !

"We arrived in Paris yesterday afternoon. I was told that Irma would see me in the evening—calling herself brazenly by the old name Irma Peterson, if you please ! —and began to say my prayers. I must say I kept a weather eye open all the time I was saying them, but I didn't even get a half-chance of doing a bunk. You see, I thought I might contact a Resistance Johnny if I got away, who might put me in touch with you boys—a long shot if you like, but a darned sight less risky than a personal interview with the delightful Irma any day. Specially with the information which I now possess ; enough to have her shot fifty times over ; and enough very seriously to inconvenience her Gestapo friends, perhaps to put them entirely out of business for a while, in England at any rate . . .

"The evening came. A resplendent officer came in and introduced himself. He was full of apologies, but Irma had unexpectedly been called away down south somewhere . . . You, Hugh, had been sighted, but something had gone wrong and you'd got away. He said, however, that it didn't really matter Irma being absent, because he had full power to give me my instructions. That man doesn't know how near he came to being kissed !

"Then he told me the whole plan, Hugh, and pretty juicy it is, too !

"You and Mat—I'm not sure they know yet about Mat, but at any rate you—were to have been arrested in that place you were at. You were to have been brought to Paris : your mission, Hugh, is either known or guessed at pretty accurately. And here *you were to have been allowed to escape.* Because your part in the Gestapo scheme of things—and I can trace Irma's hand in the idea—is to lead the enemy to the leaders of French resistance whom they can't identify. And through you, therefore, the Gestapo hoped to smash all that is patriotic in France, and then pick you up as well . . ."

" Just a second, Algy." Drummond spoke seriously. " Were they going to shadow me, or what ? "

" Oh, no. Much fruitier than that : and here's where Darwin—me—comes in. They had a tame Frenchman, that swine Emile, in on the fringe of the Resistance organisation here in Paris, as their spy. But he wasn't high enough up really to be in the know, and he wouldn't be able to worm his way into your confidence. On the other hand, he could introduce an Englishman masquer-ading as a secret sevice johnny to one or two of the right people, and if that Englishman arranged your escape, you'd be all the more inclined to trust him . . . and so would the resistance boys. The escape idea went bust when you got away, but the game could still be played under slightly different rules. Emile could bring me along to those he knew, and I would say I was detailed to help you and keep an eye generally on your comfort and safety. Nothing improbably in that. So when you arrived in Paris, I'd be put in touch . . . and could report to *them* everywhere I went and everyone I met. Juicy, eh ? You see, the thing they were terrified about was that you might get to Paris under your own steam, and that they'd never catch up with you or with your contacts."

" Irma all over ! " remarked Drummond.

" And very nearly got away with it ! " said Harlow, ruefully. " I must say, Hugh, that woman's got a large initiative ! "

" Yes," agreed Drummond dreamily. " Yes . . . but it looks to me as if the luck has changed—against her ! "

" That's not quite fair," Harlow smiled. " Admitted Algy had a bit of luck, but after all he did deserve it . . ."

" Yes," said Drummond, with a grin. " Yes . . ."

"Perhaps I can finish the story best," suddenly said Michel. "This Algy . . . may I call you that . . . ?"

"My goodness, yes!"

"Algy was brought to me, through a chain of others, one of whom Emile knew. I swallowed the story whole. Emile is a good bluffer. Well, Jean-Marie had warned me he was bringing you this afternoon, so I kept them here to greet you on your arrival. But this morning Algy found an opportunity to speak with me privately, and sketched the real situation. Emile now, of course, knows much too much," he continued in a matter of fact voice, "he will not be allowed to report to his German masters; he will be executed. But, inconvenient though it is to have him around at the moment, I do not want him warned that his game is up while he still may be useful. You see, I think we are in a good position perhaps to reverse the Gestapo plan, and to turn it to our own advantage. I don't quite know how yet, but perhaps . . . Hugh . . . ? you will think over it to-night?"

"Most certainly, Michel."

"And I suppose we should condemn this Irma Peterson to death?"

Nothing less dramatic than the way in which he said these startling words could well be imagined. It was merely a quiet statement of what appeared to be a rather unpleasant duty. The other three in the room looked at him with interest.

"What happens then?" asked Harlow.

"Oh, she will be informed of the Council's decision— the Council of Resistance must decide, of course. And then, at the first opportunity, the sentence will be carried out."

Hugh Drummond hesitated: then he decided to risk offending this charming but surprising Frenchman.

"All perfectly legal?"

"But naturally!" Michel smiled to him. "The Council represents the will of the people. The Council is acting until a Provisional Government can be set up in France itself, pending free elections. Therefore the Council has the right to take measures which it deems necessary to protect the people, and to pursue our war . . ."

" Yes . . ." said Drummond.

There seemed nothing else to say.

XXIV

HUGH DRUMMOND AND IRMA PETERSON FALL ASLEEP

TIRED though he was, Hugh Drummond did not immediately go to sleep when finally he got into the extremely comfortable bed which Michel had provided. Harlow was breathing long and evenly almost as soon as his head touched his pillow; but much as Drummond would have liked to have followed his example, he found that slumber eluded him. The totally unexpected arrival of Algy Longworth, and the story of how this arrival had come about, was too fully occupying his active mind.

Algy had undoubtedly excelled himself, there could be no question as to that. He had certainly had the luck on his side, but as Mat Harlow had generously pointed out, that fickle friend only remained a friend as long as one actually courted her favours, and Algy had taken plenty of grave risks in doing just that. One thing seemed very clear to Drummond as he lay there in the darkness : Algy Longworth must be returned to England just as soon as it was humanly possible, and he must be most carefully protected for every moment that he remained in France. Undoubtedly the knowledge which he had acquired in the course of his adventures would be of the greatest possible use in certain quarters both at the War Office and also at Scotland Yard, and might be the means effectively of stopping a very dangerous leak . . .

That seemed to put paid to any idea, as suggested by Michel, of using Emile before destroying him. Emile let loose without Algy Longworth would merely be a danger, and in view of the treasure of knowledge which

Algy was carrying in his brain, a meeting between him and Irma, which could only result disastrously, could not be risked. It seemed a pity—not that Drummond had any clear idea exactly how the man could be used, but the basic thought of turning the tables to their advantage appealed to him just as it obviously did to Michel—that the traitor Emile could not be used against those to whom he had sold himself, but the difficulties appeared on the surface to be too great . . .

Unless, of course . . . by jove, was this the germ of an idea ? . . . unless a meeting between Algy and Irma was made impossible . . .? After all, Algy was very well in with the rest, with the Gestapo boys . . . and Irma, even if she saw them now, would only think that the real Darwin had arrived and been put on the job . . . the only thing that could put Algy in the cart would be for her to see him, recognise him, and expose him . . . but suppose that was made impossible, perhaps by the abduction of Irma by the Resistance chaps to stand her trial in person ?

Hugh Drummond could not restrain a short laugh. That would be a fitting end for this woman who had for so long preyed on her fellow human beings, to face a firing squad of patriots ! And as this thought came to him, his mind also realised for the first time what a perfect, natural Nazi this woman was, who had tried to impose her selfish, grasping will on all around her ! It was very natural, perfectly in character, that she should have thrown in her lot with those gangsters in Berlin, although he was prepared to wager that it was costing them a pretty penny to keep her allegiance even comparatively loyal !

Hugh Drummond felt himself getting drowsy. It would be better to get some sleep now, and return to consideration of the matter duly refreshed in the morning, and in consultation with Jean-Marie and Michel. One thing had to be done : Algy must be sent home as soon as possible, because the longer that leak was left open, the better it would be for the enemy. He would ask Jean-Marie about that in the morning : Jean-Marie would know, he seemed to make a practice of visiting England !

Anything they could do at the Paris end must be contingent on the earliest day that Algy could be got off home ; that departure must not be delayed . . .

Hugh Drummond fell asleep . . .

At almost the identical moment that Hugh Drummond closed his eyes in sleep, Irma Peterson returned to Paris. She was not in the best of tempers : in the first place, the partially armoured car in which the Gestapo had insisted she should travel was by no means comfortable, and she was tired ; in the second, she had found on her inspection in the south a state of affairs which did not strike her as satisfactory in any way; and in the third, her Gestapo opposite number was not waiting to receive her. Added to which the purely feminine irritation of knowing that she was looking far from her best did not help her equanimity.

She sent imperiously for the Gestapo officer, consumed a little refreshment, and set about repairing the ravages of travel on her appearance while she was waiting. When he arrived, she was seated smoking a cigarette through a long holder, and looking as usual the picture of dark beauty.

"Good morning, fräulein!" he spoke hurriedly, apologetically. "The fools never informed me that you were expected so early! They shall be punished! I would never have kept you waiting had I but known . . ."

She stopped his flow of excuses with a gesture.

"Has Darwin arrived?"

"Yes, yesterday . . ."

"Where is he?"

"I sent him off on the job with our man—the man they call Emile. You see, I thought it would be better not to waste time . . ."

He spoke anxiously, nervously, as if a little doubtful about the reception of this piece of news. But he was relieved to see a faint and not unpleasant smile play about her lips.

"Thank God there is someone here who is not afraid

to take the initiative! You will scarcely credit what I found down in the south!"

"As bad as that?"

She laughed mirthlessly, and involuntarily the officer shuddered. Hardened though he was to all forms of inhumanity, the freezing cruelty which sometimes displayed itself momentarily in an action or the voice of this so lovely woman almost shocked him.

"They had Drummond—cold. The Resistance were being kind enough to deliver him practically wrapped up in tissue paper—quite unconsciously of course. Your local people, up to the moment when he arrived, behaved quite intelligently: they had previous knowledge of the rendezvous, and they managed to be there, in full possession, right under the noses of the local resistance troops . . ."

"I wish you wouldn't call them that! They are . . ."

"Face facts." She spoke bitingly, "that is precisely what they are: troops. Badly armed, but troops which have got to be extermintaed in battle just the same! Drummond came to the door, after the man who had brought him had checked that all was well with the unsuspecting Resistance leader. And then what happened? Your fool of an officer, who'd obviously been reading too many thrillers, threw open the door like a scene in grand opera, and welcomed him!"

"No!"

"Yes."

"What happened?"

"What always will happen in such circumstances. Drummond hit him, and escaped in the confusion. There was a short, sharp battle, and you lost several valuable men."

"I will have that officer shot!"

Irma Peterson smiled.

"No need," she said, "unless you like shooting dead men. The Resistance got him through the open door."

She paused, took another cigarette, and lighted it.

"So the total result," she said quietly, but a trifle ominously, "is that Hugh Drummond is still at liberty, is now warned against taking too much for granted, and is going to be just about twice as difficult to find again."

" Unless Darwin . . . ? "

" Yes, unless Darwin pulls it off."

The Gestapo officer looked at her covertly : she had not been unpleasant to him personally, but he thought she looked as if she might be at any moment. This was highly undesirable : not only had he the greatest respect for the sharpness of her tongue, but also he knew very well that this woman was held in the very highest esteem by his Chief, and even by Berlin. It would not do at all to fall out with her. Perhaps just a little flattery might help . . .

" That, fräulein, if you will permit me to say so, was a brilliant idea of yours . . ."

" What was ? "

" To bring the man Darwin here."

" It was an obvious move ! " But she smiled at him. " If you let Drummond slip through your fingers when he arrives here in Paris, I'll never forgive you . . ."

" Have no fear ! " he put in hastily.

" I must see Darwin. Who briefed him ? "

" I did."

" Nevertheless, my friend, I think it would be as well if I saw him. Can you get a message to him ? "

" Yes. Through Emile."

" Tell him to report as soon as he can. He does not know Drummond very well. It is useful to know Drummond if you have to deal with him, because he is by no means as simple as he likes people to think that he is. And it is just possible Darwin may under-rate him . . ."

" Why should he do that ? I warned him well . . ."

She laughed again, genuinely this time.

" Darwin played a little trick on Drummond, and found it a ridiculously easy task . . ."

The officer sat up with a jerk.

" Drummond knows this Darwin ? "

She smiled.

" Don't worry : Darwin did not look in the least like

himself that day. But he is a conceited fellow, and I feel it would be best if I were to warn him against taking things too easily and confidently with that cursed Englishman . . ."

"Very well. I will send a message to Emile in the morning . . . this morning." The officer rose. "You must get some rest, fräulein. It is already getting light. May I have the pleasure of taking you to lunch to-day . . . I know of a new restaurant run by an excellent fellow, who is a friend of mine : he is sometimes really quite useful. Will you give me the pleasure . . . ? "

She also rose from her chair, tall and graceful.

"Thank you. But not too early . . ."

"Of course not. Shall I call for you at one . . . or one-fifteen ? "

"Make it one-fifteen."

"I shall be here. Sleep well, fräulein . . ."

She smiled to him. She watched him as he left the room. Not a bad fellow at all, really. He looked well in his uniform. And he was not merely one of those stupid cogs in a machine, which so many Germans were. He had displayed initiative in not wasting time, and sending Darwin out at once. That, specially in the circumstances, had been a good move : Drummond was already no doubt making his way to Paris, and if Darwin could be well installed by the time he arrived, and have gained a little of the confidence of these stupid French, so much the better. But it was essential that she herself should see him : she knew his weaknesses, and she knew only too well just how dangerous Hugh Drummond could be if someone took him for the amiable, casual individual which he so delighted in impersonating . . .

Irma Peterson went slowly to bed. She was thinking of Hugh Drummond, and a frown disfigured her lovely forehead. He had not, up to now, shown any of those qualities which had outwitted and finally destroyed her beloved Carl, except perhaps courage and in the case of the stupid Gestapo officer down south—promptitude. But that, she told herself, was no reason to fall into the very same trap against which she was about to warn the man Darwin. Hugh Drummond might be playing a deep game, and until he was safely in his grave, he must be credited with the ability to engineer a surprise. She thought of Carl Peterson, and then again of Drummond : she bared her teeth in an anticipatory smile : she would ask for the privilege of attending Drummond's investigation by the Gestapo when finally he had unconsciously delivered up the members of his Council of Resistance, and when all his knowledge would be dragged out of him until his mangled body could stand no more, and he was dead. She would give herself the pleasure of suggesting certain little tricks which would assuredly make him speak ; and then, if they did it cleverly enough, would come the glorious moment when he knew no more to tell, *and still they went on* . . .

Irma Peterson got into bed, and laid her head upon the pillow. Only one thing would give her pleasure now, and that was if Drummond could only know that she was here in Paris up against him, that her wits were pitted against his in mortal combat, that the dice were heavily loaded in her favour and that he was about to be caught like a miserable rat. She played with the idea of writing him a note, and giving it to Darwin to plant on him. But she rejected that idea quickly : it was just the sort of thing which she must impress Darwin against succumbing to, this temptation to tease the victim before he had accomplished her purpose and was safely in the hands of the Gestapo. No, given even normal luck, Hugh Drummond could not escape this time : at last he was to pay for daring to lay his vile and violent hands on Carl. It was a just and a satisfying punishment. It was a punishment which really fitted the crime. It was going to be the most glorious moment of her life, because she would at least have avenged her beloved : and it should be possible to make the agony last for several days . . . for the first occasion in her life Irma Peterson thought of the great physical strength of Hugh Drummond with approval . . .

She closed her eyes. The pale light of the early morning was weakly illuminating the room. Her black hair framed the startling pallor of her beautiful face. She looked gentle and peaceful . . .

The pale light of the early morning was quite impartial and weakly illuminated the interior of the room not a mile away in which Hugh Drummond slept. His rugged countenance was no particular ornament to his pillow. He opened his mouth.

A magnificent snore reverbated through the room.

XXV

HUGH DRUMMOND CONVINCES HARLOW

DRUMMOND and Harlow slept well into the morning. While they were shaving, they had a brief discussion on their impressions up to date, and both were gratified to find that their opinions were really identical : both were much impressed by the organisation behind all the heroism that they had seen : and also by the temper of the people . . .

Before they had made their appearance, Jean-Marie came in to ask if there was anything they wanted, as he was going out into the city. Drummond put to him the question of getting Algy Longworth back to England as soon as possible, and explained his reasons for considering this a matter of urgency. Jean-Marie readily agreed : he would make himself responsible, he said, and Longworth would be given the first priority, but he warned Drummond that he thought it would be impossible to arrange a passage in under two weeks. In a sense, Drummond was pleased : not only was it pleasant to have Algy around, but also his conscience was clear now to think up some scheme with the others, which could put Emile to use . . . provided that it could be completed in those two weeks. The idea of abducting Irma Peterson was proving a very real temptation . . .

The morning passed idly, because Michel was busy. But neither Drummond nor Harlow regretted this enforced rest : the happenings of the last few days were beginning to take their toll, and a lassitude born of reaction was making itself felt. During the morning, however, Algy Longworth did contrive a few minutes alone with Drummond, and informed him that Emile was getting a trifle restive : he had confided to ' Darwin ' that somehow he must make an excuse to be allowed out within a day or so, as it was necessary for him to keep in touch with his go-between and find out if there were any fresh instructions for them from Headquarters . . .

Michel had better know about that : Drummond undertook to inform him.

But they did not see Michel, nor his family at lunch. After the rather frugal meal, Drummond and Harlow decided to make the best of an opportunity which migh not occur again, and they retired to their room, and their beds. Drummond lay fully clothed on top of the eiderdown, smoking languidly, and rather enjoying the thought that here he was in Paris, safe and enjoying his luxurious surroundings, while all over the city—maybe all over France—the dreaded Gestapo were engaged in making an anxious search for him. Makes one feel quite important, said Drummond to himself : makes one realise, too, what a valuable thorn in the German flesh these excellent patriots must be, defying the will of the oppressor at every turn . . .

The door opened, and Michel came into the room. Drummond and Harlow, sitting up to greet him, saw at one glance that something was very wrong. His face was pale and he was out of breath as if he had been hurrying.

" What's up, Michel ? " asked Drummond.

Michel closed the door of the room carefully. He then moved over to the communicating door leading to Longworth's room, opened it, satisfied himself that the room was empty, closed it again : and it was only then that he spoke.

" Bad news. Jean-Marie has been arrested."

" What ! "

Drummond and Harlow scrambled from their beds.

" How did it happen ? "

" Just pure bad luck ! " Michel sighed. " He was sitting at a café, enjoying an aperitif, when the Germans staged one of their round-ups. I don't know if they were looking for anyone in particular : sometimes they do these things just for the nuisance value. Probably they were just after a few more poor souls to deport to Germany for forced labour. Anyway, they bundled all the able-bodied men they found in their net into police vans, and have rushed them off to prison."

" Will they know who he is ? " asked Harlow quickly. Michel smiled quietly to him.

" I doubt whether they'll know what they've got," he replied. " If they don't, then we should be able to get him out in a few days. But in his case there is a danger that they may find out, because he was caught once before, and the Gestapo have a very complete dossier about him. If one of those Gestapo brutes happens to wander through the prison, and happens to recognise him from the photograph they have, then . . . then one can only wish a quick death for him."

" That's not a very likely happening, is it ? "

Drummond asked the question more to offer a grain of comfort than for any other reason : he knew only too well, from the reports he had been allowed to read in London, that Michel's remark about the best thing for Jean-Marie being a quick death was only too true.

" It depends. That again must be a matter of luck. But I wish to goodness that dossier was not in the possession of the Gestapo . . . without the danger it represents, Jean-Marie might at the worst be sent to work for the Germans, but I think we could get him out before that. The danger lies in the Gestapo taking him from the civil prison where he is now . . ."

There was an awkward pause.

" He's such a grand man ! " said Harlow suddenly.

" One of the very best," agreed Drummond.

" Gentlemen," said Michel solemnly, " I know you will

respect my confidence when I tell you that he is much more than that. In any case you must have suspected it. Jean-Marie is one of the really big men of our organisation, and we simply cannot afford to lose him. Still, don't let us be pessimistic : we have survived worse blows than this, and he is not yet lost . . . Forgive me, but I must go to arrange a few details : there are one or two things he will need to-night . . ."

"Can you reach him ?" asked Drummond in surprise. Michel smiled.

"Until they get into the hands of the Gestapo, and sometimes even then, we can always reach our friends . . ."

Michel left them. Neither Drummond nor Harlow spoke. The news had come as a severe shock : the supreme confidence of these Frenchmen with whom they dealt made any set-back even more shattering ; and Drummond in particular, after the trend of his recent thoughts, felt almost ashamed. But a new line of thought abruptly forced itself upon his mind, and occupied it so completely that he failed to hear Mat Harlow speak to him.

Harlow looked at him in surprise. Hugh Drummond was wearing a heavy frown, was almost scowling. Better leave him to it, thought Harlow : something pretty important must be under examination by Drummond's brain . . .

"Mat !"

Harlow jumped. His name had been almost barked out, and as he looked at his friend, Harlow caught something of the suppressed excitement which was very evident in Drummond's expression.

"Yes ?"

"Mat, I believe I've got it !"

"Got what ?"

"Rally round, old bird ! I don't want to talk too loud."

Hugh Drummond was sitting on the edge of his bed : he made room for Harlow, who moved over and joined him. Drummond continued in a low voice.

"Jean-Marie has got to be got out, hasn't he ?"

"Sure . . ."

"I mean, you can't let your host be manhandled by Germans, can you?"

Hullo, said Harlow to himself, what *is* this? Sounds like as if old Hugh was trying to wangle something . . .

"Apart from the fact that he's not our host, agreed."

"Part host, then?"

"Okay. Part host."

"It's up to us to do all we can to help, isn't it?"

"Certainly."

"I think I'd better go and destroy that dossier which is hanging over our pal's head. Then he'd be safe for his own boys to pull out . . ."

"*Hugh!*"

"Yes?" replied Drummond meekly.

"You've got a mission."

"I know I have."

"You've got to complete that mission. It says nothing about attempting to commit suicide first."

"You do put things well!" Hugh Drummond grinned. "Succinctly, that's what I like. But it says nothing about not helping those who are our proved friends, does it?"

"No . . ." admitted Harlow suspiciously.

"And if there's no danger attached, and in fact positive gain may result, it would be criminal not to do it, wouldn't it?"

"You'll never convince me of that!"

"What, that it would be criminal?"

"No, no . . . that there's no danger attached."

"I think I can," said Drummond quietly.

There was so much confidence in his voice that Harlow looked at him sharply, wondering if he could glean any clue from his expression. On the face of it, about the only thing that you could not argue in favour of this suggested escapade was that it could be undertaken without danger. It would be a fine thing to do, it would help the men who had received them so unquestioningly and who were so obviously contributing so successfully to harassing the common enemy, it might even yield tangible results in favour of the Allies . . . but it certainly was not safe. In fact, Harlow could not imagine how on earth it could be accomplished at all . . .

" Don't be daft, Hugh . . ." he began.

But Hugh Drummond had an obstinate look in his eyes, a look which Algy Longworth or Peter Darrell could have told Harlow would take a tremendous lot of shifting.

" Look, Mat," he cut in, " we know that at this stage the Gestapo will allow me to escape if they catch me . . . remember what Algy said ? "

" They were going to. But now it's different . . ."

" Why is it different ? "

" Well . . ."

" I don't see that it's different at all. We've only got to plant two things in the great mind of the Gestapo, and we've got the means to manage that . . ."

" Emile ? "

" Yes."

" What are the two things ? " asked Harlow after a short pause.

" The first, that I have not yet met the big boys and have not yet had time to see the inner workings of the Council of Resistance, *but that I'm going to very soon*. The second, that Emile and ' Darwin ' need a bit of consolidation with us, and with men like Jean-Marie and Michel, and that the credit for my escape would put them right with us . . ."

" Just a moment, Hugh. I agree your first point is a darned good one. But your second stinks : they can't get the credit for your escape without taking part in it. Michel won't let Emile out of this house now that he's entered it and knows about it, and Algy can't go back because he's sunk—and you'd be sunk—the moment Irma Peterson sets eyes on him, which would inevitably be almost at once."

" Not if she wasn't present to set eyes on him."

" Eh ? "

" Not if she wasn't there."

" What do you propose doing ? Inviting her out for a little dinner and dancing ? "

Hugh Drummond laughed.

" Almost that. Inviting her out, anyway, and taking no refusal. I think our resistance pals would like to entertain her for a little while—specially if it would help Jean-Marie . . ."

In spite of himself, Mat Harlow was beginning to be impressed. He had at first thought the scheme completely scatter-brained, but now he was beginning to fall for it. Its very audacity appealed to him, but he told himself severely that he must remain strongly critical : his value at that moment lay in keeping his head and his common-sense, and not following his natural inclination to plunge whole-heartedly into approval.

" You'll never get Michel to agree."

" Why not ? You saw the state he was in when he told us about Jean-Marie."

" Yes, but he daren't release Emile now . . ."

" He might. Don't forget, some possibility—of using Emile, I mean—was in both his and Jean-Marie's minds last night . . . that's why they didn't immediately dispose of him."

Mat Harlow felt himself weakening : he took a firm pull.

" That was different . . ."

" Don't keep saying things are different ! " snapped Hugh Drummond, but there was an understanding smile in his eyes.

" It was different. Probably no more than making him write a message was in their minds : but this entails letting him loose—he's got to be let loose because he's got to take part in the pre-arranged escape . . ."

" All right. But what does letting him loose entail ? "

" Scattering the news about this house, about Michel and—my goodness, yes, *about Jean-Marie* . . ."

Harlow looked quickly at Drummond : he found himself hoping that somehow or other his friend could see his way through that objection, but it loomed horribly large to him. If Emile reported the identity of the prisoner, then the Gestapo would act at once and without hesitation, since in their eyes it could not affect the Drummond case, and the whole object of the adventure would be defeated.

"Emile would be quite unable to expose Jean-Marie, since he has no idea Jean-Marie is a prisoner . . . and he will be kept in ignorance of that lamentable fact."

Mat Harlow's hopes began to rise again.

"True. But he will describe him . . ."

"Not so well as that photograph in the dossier. Even if his description is superb, the Gestapo will start looking for Jean-Marie in Paris, not in a prison, because Emile will tell them he is free in Paris . . . it's an added point for, not against."

Mat Harlow smiled.

"Let's go back," he said. "You were going to tell me what letting Emile loose entailed . . . ?"

"So I was. It means this : the evacuation of this house and of Michel and his family, and that's all. Michel would have to lie low for a bit, but I imagine it would not be the first time he has had to suffer that inconvenience. And the evacuation of the house would not, I imagine, be much more than a temporary inconvenience either ; because we know that they are all prepared for it at any moment, and alternative premises are no doubt ready and waiting. Obviously, Mat, mere inconveniences are not going to stop them doing all in their power for a personage such as Jean-Marie."

Mat Harlow felt it his duty to reiterate one important point.

"It all sounds perfectly swell, Hugh," he said quietly, "and in theory it can't go wrong . . . or so we are rapidly convincing ourselves. But there *is* the hell of a risk : have you forgotten the stories you told me about the Gestapo when we first met in London ? They are utterly unreasonable, inhuman brutes. Once they get you, they may do anything to you . . . and they may change their mind about letting you escape. If they do, you're done, with nothing accomplished and your mission unfulfilled . . ."

Hugh Drummond grinned.

"Thanks, pal. But there's a risk to anything, and the only way to judge whether or not the risk is worth taking is to weigh the probable results against it. Because we mustn't forget that they probably won't change their minds : with the real Darwin, it would be a whale of an idea. Anyway . . ." he laughed again, " I've taken worse risks in my life, and I'm still in one piece ! "

He spoke quietly, completely without pride : there was no suggestion of conceit in the way in which he spoke the words.

There was a pause. With a rising heart, Mat Harlow felt himself defeated.

" There's only one thing that rather bothers me," said Drummond thoughtfully, " and that is, how on earth am I going to get at the dossier once I do get captured . . ."

" Oh, that's easy ! " exclaimed Harlow impulsively, " All Algy has got to do is to plant the idea that it might be a good idea to have a run through the men they already have particulars about, in case you could be persuaded to place the present whereabouts of any of them . . ."

" I don't like that word ' persuaded '."

" Let him arrange it as an afterthought, just before the ' escape ' is to take place . . ."

" Here, who's planning now ? "

Harlow burst out laughing.

" It was the best way I could help . . ." he said apologetically.

" I know it was, old top ! " said Drummond quietly, " and don't think I didn't appreciate it. And thanks a lot for this last idea . . . I do believe you've got it ! "

" Hugh . . ."

" Yes ? "

Harlow seemed embarrassed.

" Hugh . . . couldn't I come too ? "

Drummond found himself totally at a loss for words with which to reply. He was deeply touched : Mat Harlow, making his request, was so obviously sincere . . .

He shook his head.

" No Mat : that *would* be madness. You see . . ."

" Oh, I know ! " Harlow sounded disappointed but resigned. " We're on a job, and we can't put all our eggs into one basket. And if anything did happen to you, there's always Algy to act as understudy for the British side. Quite apart from the fact that just as the odds are on the Gestapo staging your release, they'd be heavily against the same concession for me. Finally, it's an advantage that they probably haven't yet guessed of my existence ! "

" In a nutshell," agreed Drummond.

" How are you going to destroy the dossier when you get it ? I mean, they'll take everything off you when they take you . . . ? "

" That," said Hugh Drummond, " is one of the things I am now going to discuss with Michel . . ."

He rose to his feet. He took out a cigarette and lighted it. With a smile to Harlow, he left the room.

XXVI

OLD ACQUAINTANCES MEET

THE weather had been mild up to now, but that day it was excelling itself. True, the rays of the sun had lost a great deal of their warmth, but the sun was doing its very utmost to make up for that deficiency by shining for all it was worth from a cloudless sky. The trees of the Champs Élysées had taken on their autumn colouring, indeed had lost a good deal of their leaves in the November winds, but they nevertheless still contributed to the beauty of this thoroughfare, although they rustled restlessly in keeping with the mood of the people . . .

It was a day on which the light-hearted Parisiens should have been gay and care free : but all the efforts of the sun could do little to alleviate the strain and tension always to be observed lurking in the eyes of the men and women who passed by . . .

A large black car drew up on the right hand side of the Avenue, just a little above the *Rond Point*. It was driven by a chauffeur in black German uniform, and another man in the same uniform travelled by his side. Both were rather ostentatiously wearing heavy automatic pistols.

A lady got out of the car. The man acting as footman, or perhaps more correctly as bodyguard, alighted also and strolled round the car on to the pedestrians' walk. But he did not follow the lady as she crossed this, and made for the famous perfume shop known as Guerlain's : he merely watched her keenly, and all those around her. She was evidently a person of some importance, but not someone who was apparently likely to provoke assault . . .

Irma Peterson entered the shop. She paused for a moment, and looked around her. The place was fairly full, but chiefly of women. They were making various purchases, and for the moment none of the assistants was available to attend to her . . .

Well, she was in no hurry. Darwin, in choosing this shop for their meeting place, had made a good selection : it was the sort of place where she could waste time without drawing attention to herself almost indefinitely ; and she quite understood that having once contacted the Resistance people, he could not risk coming to any of the houses known to be the haunts of the Gestapo. Her officer had demurred slightly, but had been easily over-ruled : obviously she was perfectly safe, since she was quite unknown in France. And anyway, she wanted to visit Guerlain's : there was the necessity to replenish her supply of that admirable perfume *Vol de Nuit* . . .

The name of the scent reminded her of the Countess Lilli and Captain Hugh Drummond. A pity the big fool had finally stumbled through that very pleasant character : she had enjoyed playing the part, and it had undoubtedly been profitable. Still she could no doubt assume another equally pleasant rôle on her return to England. For a minute she allowed herself to wonder where Hugh Drummond had got to at that moment : perhaps Darwin would be able to throw some light on the matter. He had been very insistent in his message that she should meet him that morning, had sounded very much as if he had something of importance to communicate.

A large man brushed passed her : she scarcely noticed

him except to feel a subconscious surprise that a man so poorly dressed should enter such fashionable premises : perhaps he was just on business connected with the trade.

She looked around the shop. It appeared to be very much the same as she remembered it from before the war : the same galaxy of perfumes, although less displayed on the shelves, the same choice of lipsticks, the same—outwardly at least—tastefully decorated boxes no doubt containing face cream and powder. For a moment, Irma Peterson could not help contrasting the apparent abundance as compared to the visible stock of a similar establishment in London : but when she heard the woman next to her being refused a second bottle of something or other, and realised that Guerlain's were rationing their clients, and apparently judging from the remarks of the customer—rather severely. She smiled to herself : it was going to be fun having that *Vol de Nuit* again—no scent so admirably suited her . . .

She heard a man's voice ask for *Vol de Nuit* : the voice came from just behind her.

She looked round idly : she had now been in the shop some little time, and it mildly irritated her that someone—especially a man—should have found an assistant before her. They should really take their clients in their proper turn . . .

She found herself looking at the back of the poorly dressed individual who had brushed passed her : she noted, without particular interest, that this man had very broad shoulders. She looked around the shop again, to see if any of the other assistants appeared as if they were about to be disengaged. She heard the man ask how much it would be . . .

Irma Peterson spun round and stared at the back of the big man again. There was something vaguely familiar about it : she was conscious of a strong feeling that she had seen it before, only clothed very differently. But it was not this sensation which had suddenly riveted her attention : it was the voice she had heard . . .

The man spoke French very badly. True, she was no scholar herself, and she could not be sure that he might not be talking with a heavy provincial accent, or even largely in some incomprehensible—to her—*patois*. But all the same, surely he was speaking with a foreign—with an English intonation?

She looked at the assistant who was serving him. Confirmation of her suspicions was written all over the startled face of the pretty girl. The girl leant forward and started to speak slowly and softly to her client: unobtrusively, Irma Peterson edged up close to the back of the man.

"If I were you," she could just hear the assistant say, rather in the tones of a French mistress giving a lesson to a child, "I would get out of Paris quickly. Paris dangerous. Country much safer. Find friends more easily."

Quietly, Irma Peterson edged round to the side of the big man, who had now taken his parcel and was fumbling with his money. She studied his profile carefully: she looked at his hair.

He was wearing rather a crude wig. His face was quite cleverly made up, but it was the work of an enthusiastic amateur rather than of the expert.

Irma Peterson's lips parted in a smile of triumph: no wonder those great shoulders had appeared to be familiar!

Hugh Drummond had evidently not yet seen her. If only Darwin had been punctual! For Irma Peterson knew that she had to make a very important decision, and she knew also that she had only a very few minutes in which to make up her mind: just the time in which it would take Drummond to sort out his money, pay for his purchase, and leave the shop. And whatever Darwin had to report might affect that decision vitally.

Irma Peterson slipped out of the shop. She saw that her bodyguard had strolled over the pedestrians' walk and was now within a few yards of her. She beckoned to him.

It took her only an instant to give him the necessary instructions. He nodded, and went quickly to the chauffeur. Then he returned, and stood a little to one side.

Irma Peterson waited for Drummond while her mind grappled with the problem. Should she seize him now, when she could, or should she let him go, in the hope that Darwin had already made his contact? Did she dare do that, and let him disappear again perhaps never to be picked up by Darwin, should he not already have found him? If only that unpunctual creature would turn up even now, there might still be time . . . what could have happened to him? Casual, yes, but he was not normally unpunctual . . .

Irma Peterson made up her mind. Hugh Drummond must not be allowed to get away. No real harm would be done even if Darwin had already contacted him, because the original plan could always be put into operation . . . the risk of allowing Hugh Drummond to walk off into the vastness of the great city was more than she was justified in taking . . .

He came out of the shop, and stood for a few moments as if wondering in what direction to saunter away: no doubt, in peace time, thought Irma Peterson, he would have strolled across the Champs Élysées, after the strain of purchasing a bottle of scent, and indulged in a short one at the Travellers' Club. She would almost have taken a bet that the idea was in his mind now. She allowed him to take a few steps along the pavement, and then nodded.

The uniformed German caught the signal. He quickly caught up with Drummond, and touched him on the arm. Hugh Drummond stopped, looked at the man, and smiled a trifle vacantly.

Irma Peterson, close by, watched in some amusement. She was interested to see how Drummond would attempt to extricate himself from what must be an unpleasant situation. She glanced around, and saw that her chauffeur had left the car and was rapidly approaching. Good: they would shoot if Drummond took to his heels, they were crack shots, and they had been told—in the brief moment when she had been able to give her instructions—only to wing him if he attempted to bolt. She could well afford to watch and enjoy his embarrassment . . .

The German said something to him—Irma Peterson knew it was an order to walk to the car. Hugh Drummond just grinned vacantly at him and made an odd sort of gurgling noise . . .

Irma Peterson stared : what on earth had happened to him ? She expected something better from this man of action . . .

The German repeated his order tersely, and indicated the automatic in his hand. The chauffeur had now joined the two : one or two pedestrians were beginning to notice the little group, were beginning to sheer away with pitying glances towards the Englishman . . . Hugh Drummond gurgled again, pointed to his ears and mouth, shook his head, grinned pleasantly, and then emitted a sound which bore a remarkable resemblance to a hiccup . . .

Irma Peterson had seen enough : she walked quietly up to them.

" Good morning, Captain Drummond ! "

She laughed : Hugh Drummond positively jumped. His eyes seemed to be about to fall out of his head, and his mouth opened in surprise. Irma Peterson congratulated herself on seeing him so taken aback : she would enjoy remembering him like that . . .

" So you can hear *my* voice all right ! and no doubt you can speak to me as well . . . ? "

" Christopher Columbus ! " said Hugh Drummond.

" I beg your pardon ? "

" I shouldn't bother ! " said Drummond, apparently quite cheerfully. " Just mildly relieving my feelings, that's all ! "

" The man with the gun—just in case you can't understand German—is requesting you—pointedly—to walk to that black car over there." Irma Peterson smiled pleasantly, " I think he is getting just a little impatient. As he looks rather as if he would enjoy pressing the trigger, I think if I were you I should obey him."

Hugh Drummond looked round him quickly : for an instant she thought that he was contemplating flight. So did the two Germans, for they closed on him menacingly. Drummond glanced at them, and then turned back to her.

" Good shots, these Johnnies, aren't they ? "

" I am given to understand that they are absolutely first class."

" Yes, I've heard so too. So there doesn't seem anything for me to do for the moment but accede to their wishes, does there, Irma my dear ? "

She flushed. She could not help admiring his control over himself, much as she disliked acknowledging any quality in his character. And his free and easy use of her christian name in almost affectionate tones, or so he made it seem, annoyed her . . .

She turned on her heel and walked to the car. Drummond followed, closely attended by the two uniformed Germans. Drummond was pushed into the back : one of her bodyguard took up his position on the small seat opposite him, and Irma Peterson got in beside him. The chauffeur took his place and drove off, only just in time : the few spectators of the scene were beginning to look menacing, were quite openly saying unpleasant things. She wondered how they dared . . . in the face of armed authority as represented by the black uniformed men . . .

" I seem to have got the sympathy of the audience . . ." murmured Drummond. She was curt with him.

" You'll need it."

" Just as charming as ever, I see, Irma ! But I must congratulate you on your looks : your real, dark self, you know, suits you far better than any of your blonde artifices . . ."

" That will do, Captain Drummond."

" Will it ? What a pity ! I was just getting really under weigh, and I'm quite sure I should have said something really delightful in my very next sentence. Are you sure you wouldn't like to hear it . . . ? "

She ignored him. But it is an extremely difficult thing to ignore a determined conversationalist in the close proximity of a closed car.

" What a lovely day ! I think Paris is looking quite beautiful, don't you ? In spite of these comic opera German uniforms . . ."

She did not reply.

" Did it cost much ? "

" Did what cost much ? "

She was startled into the reply by the unexpectedness of the question.

"To have your nose straightened?"

She decided to ignore him again.

"I do wish you'd tell me," said Drummond almost plaintively, "because Peter and Algy—you remember them of course?—were really quite worried about it. Personally-I hope it didn't cost much because I don't think its an improvement—that slight touch of Old Rome gave you a certain distinction, I thought. But just for the sake of the others, won't you tell me? They'll be so disappointed if I don't know when I see them again . . ."

"You seem very confident that you will see them again."

"Naturally. Surely you know me well enough to know that I'm no pessimist!"

"Let me give you a piece of advice, Captain Drummond," she spoke coldly. "Save your breath. Gestapo investigations are apt to take a very long time, and you may want to do a lot of . . . shall we call it talking?"

Hugh Drummond grinned.

"By all means let's call it talking. But won't you . . ."

"We are just arriving," she interrupted him, "and I should like to impress upon you that you have no chance of escape whatsoever. You may hate and despise the Germans, but they have one tremendous quality—they are very thorough. The arrangements for receiving and retaining visitors in this place are fool proof. You had better accept your defeat in the best spirit which you can muster . . ."

Hugh Drummond laughed, although she thought she detected a forced note—of anxiety?—in the sound.

"But that's just what I am doing!"

They had pulled up for a moment to allow the great doors to be opened : then the car drove through into the courtyard. She gave a curt order to her bodyguard, and left the car. As she walked to the door, she glanced over her shoulder and saw Drummond being unceremoniously hurried towards another . . .

It did not take her long to explain what had happened. The Gestapo Officer was delighted, and complimented her. She waived aside his congratulations.

"I could not, of course, wait for Darwin. Please send

for him at once. He must risk coming here—to-night in the dark should be safe enough if he dares not come before—because we must all meet and discuss this new development. Everything depends on his report. I shall go to my appartment, and wait to hear from you."

" Very well, fräulein . . ."

Irma Peterson returned to the car. She then drove straight to the apartment which had been put at her disposal. She curled up in a comfortable sofa, and closed her eyes . . . she wanted to think . . .

About an hour later the telephone bell rang : lazily she reached for the instrument and answered it. She heard the voice of the Gestapo officer.

" Although this is a private line, I cannot speak too clearly, fräulein . . ."

" Go on."

" The . . . Frenchman . . . is here. With me now. Our Frenchman."

" Yes . . . I undertsand."

" He was surprised that you had not met your friend, because he left in plenty of time to keep the appointment . . ."

" Why didn't the Frenchman go with him ? "

" Because it was thought that I should be informed of a new development. I agree that he was right to come straight to me. The point is this : my visitor to whom you introduced me an hour ago is due at the meeting—an important meeting where he will meet *interesting people*—to-night. Our friends had made contact with him, but welcome the happenings of this morning because their position is by no means secure, and if the original idea is now carried out, it will obviously help them enormously. But, as the appointment with the interesting people is for to-night, we must act quickly . . ."

" Yes," said Irma Peterson.

She paused a moment, thinking fast.

" Yes. I think I had better come over at once."

" You will of course, take the arranged precautions ? "

Irma Peterson frowned petulantly.

" I hardly think it necessary ! "

"I must insist, fräulein. I am responsible for your safety, and you agreed to follow my instructions."

"Oh, very well! And listen . . ."

"Yes?"

"He—your visitor—was buying scent. He bought a bottle of the perfume I use. I think I would like it . . ."

She heard a laugh at the other end of the line.

"I have the things that were found in his pockets before me now. I have the bottle: I will keep it for you . . ."

"Thank you . . ."

She replaced the receiver, and rang the bell. A tall, dark girl of about her height entered the room. Irma Peterson started to remove her dress.

"Here, Carlotta, take this dress and put it on. You will find my hat and furs downstairs. Then take the black car —you will find it waiting for you—and go for a spin. Anywhere you like—the Bois should be looking nice on a day like this . . ."

"*Si, signora* . . ."

Irma Peterson lifted the house telephone: she gave some brief instructions, and replaced it on its hook. It was a nuisance having to change her dress and her car every time she went out, particularly since to take precautions in Paris—who knew she was there, or who she was?— seemed really quite unnecessary. But if the Gestapo were fussy about her safety—and they certainly seemed to have a very real respect for these Resistance groups—well, it was at least a compliment, and she must humour them. The idea was a good one: that a decoy, dressed in the clothes she had last been seen wearing, and travelling in the car she had last been seen using, should precede her by a few minutes every time she left the house: and that she should then follow in a very different car very differently attired: But still, it was really very much of a nuisance.

She put on a light suit, and took a fur cape from the cupboard.

As she swung it round her shoulders, she looked out of the window. She saw the big black car, complete with armed chauffeur and bodyguard, sweep out into the street and glide off in the direction of the Bois. Carlotta would no doubt enjoy herself : that girl certainly had a soft job . . .

Irma Peterson returned to her sitting room, and again went to the house telephone : an obsequious voice apologised for the delay, but the call on the second car was unexpected : however, it would be ready without fail in just about half an hour, perhaps before. Impatiently Irma Peterson lit a cigarette, and cursed the ridiculous caution of the Gestapo . . .

The big black car swung down a sidestreet. Another car, following, drew alongside suddenly. Silenced automatics spat. The uniformed driver collapsed over his wheel, and his companion crumpled even before he could reach for his own weapon.

A man swung athletically from the other to the big black car, and brought it to a standstill. It was the work of a moment to transfer the terrified girl from the black car to the other, which at once made off.

It did not take much longer to drag the two bodies into the interior of the black car, and to drive it off in its turn. The new driver smiled to his companion.

"Very pretty," he said, "and don't look so nervous—we also drive on the right in America ! "

The telephone bell rang. Michel answered it.

" *Tout va bien,*" said Harlow's voice.

Michel turned, and smiled to Algy Longworth. " Okay ! " he said.

But Longworth was already on his way out of the room.

XXVII

ALGY LONGWORTH TAKES HIS OPPORTUNITY

EMILE looked at the German officer impatiently. In spite of himself, he envied the outward calm displayed by his companion, but all the same the circumstances were such that this exaggerated control was really insupportable. Surely this woman had now had plenty of time to make the journey from her apartment to this headquarters? What harm could there be in ringing again and administering a tactful rebuke for her dalliance : he was tired of explaining that on time depended the success of their plan. And, were he to be quite frank, Emile was extremely anxious to get this Drummond job to a successful conclusion just as soon as possible : he was certainly being very well paid, but he was nervous in the company which he was now forced to keep. He could well imagine the value of his life if such as Michel were ever to discover that he was not really working for Resistance . . .

Her unpunctuality was really intolerable : what could she be doing to be keeping them waiting in this high-handed fashion. Who was she, anyway, this Irma Peterson who could keep the Gestapo uncomplaining while, no doubt, she merely titivated, perhaps trying a new tint of powder . . .

" This delay is dangerous to our plan . . ."

" To *her* plan," corrected the Gestapo official. " We cannot move without her approval . . ."

" But she will give it ! As you say, it is her plan. Every minute makes the risk of missing the opportunity greater. This Council meets very seldom, and takes the greatest precautions. Unless I can get Drummond back quickly, he may miss to-night's meeting, and if he does we will have to wait weeks . . . perhaps even months . . . for another opportunity. Think, just think for a moment : he will lead you to-night to all the heads of resistance gathered together under one roof ! By to-morrow you can have him back here and do what you like to him, and you can have smashed organised resistance in France because you can have all its leaders in your power ! "

He paused. Surely this bonehead would understand that argument ? But he was damped to see the impassive expression on the face of the man seated at the desk.

" Who is this woman," he burst out, " who can take such liberties with the Gestapo ? Who is allowed to follow her feminine whims and jeopardise . . ."

" Enough ! "

But Emile was determined.

" You've got to listen to me ! I can take Drummond now to his French friends in that house in the eighth *arrondissement*. We may be still in time for him to keep the appointment they have made for him. You will have the house under observation : you will follow him to the tryst. Then, when you know where it is, you can swoop. If anything goes wrong, I shall be there to guide you, and that cannot fail because I shall be the hero who has rescued Drummond from your clutches, and I shall be completely trusted. Is it foolproof or is it not foolproof ? "

The German smiled.

" It is foolproof, and it is *her* plan," he said coolly.

" Oh . . . ! Why should she be allowed to ruin her own plan ? "

" You are getting over-excited," smiled the man at the desk. " That is a failing due to your nationality. Keep calm. Look at me ! Keep cool. I tell you the plan will not be ruined . . . I wonder where the Englishman is . . . ? "

An underling entered the room. Subserviently he approached the desk, and spoke a few words softly to his officer.

" Show him in . . ." The man at the desk turned to the Frenchman. " Darwin has just arrived. Now we shall know why he was late . . ."

Algy Longworth was ushered into the room.

" Good morning, Mr. Darwin . . ."

" Good morning," said Longworth briskly. " Hullo, Emile. Got it all set ? Because if you have, we better get going . . ."

Irma Peterson lifted the house telephone once more. She spoke acidly to the voice which answered her. She was assured that she would have only a very few minutes more to wait . . .

" You failed to keep an appointment this morning, Mr. Darwin."

"I know I did," said Longworth to the man at the desk, "but I ran into some of our pals, Emile. I couldn't be rude without having an aperitif in the sunshine under the noses of the Gestapo. It seems to be a favourite sport among Frenchmen in Paris."

The German flushed angrily. But Algy Longworth gave him no time to voice his disapproval.

"And I'm extremely glad I did. We've only got a very short time, Emile, and if we don't go at once Drummond will be sneaked off to his meeting and we'll be left behind . . . that is, if they ever let us go . . ."

"Drummond has been arrested," said Emile sharply.

"What !"

"This morning. By your clever Miss Peterson !"

The German held up his hand.

"You will not speak in that tone about the fräulein !" he said curtly.

"I don't advise you to, in her hearing, anyway," grinned Longworth. "Where is Drummond now ?"

"Here, Mr. Darwin."

"In this house ?"

"Yes."

"Then he must be released at once. There is absolutely no time to lose. This is the chance of a lifetime ! Golly—the whole bag with one shot !"

"You see ?" said Emile violently. "You hear what he says ? And still you sit there, and do nothing !" He turned to Longworth. "I've been trying for the last half-hour to persuade this officer . . ."

"Enough !" interrupted the German. "We are waiting for Fräulein Peterson."

"Oh, I shouldn't do that !" Algy Longworth laughed lightly. "Might wait a week ! Don't forget I know her better than any of you, and she's notoriously unpunctual . . . that's why I didn't bother very much about my date with her this morning . . ."

The German officer, for the first time, was visibly shaken. The force of the arguments put up by the other two had not escaped him, and he was as anxious as they were that nothing should be done to jeopardise the admirable plan. The prospect of capturing all the principal men of the resistance groups in one fell swoop was one which made his mouth water. But Fräulein Peterson had already shown herself a domineering personage : she was obviously well in with Berlin, which meant that she had to be treated with a great deal of respect : and she was painfully outspoken if anything was done contrary to her taste, as he knew by experience in the early hours of one morning when she had returned from the south . . . she had said she would come at once, what could be keeping her ?

He was a little upset by Darwin's statement about her unpunctuality. Darwin must know : he was the only one among them who really knew her at all. He was tempted to ring again : but he decided against this : he did not want his head bitten off, especially in front of these two, even at the end of a telephone. It would be very bad for discipline, and these two treated him much too casually already. An idea, a comforting idea, came into his head.

Just as he looked up at his companions, Darwin spoke.

" Look here," he said, " can't we take advantage of this . . . this unfortunate arrest ? I mean, Drummond can't be just let loose in the street. Even his monumental intelligence couldn't fail to think there was something pretty fishy about that. Why couldn't we revert to the original plan ? Stage an escape, what ? I mean, that would help me and Emile a lot : we're not awfully well in yet, you know . . ."

The German smiled.

" That is precisely what I had decided to do."

" Really ? " Algy Longworth beamed at him. " Great minds think alike, what ! Well, let's get going . . . have you fixed the details ? "

" No ! " said Emile angrily. " No ! he won't move until . . ."

" Enough ! " said the man at the desk sharply. He made a mental note that this Frenchman should be taught a sharp lesson in deference to his German superiors . . . but later on, when he had done his job. " I have decided to make the necessary arrangements now. The new guard is just going on duty. They will be warned of what is to occur, they will be told to shoot, but to shoot wide—have no fear, they are all picked men. I will get Drummond into the room here, you two will burst in and bundle him off, down the back stairs, to the car which will be empty and ticking over just outside the house. And here . . ." he opened the drawer of his desk, and pulled out two small pistols " are your arms. They are at present loaded with blank, for sound effect in the escape."

He laughed happily : he had enjoyed thinking all this out, when the plan had been first suggested, and preparing it : he was glad it was going to be staged after all. Before the war, he had often thought that he would make an admirable theatrical producer. " When Drummond sees me fall, he will really believe in the whole thing. Here are also some real bullets : I hope you won't, but you may need them later on."

While he was speaking, he had rung the bell. An officer entered, and was instructed to parade the new guard in the courtyard. Longworth and Emile were taken down by the way they were to use in rushing Drummond out, and were shown to the men composing the guard while these were being given their instructions. Then they returned to the office.

" No time like the present ! " smiled Algy Longworth, " send for Drummond . . ."

An obstinate look came into the German's expression.

" We will wait for Fräulein Peterson," he said stubbornly.

An exclamation of annoyance escaped Emile, but the German was glad to notice that the Englishman's cheerful countenance did not alter. He was prepared to approve of Darwin, until he heard him speak and realised the import of his words.

" Just as you like," said the pleasant voice. " Call me in about a week's time, when all the resistance leaders have got safely back to their normal safe haunts and are carrying out the measures they have decided on this evening, to harass and impede the German war machine. I should imagine

Berlin will ask some pretty awkward questions which it won't be too easy to answer . . . if you're able to think of any answer at all."

The thrust was a powerful one. Algy Longworth watched the German out of the corner of his eye : he was anxious to get the plan into operation as soon as possible because—although no direct threat to himself and Drummond could come of it—at any moment the abduction of Irma Peterson might be reported, and that might lead to delaying complications . . .

The man at the desk was struggling with his commonsense and the effects of his strict training. His commonsense told him that he must believe the information given to him by these two agents, and that, therefore, he must concede the urgency. But his training told him that, well though he might have done to rise to his present position of comparative authority, he should not act on his own without the concurrence of his superiors. Then suddenly a comforting thought came to him : what was it that Irma Peterson herself had said to him, that morning when she had returned so very dissatisfied from the south ? " Thank God there is someone here who is not afraid to take the initiative.' Yes, she had said that . . ."

He looked up at the men standing before him. His training shot its last, weak bolt ; but he knew that he had succumbed to the temptation . . . it was a temptation, for it might mean a lot of personal credit for him, perhaps a decoration, possibly promotion . . . ?

" What shall I say to him if I do send for Drummond ? "

Algy Longworth was quick to recognise the white flag. He was also quick to seize the heaven-sent opportunity. He had been wondering just how to suggest that Drummond should have access to those all-important files . . .

" Why not let him have a look at the portrait gallery ? He may already know one or two of your suspects—then while you're talking Emile and I will sneak in . . ."

The German capitulated.

" Very good. Go and wait in the next room. Come in when I give the signal . . ."

" Which is ? "

" I shall have a fit of coughing," pompously declared the German.

" Right, but mind your tonsils . . ."

Algy Longworth and Emile retired. Longworth grinned at Emile.

" If he doesn't have that spasm soon enough for us, we'll jump it on him," he whispered encouragingly. " He can't stop us now : all the orders have been given."

Emile smiled. Longworth moved over to the window, and remained with his back to Emile for a few moments, looking out, but his fingers were busy.

His mind was made up, the German acted with promptitude. It was not long before Hugh Drummond was brought to the room, and stood before him.

" Captain Drummond," he said curtly. " You have been treated well because you are an Army Officer. But I must warn you that you have seriously jeopardised your position, and put yourself outside the protection of the rules governing prisoners of war, by forcing your way into German occupied territory in civilian clothes. We would be perfectly within our rights if we shot you now, out of hand : particularly as we have information that you have been mixing with those French rebels and anarchists who so outrageously claim to be patriots."

" We had an expression for all this at school," said Drummond with a smile.

" Eh ? "

" We called it stale news. But don't let me stop you : you're putting it beautifully."

The German flushed : these Englishmen really were most trying : their flippant attitude towards even the most serious things was irritating, and he toyed with the idea of calling in a specialist and teaching this stupid lump of humanity a lesson . . . but no, there would be plenty of time for all that later . . .

" You are to be given a chance, however, of redeeming yourself at any rate partially, although I will make no definite promises. You are, as you may have guessed, in the hands of the Gestapo. We could, however, just hand you over to the military as an officer whom we arrested trying to escape through France. You would then be treated with all the courtesy due to a prisoner of war. Naturally, however, we of the Gestapo would require some consideration for such generous treatment."

" You overwhelm me . . ."

" I am glad," went on the German quickly, " that you appreciate the really exceptional favour which is granted to you. And all that we ask of you in return is to tell us one or two very simple little things . . . for instance, these two photographs which were found on you . . . they are portraits of . . . whom ? "

He held up two photographs of men. Hugh Drummond seemed to hesitate . . .

" We of the Gestapo are accustomed to having our questions answered, Captain Drummond. I hope I need say no more than that . . . I really should hate to give a certain order to the guards on each side of you," he went on in a softer voice : " Let me remind you that these photographs are signed . . . and that we have comprehensive files . . ."

" D'you know those men ? " asked Drummond.

Really, this man was too easy, the German told himself. He had always doubted the stories he had heard about Bulldog Drummond . . .

" Yes," he lied.

" Then," said Drummond cheerfully, " there's no point in my telling you, is there ? "

" I'm afraid I must insist . . ."

" Oh, well anyway there's no harm done if I do. One's Albert, the head of resistance in Lyons . . . yes, that one. And the other is Marcel, who does the same job in Nantes . . . but if you know them, why bother me ? "

The German smiled ingratiatingly.

" Thank you, Captain Drummond. Merely a little test to see if you would tell me the truth. I am really personally glad that you are going to co-operate : I should hate to see so gallant an officer in any more uncomfortable position than that of a prisoner of war. Now just a few more little tests . . ." He opened a file which was lying before him on the desk. It was filled with forms, to each of which was attached several small photographs. He pushed them over towards Drummond. "Would you mind looking through these, and telling me what you know about any of the men you may perhaps recognise from portraits . . ."

Hugh Drummond took up the file, and the next moment very nearly dropped it. For the door opposite him had opened and Irma Peterson—as large as life and apparently in the very best of health—walked into the room.

The Gestapo officer looked round quickly : as soon as he saw who it was, he got up quickly, and went towards her. But as he did so, he spoke :

"Carry on, Captain Drummond . . . I won't be a minute . . ."

Hugh Drummond looked down again unseeingly at the sheets in his hand. Something had gone wrong, something had gone desperately wrong. Somewhere very near, he knew that Algy Longworth was lurking, waiting for him to give the signal that he had completed the job, that Jean-Marie was safe from recognition, and that the escape could now be staged. But the whole plan was contingent on Longworth not being recognised, and by this time Irma should have been safe in Michel's reliable hands . . . what on earth could have happened ?

Hugh Drummond forced himself, although still a trifle dazed by the totally unexpected appearance of Irma Peterson, to concentrate more fiercely than he had ever before concentrated in his life. Mechanically he passed one sheet over the other in his hands, until he recognised the photograph that was uppermost to be the likeness of Jean-Marie. As his eyes focussed the pictures, his mind cleared. There was still a chance : everything would have to be hurried now, and everything depended on Longworth realising the unexpected danger and acting promptly.

"Good morning once again, dear Irma !" boomed Drummond in a loud, penetrating voice.

The German officer jumped. Irma Peterson looked up impatiently.

"I have nothing more to say to you Drummond . . ."

"Oh, but I have to you ! " Drummond still boomed out his words : now he bellowed with laughter. "D'you remember a certain box in a certain theatre, at a certain charity matinee not so long ago in London ? Well, go on, do you remember that ? "

She paid no attention, but continued talking to the German officer.

"D'you remember a lovely blonde who asked me if I could possibly find her a bottle of *Vol de Nuit* " ? roared Drummond.

She looked at him sharply : she could not withhold a smile from her lips . . .

"Yes, I do."

"Well, like a damn fool, I went and bought her a bottle this morning, and look where it's landed me ! " he laughed tremendously. "Oh, well . . . even if it's the last thing I do, although I hope to find myself better off almost *at once* . . . you'd better have it, Irma. Here it is on the desk. Here . . . catch . . . ready ? . . . hoopla ! "

Surprisingly, Irma Peterson caught the flying package.

"Thank you, Captain Drummond . . ."

"Oh, well caught, girl ! I'm dashed if I've ever seen a better catch . . ."

He got no further. The sound of a door being wrenched open behind him was almost simultaneous to the crack of a pistol. The Gestapo officer doubled up, a look of pained surprise on his face. He sank to the floor.

"This way, Hugh ! "

It was Algy Longworth who spoke, and it was Algy Longworth who guided Hugh Drummond out of the room. The whole thing was done with such speed that Irma Peterson had not recovered from her surprise before the room was empty.

But as they disappeared she recovered her wits.

"Stop them ! " she screamed. "Stop them ! "

The two soldiers who had been guarding Hugh

Drummond smiled indulgently. One of them spoke. "It was all arranged!" he said with great humour.

"Fool!" she cried, "was it all arranged that your officer should be murdered!"

"Murdered?" said the other: looked at the prostrate form: then continued with pride. "He is a very good actor . . . I have seen him at the concerts in the officers' mess . . ."

For answer, Irma Peterson pulled the man over on to his back. A startled exclamation escaped the two soldiers: there could be no question at all that their officer was very dead . . .

Irma Peterson rushed to the window, struggled with it to get it open, and then screamed a warning to the guards below . . . but even as she did so, she knew that she was too late, for she heard the roar of a car gathering speed outside . . .

Irma Peterson rushed from the room.

XXVIII

MICHEL MAKES A FINAL DECISION

As they swept up the Boulevard des Capucines, Algy Longworth leant over and spoke in Drummond's ear. The latter, who was driving, took his foot off the accelerator for a moment, in order to hear better.

"They know all about it by now. You can bet that Irma talked quick. I think the sooner we ditch the car and disappear on foot, the safer it will be . . . now we've got our start."

Hugh Drummond fully agreed. He had been apprehensive for several minutes now of hearing the roar of a pursuing Gestapo car. But there was just one fly in the ointment.

"Emile?" he asked, raising his eyebrows.

Algy Longworth smiled reassuringly.

" All right. I've been watching him, and he's about the only man alive who doesn't know by now that the whole thing hasn't been on the level . . . he even thinks my shooting was with blank, and that the standard of acting in the Gestapo is extremely high . . ."

Longworth laughed happily : it pleased him to think that Irma's arrival had granted him the chance to rid the world of one of these wretches . . . for he could not have used the gun so kindly presented to him had Irma not arrived so unexpectedly to expose the plot.

Drummond pulled the car into a side-turning, and drew up abruptly. The one or two pedestrians quickly scattered ; a German car, and specially one containing men in plain clothes, was no object to remain near in Paris if you could possibly get well away from it.

Emile, surprised, asked what they were up to. Complainingly, he followed them from the car and away down the side street. Drummond briefly told him that the Gestapo were bound to send fast cars in pursuit, and that it was better to have nothing to do with them. Emile, who did not relish the long walk in front of them, told Longworth privately that he thought this was carrying realism too far ; but Longworth explained that Drummond must be humoured if they were to get the full benefit and credit for the escape. Emile, reluctantly, agreed that this was true . . .

The wisdom of Longworth's advice to Drummond was quickly apparent. They had not gone very far when a low Citroen—and the low black Citroen automobiles were a great favourite with the Gestapo—flashed past with keen-face men sitting alert and very obviously on a search. Several more were sighted during their walk. They could only be on the job of tracking down the fugitive car, and one incident convinced Drummond that it had been found. One of these Citroens, just as they were entering the Champs Élysées, slowed down most unpleasantly almost opposite them and gave Drummond and Longworth a bad moment. But Hugh Drummond saw that the man beside the driver was wearing headphones, and was obviously receiving instructions over his wireless-telephone : the car had only slowed down in order to turn, and race off in the direction in which it had come.

" The sooner we're home the better ! " was Longworth's only comment, and Hugh Drummond was very much in agreement. He had only been in the hands of the Gestapo for a very short time, but it had been quite long enough . . .

Algy Longworth made to turn left away from the Champs Élysées.

" It is shorter to go straight on, and turn further up . . ." objected Emile.

" Not to where we're going, old cock ! " smiled Longworth. " Michel has evacuated the other place as no longer being safe . . ."

Emile sidled up to Longworth, his face troubled. He managed to talk to him unheard by Drummond.

" But this is serious. It is to the original house that they will send the escort . . ."

Longworth nearly laughed, not so much at the anxiety of this man he despised, but at the strange use of the word ' escort '.

" It's quite all right," he said out of the corner of his mouth. " I've fixed it all. Explain later . . ."

And with that, Emile was forced to be content.

A few minutes later, led by Longworth, they turned down a mean little street. Longworth nodded cheerfully to a pretty girl at the seat of custom in her newspaper kiosk : she smiled back.

" Just a shot in the dark, or do you know that lovely ? " inquired Drummond.

" One of Michel's look-out girls," said Longworth casually, " as a matter of fact, she's his daughter."

They stopped at a drab looking house. Longworth knocked. Michel himself opened the door to them.

" Welcome home ! " he smiled.

Drummond entered first followed by Longworth. As Emile entered, and Michel closed the door, two men took the traitor firmly by the arms. Emile uttered a startled exclamation, but one glance at the expressions on the faces of his captors, and also on the stern faces of the other three, told him the whole story. He swayed, and would have fallen but for the men on each side of him ; he turned white as ivory, without even a spot of colour in either cheek : all the blood seemed to have been drained from his face.

"Take him away," said Michel curtly, "and deal with him . . ."

Emile did not plead for mercy : perhaps he knew only too well how useless that would be. He made one violent attempt to break loose from his captors, but they were much too strong for him. Suddenly, however, his eyes burning wildly, came to rest on Longworth. And then he committed his final disloyalty.

"That man !" he screamed hysterically, "You think Darwin a British agent ! He is not ! He is paid by the Gestapo !"

"Longworth is the name," said Algy Longworth quietly, "and if I ever get any money for anything I've done for the Gestapo, I'll start a fund for the women they've widowed . . ."

"Take him away," said Michel in disgust.

He turned his back on him, and moved towards a door, followed by Hugh Drummond and Algy Longworth.

Inside the room which they entered, Mat Harlow jumped to his feet. Impulsively, he shook hands with Drummond, a broad grin on his good-humoured face.

"I'm just so glad to see you," he said, "I could do a solo dance ! Everything okay ? "

"Only just !" Drummond laughed. "What about Irma ?"

"She's not in the least what you led me to expect. All the wind seems to have been knocked out of her : no life, no quick repartee, and frankly I don't think she's as good looking as you both make out : she was certainly much better as a blonde. All she does is to sit in a corner and moan, and insist that her name is Carlotta."

"It probably is," said Longworth lightly, lighting a cigarette.

"What ? "

Drummond grinned pleasantly.

" All's well that ends well, Mat. But you didn't get hold of the right Irma. Never mind : her turning up rather helped us, really through a bit of quick thinking by Algy . . ."

" Stuff ! " announced Longworth, " You started thinking seconds before I did."

" I had the advantage—and shock—of seeing the lady walk into the room. Anyway, Mat, before I start, tell us exactly what happened your end ? "

Harlow had listened to the conversation with increasing amazement.

" Why," he said, " the car and the lady were pointed out to me, Hugh, as you well know, by yourself—just before you walked into the web. We followed the car to the Gestapo, and then to what must be her apartment. We tried to get her going there, but we just didn't get an opportunity. We were in luck all the same : out she came again, and this time turned up towards the Bois, which gave us our chance in one of the small streets. We came alongside, and the boys were grand, everything went according to plan. We got both the car and the girl . . ."

" Yes, but which girl ? " said Longworth with a smile.

" Listen, I'll swear it was the same girl you pointed out to me. Dressed in the same dress, same furs, same hat . . . everything ! And in the same car with the same body-guard ! "

" I think," said Drummond, " we'd better interview this . . . Carlotta."

" I shall be delighted," said Longworth quickly.

" One moment." It was Michel who spoke. " Forgive me, Hugh, but have you anything—strange—in your pockets ? "

" Eh ? No . . ." He felt carefully in all his pockets. " No, nothing. But . . . oh, I see ! " He laughed. " You mean these ! "

Drummond picked up the Gestapo file of suspects from the table on which he had placed it when entering the room, and handed it to Michel. The effect on the Frenchman was instantaneous : his eyes shone as he turned over the pages, and then he advanced quickly on Drummond. Before the big man knew what was happening, he had been kissed on both cheeks.

"Excuse me reverting to type!" said Michel, laughing, a hint of happy tears in his eyes; "but you have done a tremendous service, Hugh, to . . . to France!"

In that moment Hugh Drummond not only felt really proud, but also that any personal risk had been more than repaid.

"The boys have a fire down in the cellar," went on Michel quickly, as if to cover any embarrassment which he might have caused. "I will quickly go and stoke the flames with these. The sooner they are destroyed, the better. I will join you in Carlotta's room . . ."

He hurried out.

Hugh Drummond caught Algy Longworth's eye: that insufferable jester looked on the point of being mischievous. Drummond spoke quickly:

"Come on, Mat . . . where's Carlotta?"

The American still looking mystified, led them to a room in which a tall, dark girl—certainly no beauty in her present condition, since she had been giving way to hysterical tears—was being guarded by two armed Frenchmen. The story was very simple, and she told it with no attempt to conceal anything. Hers was a very minor job: just to act as decoy. She would never have taken it had she thought there was the slightest danger of anything happening to her. She was an Italian girl, and her German friends had assured her that it would be great fun, well paid, and perfectly safe . . .

"Might be the story of her miserable country!" remarked Longworth, when they were all back in the sitting-room.

Mat Harlow was very depressed, and Hugh Drummond noticed it.

"Don't take it too hard, Mat!" He smiled affectionately at him. "It was in no possible way your fault: if I or Algy had been on your job, we'd have made the same mistake, even knowing the woman."

"What happened your end?" asked Michel.

"Up to the last few appalling minutes, everything went

perfectly. But I think you'd better start, Algy . . . all that happened to me at the beginning was that Irma fell for the bait and abducted me. Over to you, Algy ! "

" When I arrived, it was clear that the blighter Emile had swallowed your story, Michel, and was pressing for Hugh's immediate release," said Longworth. " I added urgent pressure. We had a wee spot of difficulty because the Gestapo blighter obstinately wanted to wait for Irma, and as I was under the misapprehension that she couldn't turn up, I didn't want to waste any time. I'd have been even more urgent if I'd known the truth ! However by a mixture of flattery and sheer downright common sense—and by playing the incessant tune that you boys wanted to take Hugh off to a meeting of your council almost immediately—we got him finally to act. Over to you, Hugh ! "

" I had enough time to see how prisoners—not even prisoners, darn it, but only suspects who may be perfectly innocent—are treated in that place." He shuddered involuntarily. " Then I was taken up to the Gestapo blighter. He fell for those photographs ' found ' on me in a way which would have delighted you, Michel. I—apparently reluctantly—gave him the names and places you had told me."

" Good ! " remarked Michel with satisfaction. " Two leading collaborationists are in for an unpleasant surprise very soon, and I doubt whether they'll live to clear themselves ! "

" Great Scot ! "

Hugh Drummond looked at Algy Longworth sharply.

" What's the matter, Algy ? "

" I shot the blighter ! The information will have gone with him ! "

" No ! " Drummond smiled, " I saw him making notes. His successor will find them, and don't forget my guards were witnesses."

" Thank the lord for that ! "

" We progressed to the real file," continued Drummond " and he handed it to me. I had noticed the scent bottle on the desk within reach; our gamble had come off, but of course it was odds-on anyway that they'd keep the things found on me together. I had only to find the form concerning Jean-Marie, reach over for the bottle, do the trick and then give the signal to Algy to get going. Frankly, I was in very high spirits as I began to look through that file—and then, in walks Irma Peterson!"

"I should have fainted," remarked Algy Longworth. "As a matter of fact, I very nearly did when I heard you talking to her, Hugh!"

"That was my only way of telling you what had happened, Algy." Drummond laughed, "to bellow at her and hope to high heaven you'd hear. And I had to tell you that our only chance was to act at once . . ."

"Yes, I got that bit!"

"Bless you! The moment you appeared, and she saw you, the game was bound to be up, unless it was just a fleeting glance . . ."

"So," said Longworth, "we anticipated the curtain and went like a thunderbolt right through the escape scene, before the producer or his unexpected and unwelcome assistant could stop the show."

"But you never used the bottle!" said Michel, interested. "You brought back the documents intact . . ."

"They were in my hand," said Drummond, "so I thought they'd better stay in my hand. Sorry to have given you the trouble of filling a flagon of Guerlain's *Vol de Nuit* with your own concoction, but all I could think of was to distract her attention for Algy to make his entrance, so I . . . . I gave it to Irma!"

"My goodness!" remarked Michel. "She's in for a surprise when she tries to use it!"

"A painful surprise is my hope!" said Drummond. "I hated abandoning the real bottle—seemed such a waste! But I hope the little girl who served me in the shop finds it and keeps it for herself—she was sweet! Gave me some jolly good advice when she realised I was an Englishman!"

"Papa!" said a voice from the door. "May I speak to you?"

Michel was already on his feet as the others looked round. Drummond saw, standing at the door, the pretty girl whom he had seen in the newspaper kiosk.

Michel and she talked in low tones, and rapidly, in French. Michel turned quickly back to the others.

"Hugh and Algy! Will you please look through your pockets quickly. And tell me if you have any strange object that looks rather like a watch . . ."

Mystified, the two Englishmen did as they were asked.

"Nothing," said Drummond.

"Nothing!" echoed Longworth.

Michel breathed a visible sigh of relief.

"Micheline—this is my daughter—has been on the look-out. She has seen strangers outside, apparently very interested in the time. They appear to be looking at their watches very frequently, as if they were waiting very impatiently indeed for someone who is late for an appointment. Of course that may be the real explanation, although it is suspicious that two or three men should have chosen the same street—and this street—for their assignations with unpunctual people. But it means more to us than that, and when we see such a sight we are at once on our guard. You see, the Gestapo has a nasty little instrument, which looks rather like a watch, and which automatically emits a signal on a certain wave-length for several hours on end. If it is planted on someone, the exact whereabouts of that person can be picked up by the Gestapo agents if they are within a short radius of about a hundred metres, by comparing two or three readings from different positions on their own watch-like receiving instruments. You see now why I am disturbed: what more likely, in view of the use to which they had planned to put him, than that they planted one of these emitting sets on Hugh?"

There was a stunned silence.

"They stripped me when they searched me," said Drummond suddenly.

"Were your clothes always in the same room?" asked Harlow.

"I think so, but I can't be sure," said Drummond

slowly. "I'm afraid I didn't keep my eye on them . . ."

He suddenly whipped off his jacket. Harlow took it, and began to search it very thoroughly, feeling all over the lining. The others seized garments as Hugh Drummond pulled them off, and subjected them to as careful a scrutiny.

An exclamation from Harlow stopped them all abruptly : they stared at him. He had pulled out his knife, and ripped the lining of Hugh Drummond's jacket. He pulled out, before the startled eyes of his small audience, a small object like a very thin, full hunter watch, which had been cunningly sewn in.

"I'm not surprised you didn't feel it ! " he said quietly. "Well out of the way and as light as a feather ! "

Michel literally leapt upon him, and snatched it away. It was the work of only a few moments to lay it on the stone base of the empty fireplace, and smash the delicate mechanism to small pieces with the heavy poker.

Michel turned towards the door.

"Micheline ! " he called.

The girl, perhaps when Drummond had started to tear off his clothes, had returned to the passage outside : but she had left the door open, and she reappeared immediately.

"Join your mother *at once*. She is with André. I will send a message as soon as I can."

"Yes, papa."

Michel smiled to her, blew her a kiss as she went, and turned back to the others.

"Another evacuation, gentlemen. And immediately. Somehow or other the Gestapo have got on to this house, and the betting is that they now know Hugh Drummond is here." He spoke very quietly and very calmly, but he left no doubt at all in their minds that the position was serious, and that counter measures were a matter of urgency. Mat Harlow admired him intensely at that moment. " I think—in fact, I am positive—that we should split. We can come together again later. You said, Hugh, that Algy— because of his fund of useful experience and knowledge "— he smiled at Longworth—"must be got back to England as quickly as possible. I agree. I will send Algy out of

Paris now, to a place in the country where he can wait in safety for the final arrangements for his return. We will merely move house—but we must do it quickly . . . excuse me."

He left the room almost at a run.

Drummond was dressing himself again. He was frowning heavily.

" I could kick myself," he said suddenly.

" Can't think why," said Mat Harlow, with a smile. " You couldn't possibly know . . ."

" Hugh," said Algy Longworth quietly, " couldn't I . . ."

" No."

" I mean, it seems so silly for me to run away just as I'm enjoying myself . . ."

" No, corporal ! And that's an order."

Hugh Drummond looked at Algy Longworth. Algy Longworth looked at Hugh Drummond. Mat Harlow saw them smile, and realised the depth of understanding between them.

" Ay, ay, captain ! " said Longworth resignedly.

Mat Harlow helped Drummond on with his jacket.

" Hugh," he said quietly. " It's our job to see everything that we can in this Resistance organisation. I think we should split too : one of us to see what they do with Algy, the other stay here and watch Michel. As we're going to join up again very soon anyway, it won't inconvenience Michel."

Hugh Drummond thought for a moment.

" You're perfectly right, Mat. But as I got Michel into the fire, even without knowing it, I'd better stay with him."

Harlow smiled.

" Oh, no, you don't ! We'll toss for it."

" All right . . ."

Harlow took out a coin.

" Heads you stay with Michel, tails I do . . ."

" Agreed."

He spun the coin.

" You're a lucky devil, Hugh ! " Mat Harlow said ruefully. " Heads it is."

As he picked up the coin, Michel came back into the room. He was informed of the slight change in plan, and assented at once.

"All is ready," he said, "please come immediately . . ."

They followed him out of the room. Two pleasant-faced youths were introduced: Algy Longworth and Mat Harlow were bustled away with them through the back door. Michel and Drummond were alone in the house.

"Michel," said Drummond. "I just can't tell you how sorry I am . . ."

Michel, smiling, took him by the arm.

"Even Napoleon lost a battle," he said gaily, "and you have won a great victory, and only lost one of the little skirmishes . . ."

Which thought Hugh Drummond, was a really very handsome way of putting it . . .

"Come with me," said Michel. "There are one or two papers to burn, and then we must be off . . ."

He led the way down to the cellar. The fire was still burning, and there was a pile of paper stacked close to it. Drummond saw that most of this pile was composed of copies of the clandestine press which he had heard so much about, but which he had not up to then actually seen.

They burnt the lot.

"You see," explained Michel, "it wouldn't matter much they're getting them, except that they could use them to plant on our people, when they have nothing else to offer as evidence . . ." He laughed. "My mother will be furious! She is the head of the distribution department . . ."

As the last copy went on the flames, Michel stood upright and rubbed his hands.

"Well, that's done . . . now for our next home!"

They turned: they found themselves staring down the barrel of an automatic rifle. The room seemed to be filling with men in greenish-grey and black uniforms.

Michel's hand flew to his pocket. A sharp voice barked out an order to raise their hands above their heads. Slowly Michel withdrew his hand . . .

The men made way suddenly, and Irma Peterson entered the cellar.

" We meet again, Hugh Drummond ! " Her tone was bantering, but there was an underlying current of triumph to be discerned in her voice. " Won't you introduce me to your friend ? "

Neither of them answered her : for once Hugh Drummond was without words.

" So you won't talk ! " she said softly. " I wonder if you will keep up your attitude when I hand you over to certain of my friends . . . it will be very interesting . . ."

" I am afraid that you will have to excuse me, madame . . ."

It was Michel who had spoken : he met her angry glance without a sign of trepidation.

" You'll talk all right ! " she said disdainfully.

" I think not ! "

" You're very certain of yourself ! " She laughed mirthlessly. " Well, we shall see . . ."

" Yes, madame." Michel was smiling. " You will see how a Frenchman can die—so that Frenchmen and France may live . . ."

His hand, the hand which had flown to his pocket, went abruptly to his mouth. Just for a moment he stood there, still smiling : then, as he sank to the ground, Hugh Drummond saw a spasm of agony flash across his fine face . . .

Hugh Drummond went berserk : but sheer weight of numbers bore him down . . .

XXIX

JEAN-MARIE RETURNS

IT was fully twenty-four hours later before Mat Harlow returned to Paris with his two young companions, Algy Longworth having been deposited in a farm house, to live in much the same conditions as Harlow himself and

Drummond had lived for the first few days after their arrival in France. Harlow was taken to a house not very far from the cathedral of Notre Dame, and introduced to his new host, a man who went by the name of Georges. Georges, although he had a good deal in common with such as Michel and Jean-Marie, was different in that he was a short taciturn man who gave a totally erroneous impression of being too fat and flabby for much action. But Harlow had been told of a few of his exploits, and he was prepared to believe in a deceptive appearance. Harlow was received with a good deal of ceremony, just as if he were paying a social visit in times of peace; he was shown to his room by an elderly butler who looked like a duke, was asked if there was anything he wanted, and only when he appeared to be completely satisfied was he informed that if he could spare the time, his host would like a few words with him in the study. He was shown the way . . .

Georges came to the point at once.

"I have disquieting news, I'm afraid," he said. "Michel and your English friend have disappeared. They were together—the last two left in the house that had to be left—when they were last seen. There was, apparently, a little clearing up to do, and characteristically Michel elected to do it himself. I want to say at once that this does not necessarily mean a tragedy, but all the same it is disturbing. It is of course perfectly possible that for some reason they could not come straight here, but I should have thought they could have found some means of telling me that . . . that they were being delayed."

He paused, and looked at Harlow.

"You are worried?"

"Yes," admitted Georges. "Yes, I must be frank: I am worried. It is really so unlike Michel to keep us without information. He has often had to disappear before, but we have never been so long without getting a message ."

"Hugh Drummond was with him?"

"He remained with him in the house. They were the last two to be there. That is all we know . . ."

It was a very severe blow to Mat Harlow. Georges went on to tell him that Jean-Marie had been moved to the prison hospital, according to plan: the pills with which he had been immediately supplied by Michel, on the very night of his arrest, had done their work, and he was running a high and mysterious temperature. Mat Harlow found himself listening automatically. The doctors were sympathetic: while that temperature lasted—that meant while the pills lasted—they would not look too closely into the cause of illness, but would just keep Jean-Marie in a hospital bed. They had done it before—a process of patriotic half closing of their eyes—and they would do it again. It was quite easy to remove him from the hospital. The Gestapo had an unpleasant habit of raiding the hospitals, and just taking straight from their sick beds anyone for whom they were looking. That, thanks to Hugh Drummond's magnificent raid on the Gestapo files, would not now happen to Jean-Marie, said Georges. But a party apparently from the Gestapo, dressed as they were, and in a Gestapo car, would visit the hospital that evening, and in the same inhuman and boorish manner would insist on removing Jean-Marie. Georges smiled genially as he said that he hoped to welcome Jean-Marie to his house in time for dinner . . .

Mat Harlow was interested and glad to hear that the rescue of the excellent Jean-Marie was so imminent. But his anxiety for Hugh Drummond was growing. He asked Georges a few questions, but his host knew no more than he had already told him: he did assure him, however, that if nothing were heard by the following morning, extensive inquires would be instigated. At the moment, Georges explained, he was reluctant to be too inquisitive in case inquiries should only embarrass Michel . . .

Harlow made an excuse and went up to his room. He sat down in the armchair. What could have happened? Nothing really could have been more easy than the departure of his own little party from that house: surely Michel— who had been the one to insist on the urgency—could not have waited too long? The thought sickened him: he could well imagine what would happen to Hugh Drummond if he again fell into the clutching hands of the Gestapo; they would be only too eager to take it out of the man who had so successfully fooled them.

Harlow felt in his pocket, and drew out a sheet of paper. Hugh Drummond had given him that paper just before he had gone to take ' Darwin's ' place at the assignation at Guerlain's. Harlow remembered that Drummond had said to him that he could read it any time he liked, but that it would only be necessary in the event of something going wrong. He had forgotten all about it until now . . .

Mat Harlow hesitated for a few moments, staring at the paper in his hand. Then, quickly, he unfolded it.

" *Dear Mat*," he read, " *if anything happens to me, you can no longer afford to take risks. Because of the job, I mean. At least one of us must speak, and I know that one of us is enough— this is your proof that I am ready to concur in all you say. Thanks, pal, for a lovely party, and I'm damned glad we both think the same way. Hugh.*"

Oh, no, you don't ! said Mat Harlow to himself. You're a grand scout, Hugh, and I know that what you have written is pure common-sense. But if I was in trouble, do you think you'd leave me just because of the job ? Not likely ! And if you are in trouble, you won't find me not raising heaven and earth to get you out. We're pals, Hugh, and Allies : that presupposes a responsibility to help each other. I'll only use this if . . . by heaven, I needn't use it at all, in any circumstances !

He laughed. Algy Longworth was safe now, would be there to bear witness much more effectively than that note . . . if disaster really happened.

It gave Mat Harlow a great deal of pleasure to tear the note into small pieces, pile them up in the grate and burn them. Not that he was not touched by this proof of Drummond's faith in him, but it was satisfying to destroy anything which could in any way be interpreted as preventing him rushing to Hugh Drummond's help, if that odd but attractive character should by any chance require it . . .

But surely they could not have delayed too long? Harlow found himself wondering what that little clearing up to do, referred to by Georges, had consisted of? Michel had hurried them off so insistently: it was inconceivable that he should have dallied himself. Of course, it was just possible that their own departure had only been in the nick of time, but it had been carried out so uneventfully that it scarcely seemed possible . . . and as they went, they had seen no sign of danger . . .

Mat Harlow shook himself: he was getting morbid. Georges, worried though he undoubtedly was, could remain cheerful and hope for the best, so why on earth shouldn't he? What, asked Harlow of himself, would Drummond have done in his shoes at that moment? He was very short of sleep: he had not rested since he had last seen Drummond. The thing to do is to get some sleep, so that he should be fresh if he were needed.

But much easier said than done. Unpleasant, haunting thoughts of the dangers to which Hugh Drummond was exposed would not leave him, and became almost worse when he closed his eyes. This is ridiculous, Mat Harlow told himself: make your mind a blank, it should be easy enough: he is probably in no greater danger now than you are yourself: Mat, my boy, just take it easy and relax . . .

Harlow had no idea how long he had slept, when he was woken by the round little Georges. But one look at the expression on the face of his host brought him instantly to full consciousness.

" What's happened? "

" Jean-Marie is here," said Georges, in a curiously hollow voice. " Come—he wants to speak to you. But Michel is . . . dead."

" Hugh? is Hugh Drummond . . ."

" No, we do not know that he is dead. But Jean-Marie will explain what he has heard—come with me."

Jean-Marie—a frail, pallid ghost of the man Harlow remembered—was sitting in an armchair in the study. He smiled sadly as Harlow followed Georges into the room.

"I'm glad to see you . . ." began Harlow awkwardly.

"And I'm more than glad to see you Mat!" Jean-Marie's voice was strangely resonant coming from such a fever-wracked body: Harlow thought to himself that this self-imposed temperature, although it gave its victim an alarming appearance, could not be too dreadful in its effects. "And I have to thank you for your part in protecting me . . ."

"I did nothing—except make a bloomer!" said Harlow quickly.

"Michel is dead." Jean-Marie spoke quietly, undramatically. Mat Harlow was immediately reminded of his tones as he had described to them, in the little house in the south, the meaning of that fusillade of shots which they had suddenly heard. "He was brought in to the hospital in which I was, but he was dead when they got him there. Poison. He had always told me that he was afraid he might not be able to stand torture, and that they might make him speak. He said that as he knew so much, and so many people, he would never risk it, and would not be taken alive. He always carried the phial: he once showed it to me. Michel is one of our great heroes: I have no doubt that whatever they might do to him, he would not have spoken. But perhaps it is best this way . . ."

"You are quite certain that it was Michel?" asked Harlow.

"Quite certain. One of the nurses is one of us: she knew Michel. And she saw his body."

There was a short pause.

"I can't express how sorry I am," said Harlow quietly.

"I know it." Jean-Marie smiled again. "The nurse of which I speak heard the Boches talking . . ."

Mat Harlow looked up quickly.

"Yes?"

"They were saying among themselves that at least the Englishman had been taken alive. They said that he was an enormous man with the strength of ten devils, but that he had been finally subdued. The nurse said that if he alone had inflicted all the injuries for which the Germans had to be treated, then indeed their description must be right . . ."

"There can't be any doubt then, about that either . . ." said Harlow soberly.

"None," agreed Jean-Marie. "It could be no other than Hugh Drummond. And he is now in the hands of the Gestapo."

None of the three said anything more for a few moments. The certainty of all that he had feared struck Harlow a new—and he felt unreasonable—blow. At the back of his mind, Mat Harlow had always felt convinced that Drummond was in trouble from the moment that Georges had told him of the disappearance . . .

"Well," he said dully, almost to himself, "we've got to get him out."

"Exactly."

As Jean-Marie spoke the word, Harlow looked up at him quickly : he had not really been conscious of speaking aloud : for a second he imagined that Jean-Marie had guessed his thoughts.

"It is never pleasant to be in the hands of the Gestapo," continued Jean-Marie, "but for a day or two we need not be unduly anxious. If those fiends follow their usual procedure—and all Germans are very much subject to procedure—they will not question him, with all that that entails, until they have subjected him to what they call the softening process. This consists in locking him up in a cell designed to hold one, or two at the most, with three other prisoners, throwing in some filthy food once a day, and never allowing the victims out of the cells even for the calls of nature. After about a week, the prisoner is taken before the examining officers, and it is not until then that real physical violence usually begins. The idea is that by that time the victim is mentally in no condition to stand very much physically."

He paused, and asked Georges for a cigarette. The recital was evidently a severe strain on his strength.

"Sometimes the examination takes place at another place to where the prisoner is incarcerated. That is our big chance—if we know that a man we want to rescue is being moved, even in an armoured car, from one place to another. But we must know *when* he is being transported. I must not hide from you that we seldom can find out this vital information—the Gestapo houses are very much more difficult to penetrate than the French prisons, such as the one I was in, where we know most of what is going on— and the Gestapo sometimes take special precautions with particularly important prisoners . . . like never moving them, and examining them on the spot ; or if they do move them, furnishing insuperable strength in the guard."

" They'll think Hugh a particularly important prisoner all right ! " said Harlow.

" Not necessarily," smiled Jean-Marie. " I am saying nothing against Hugh Drummond when I voice that opinion. Had their plan worked, he would have been a vital prisoner, because he would have been able—if willing under dreadful pressure—to identify so many leaders of Resistance. But it didn't work, and the fact that they arrested him again proves that they recognise it cannot now work. When Irma Peterson recognised Algy, the whole thing blew up, because they know that Algy must have exposed the whole plot to Drummond. So it is just possible that they may not consider him a vital prisoner, to be treated abnormally—a thing the Boche hates doing. They may move him. And if, by hook or by crook, we can find out *when*, you may be sure that every patriot in Paris—should that be necessary—will turn out to get him safely back into our keeping."

" How can we find out when ? " asked Harlow.

" That, my friend, is the difficulty. We have also to find out just exactly where he is. Men are working on that already, reliable men. We shall find him, never doubt, and soon. Until then . . . we can do nothing."

He rose from his chair : Georges solicitously helped him. Jean-Marie smiled understandingly at Harlow.

" Good night, Mat. That no doubt seems to you a hollow wish. But try to get some sleep, for sleep makes energy, and you may be very busy to-morrow. If we get any news during the night, be sure we will wake and tell you . . ."

Mat Harlow watched him walk, not very steadily, from the room.

XXX

MAT HARLOW PLANS HIS PARTY

THE news came early on the following morning : Hugh Drummond was incarcerated in one of the most impenetrable of the Gestapo hells and he was being treated as a very special prisoner . . .

Neither Jean-Marie or Georges said very much, but their expressions were eloquent. Jean-Marie's cautious optimism of the night before had gone : he said, quite frankly, that they were up against a problem which had not previously been successfully tackled. They had no means of entry to this place, no source of information from within its walls. The Gestapo, always more difficult than the civil Vichy power had made of this dreaded house a stronghold which was theirs entirely, and into which no Resistance agent had ever succeeded in infiltrating. No prisoner taken there had been seen again, and apart from very occasional offical announcements, usually of execution, no more had ever been heard of any unfortunate imprisoned in the gaunt building . . .

" You said last night," said Harlow quietly, " that if Hugh was to be removed, and you knew exactly when, you'd feel confident of releasing him ? "

Jean-Marie looked at Harlow.

" Yes, I said that," he agreed, " I did not know at the time that he was being treated with such special attention, and this might mean that if he was taken anywhere else, the guard would be specially selected and specially strong. But that would only mean a sharper fight. I can promise you that if he is taken from that place, and if we have previous knowledge of the date and time, we will do all in

our power to get him back, and we will probably succeed
. . . I can't say more than that . . ."

He paused, and looked at Mat Harlow with renewed
interest. He hesitated, and then decided to ask the question
that was on his lips.

"Mat," he said, "you've got something on your mind.
What is it ? "

"I've been thinking . . ." said Harlow, "quite a lot.
But I want to think some more . . ."

There was a long silence. In the middle of it, Georges
produced a bottle of wine.

"Feeds the brain," was all he said as he filled three
glasses. Mat Harlow accepted his glass gratefully. But
it was quite a long time still before he spoke. The Frenchmen, busy with their own thoughts, waited patiently.

"Look here, fellows . . ." said Harlow suddenly.
"How does this one strike you ? "

Considering the amount of time that it had taken to think
out, the idea was very simple to explain. Harlow noticed
that fact as he was speaking, and it pleased him. All the
best ideas can be described in a very few sentences . . .
who had told him that ? Some author, no doubt, of whom
he knew many : but it was as true as most generalities.
In its audacious simplicity lay the strength of the plan of
action he was suggesting.

There was quite a pause when he had finished. Jean-
Marie was the first to break the silence which to Harlow
was becoming uncomfortable.

"It might work . . ." he said.

"It's an enormous risk ! " said Georges, frowning.

"Why ? " asked Harlow, a trifle belligerently.

"It has never been done before."

"That," Harlow interrupted, "is to its advantage.
You know . . . surprise."

"I mean successfully," Georges corrected himself.
"No one has got into that house . . ."

"No proof that it can't be done ! "

"No proof, as you say, Mat," said Jean-Marie, "but it
is not encouraging for the man who tries . . ."

"I need no encouragement." Harlow spoke defiantly.

"I know you don't!" Jean-Marie was smiling, "but we must look at this thing from eve y angle . . ."

"Incidentally," cut in Harlow, "no one up to now has ever tried to with such advantages . . . we've got the means, let's use them!"

"Supposing," said Georges thoughtfully, "that they check by telephone with Berlin? They might do that . . ."

"Then it blows up, and I try to shoot my way out!"

Mat Harlow laughed: he could see himself having a great chance . . . but anyway a few of the beasts would go down and out for good before they got him . . .

"I'm not so sure that they'll check with Berlin," said Jean-Marie slowly. "They are very susceptible to official documents, and if the thing is made urgent enough—you'll have to give the impression of being in an awful hurry, Mat . . ."

"Don't worry: I shall be!" laughed Harlow.

"If you domineer, rant, and promise them the fury of Berlin—of Herr Himmler himself—if there's any delay, you may rush them off their feet. Yes . . ." a light of excitement was coming into Jean-Marie's eyes as he continued to speak. "Yes, I believe you might do it . . . you might succeed in doing it . . ."

"Anyway, what's the alternative?"

Mat Harlow had judged his moment shrewdly. He knew very well that the idea he had put forward was a desperate venture—but he knew equally well that neither of his friends had anything better to suggest. He forced home his advantage.

"What's the alternative?" he asked insistently.

Jean-Marie smiled to him.

"When do you start?" he asked.

"Just as soon," said Harlow, "as you can get your end all set. And please make that fast . . . I hate the thought of Hugh being in there one minute longer than he need be . . ."

"So do I." Jean-Marie spoke seriously. "But you

must give me a few hours at least—there is a good deal to arrange. The earliest will be late this afternoon, and we must consider whether the early hours of the morning will not be better . . ." He raised his glass. " Good luck, Mat . . ."

Mat Harlow laughed gaily : the prospect of action appealed to him enormously.

" Thank you."

" Should we not inform your Algy Longworth ? " asked Georges unexpectedly.

" You bet not ! " replied Harlow quickly. " If Algy knew what had happened to Hugh, he'd be up here faster than lightning, and I couldn't keep him out of the show. That, Jean-Marie, simply must not happen : one of us three has got to get back and speak, and Algy's the man because he can talk for Hugh, and myself, and he's the only one who knows the Ireland bit. No, this is my party—and if anything goes wrong, I rely on you to rush Algy back to England . . ."

" It shall be done . . . er, I really hesitate to ask this question, it sounds so stupid—but, Mat, you do speak German ? "

" Better than my French," said Harlow simply.

XXXI

MAT HARLOW PLAYS HIS PART

MAT HARLOW, sitting in the back seat of the Citroen with which he had been provided, had to confess to himself that he was feeling extremely nervous. It was fairly early in the morning—it had been light for only about an hour, and he was never at his best until later in the day—but Harlow could not help wondering if he would ever see a later in the day. Of one thing he was quite determined : if things went the wrong way, he would sell his life at the cost of many of those who tried to lay hands on him, and the German pistol which he carried was a pleasantly massive object to the touch of his fingers . . .

Harlow sat upright : what sort of thoughts were these ! Right enough prepared, but it was nonsense even to accept the possibility of failure. Too much depended on success for him even to think of any other result : the safety of Hugh Drummond mattered to him personally far more than he would have thought possible in the short time in which they had been acquainted, but this was far more than an endeavour to save the life of a friend. Hugh Drummond and himself represented an allied team on whose report a great deal might depend, far more even than had appeared likely when they had set out from London. It was perfectly clear from all they had experienced and seen that a tremendous potential factor in the forthcoming invasion of German-occupied France was not fully appreciated at home, simply because sufficiently influential people either had been misinformed, or would not credit the truth of the evidence under their noses. But Hugh Drummond and himself were specially accredited investigators, and their report must not only be put in, but also be supported by their personal contacts and efforts . . . Mat Harlow knew enough of human nature to realise the immense difficulties of overcoming long-standing prejudice. This was just as important from the British as from the Americans point of view, and Hugh Drummond must therefore be extracted from the hands of the Gestapo in order that the team work might continue when they both finally separated to their respective countries.

Yes, that was the way to look at it. Harlow felt better, even though they were rapidly approaching the building which was their destination, and therefore zero hour. Mat Harlow had never experienced the feelings of a man waiting in a muddy trench for the last few minutes before going over the top to attack, but now he knew exactly how that man felt about it . . .

Harlow took a last, quick look at his uniform. He really looked rather well in it, he thought : the Gestapo were no laggards in military magnificence. He smiled at the ribbon of the Iron Cross which he was wearing. Jean-Marie had made a pretty speech about that when he had insisted on Harlow putting it on : it was supposed to be a decoration for personal courage, wasn't it ? Well, then . . . All the same, said Harlow to himself, pity he had been forced to don the small fair moustache.

They stopped in front of the gate of the building. One of the two French volunteers, dressed in the uniforms taken from the late bodyguards of Irma Peterson, made as if to get out, but there was no need. The gates were opened wide, and the car drove in.

They were evidently expected. Well, that meant that the first trick had been won. Georges, who spoke admirable German, must have been convincing over the telephone . . .

As soon as the car came to a standstill one of the young Frenchmen jumped from his seat, ran round the car, opened the door and stood very stiffly to attention. Mat Harlow got out, and stared about him haughtily : he hoped the pince-nez spectacles wouldn't wobble : they had been a brain-wave of the man who had supplied the uniform and altered it in an hour to fit him so perfectly, and his argument for using them was sound. There is no greater flattery than imitation, specially in the higher Nazi circles, and the man whom he was supposed to serve wore that very type of pince-nez. Besides, the more he could look like Himmler, the more he would remind those whom he must impress, of the apparent importance of his mission.

A young officer approached and clicked his heels.

" Why am I being kept waiting ? " barked Harlow, and surprised even himself by the cold aloofness of his voice.

The young officer was evidently taken aback, and not a little flustered.

" I beg your pardon, Colonel. If you will please come this way . . ."

Mat Harlow, now he was committed, rapidly began to gain confidence. He felt a sensation which he had often felt before, only in a very different sphere of activity : he felt that he was already on the field, and that the nerves of before the match had vanished as if by magic. But he was grateful for that lecture by Jean-Marie on the boorish haughtiness of German staff officers from Berlin . . .

He followed his guide to a large, luxuriously furnished room. An officer rose to greet him : Mat Harlow required only one glance to see that he was only a major . . .

"Where is your commanding officer ? " he demanded.

"I regret to inform you, Colonel, that he was killed two days ago. We have had trouble . . . I am temporarily commanding."

"You are always having trouble ! " Harlow spoke brutally, and was pleased to note that the shot had gone home. "Headquarters is by no means pleased . . ."

The Major burst into a flood of explanation. It really was very difficult, he said, to deal with an authority as weak and gutless as Vichy, and an administration so riddled with rebel elements. But they were doing their best, and they were confident that results would improve . . .

"Things are getting worse, not better," remarked Harlow drily.

The major offered him a cigar. Mat Harlow accepted it, and allowed it to have the obviously intended effect.

"However, you have done well to catch the English pig," he said more genially. "Berlin may be inclined to overlook a good deal because of that. Is he ready ? "

"Well . . ."

The Major looked awkward, as if he found it difficult to go into the obviously necessary explanation.

"You got my message from the airport ? " asked Harlow, in an ominous tone of voice.

"Yes, yes. But there is a little difficulty . . ."

"There is no difficulty at all," stated Harlow angrily. "You are wasting time, and there is no time to waste. Headquarters requires the prisoner Drummond in Berlin at once : do you think I . . . I . . . should have been sent by special aeroplane to fetch him if the matter was not of the greatest urgency ? Read that ! "

Imperiously he flung a document, which he took from his tunic, on to the desk. It would have been just as easy and a great deal nicer, to have handed it to the embarrassed officer standing close to him, but Harlow was beginning thoroughly to enjoy the rôle he was playing ! He would probably never have another opportunity of ordering the Gestapo about . . .

"Yes, Colonel."

The Major picked up the document and began to read it. Just for one second Mat Harlow found himself hoping desperately that there was no flaw in it : no, there couldn't be, after all the care that Georges—acknowledged even by Jean-Marie to be the expert in this line—had given to it.

There was something meek and obsequious in the way that the Major handled the document. No doubt, Harlow told himself, there is a great deal to be said for strict military discipline, but surely not to the extent of absolutely blind unquestioning faith in anyone of superior rank . . .

The Major looked up. He held out the document.

"Keep it," Harlow told him gruffly. "It is your authority. Is it quite clear ? "

"It is perfectly clear."

"In that case, don't keep me waiting any longer."

"You must have some coffee, at least, Colonel, before you go back . . ."

Harlow did his best to glare at him.

"I will have some coffee, yes. But only if it arrives now, at this moment, while you fetch the prisoner."

"You see, Colonel . . ."

"Why," thundered Harlow, "are you trying to delay me ? Do you doubt my authority ? "

"No, Colonel, but . . ."

"It cannot be, can it, that you doubt the wisdom of Berlin ? "

The effect of this insinuation was remarkable : the Major quite a big man, seemed to shrivel.

"God in Heaven, no ! "

"Well, then . . .?"

"You see, Colonel, of course we are disappointed." The Major spoke quickly, and his eyes seemed unable to meet those of Harlow. "We had hoped here in Paris to extract from the man Drummond valuable information about the Resistance leaders with whom he is known to have frequented. But . . ."

" You shall have him back—if there is anything left of him—when we have done with him in Berlin," promised Harlow magnanimously. " Now don't let's waste time talking any more. Give the necessary orders."

" Unfortunately I cannot."

" What do you mean, you cannot ! "

" I am not in charge of the prisoner Drummond. He is a special case. The case is in the hands of Fräulein Peterson. I am sorry, but I am powerless."

At last it was out ! The whole embarrassment of this typical German had been caused by his unwillingness to confess that he was under the orders of a woman . . .

Mat Harlow thought extremely quickly. He had always supposed that at some stage he would have to deal with Irma Peterson, but he had been unable to make definite plans to meet the contingency, inevitable though it was, in the absence of certain knowledge of the position she held with the Paris Gestapo. He knew very well that she would be an entirely different proposition to the Major, and he had an unpleasant suspicion that he really should have known all about her, in the rôle he was playing, since her appointment—so obviously unpopular—must have come direct from Berlin.

" I expected to find Fräulein Peterson here to meet me," he said sharply. " Where is she ? "

" I thought it better not to inform her of your arrival until I had seen you."

" What ! " Harlow nearly lost his pince-nez in his endeavours to look outraged : the incident startled him, and he contented himself with scathing words. He refused to allow the unfortunate officer to interrupt a flow of invective of which he was really proud.

" Listen to me, Colonel ! Please do not think I am attempting to put difficulties in your way ! " The harassed Major spoke quickly as soon as he had an opportunity. " But there were things I wanted to say to you about that woman—things which you might like to report to Berlin—which I could not say in front of her."

Harlow looked at him severely.

" Well ? "

Given the chance, the Major really let himself go. Irma Peterson was insupportable. It was not possible to expect senior officers to work under her. She was arrogant and conceited, which might perhaps be borne but only if she were also efficient, and she was not. How could she be, if it were possible for the stupid British to substitute one of their agents for her own man from her own organisation in London, for which she alone was responsible ? That fact had cost the life of the distinguished officer under whom he had worked so happily until two days ago, and whose existence since she had been in Paris had been made a misery. She could not claim the credit, although she no doubt would attempt to, for the recapture of the Englishman. Because of her senseless, idiotic theatrical plan, Drummond had been able to get away, and she was the only one present who had known what was happening. It was true that she had followed the escaping car quite quickly, and had shadowed the fugitives to the area in which they had taken refuge ; but it was the Gestapo alone, thanks to its own admirable invention, which had been able to place the exact house, and then make the successful raid. Irma Peterson, according to the Major, was quite intolerable . . .

Mat Harlow had enjoyed the speech, but he would have enjoyed it far more if he had been able to concentrate on it. That had not been possible because an idea was quickly formulating in his brain. Two birds with one stone . . . ?

He became quite pleasant and sympathetic towards the Major, to that officer's obvious and immense relief.

" We in Berlin are not unacquainted with all that you say," he told him. " Her London organisation has not been so successful as we could have hoped, and the reason is becoming clear to us. That is why I propose to take Fräulein Peterson back with me this morning . . ."

" To Berlin ? "

"Yes."

The Major rubbed his hands : he simply could not help it. " Will she go ? "

That was the very question that Mat Harlow was asking himself. But he raised his eyebrows . . .

" I fail to understand you, Major." He spoke with a return of his former asperity. " She was appointed by Berlin, was she not ? "

" Yes, yes, of course . . ."

" And I represent Berlin, here to summon her—and her prisoner—at once to headquarters."

" It only mentions the prisoner in the document, Colonel . . . ? " said the Major, doubtfully.

" If she alone is responsible for her prisoner, she must accompany him," replied Harlow with a conviction he was very far from feeling. " Failing that, I will give her orders verbally . . . the document is signed by my friend Herr Himmler himself, and he will not be pleased—he will not be at all pleased—if I have to report that she is being in anyway . . . difficult."

Mat Harlow was delighted to notice the effect he produced by the familiar use of the dreaded name.

" But come, Major ! " he spoke sharply again. " Give the necessary orders about the prisoner. Ring up the woman, tell her that she is summoned with Drummond to Berlin, and that I have my private aeroplane waiting to take her. Tell her to hurry, that I am tired of waiting. And that coffee . . . where is that coffee . . . I should like a cup of coffee ! "

The Major rushed into action. Orders were given right and left, and Harlow listened to his end of the telephone conversation with Irma Peterson. The name of Himmler seemed to have a remarkable effect on her as well, and the Major used it a trifle unscrupulously in his expressed anxiety to be rid of her. He stated that he had the official document containing the order in his possession . . .

Diffidently, the Major spoke again over the coffee.

" I am in charge here in Paris, Colonel," he said quietly, " and I know the local conditions—forgive me—better than you do. I cannot allow you to take the prisoner to the airport in your car . . ."

" He will be powerless manacled and shackled . . ."

" I fear nothing from him. But one cannot take too many precautions when dealing with these so-called patriots. I will provide you with an escort, and the prisoner must travel in an armoured car . . ."

Mat Harlow gave in gracefully : there was in any case, nothing that he could do about it, and Jean-Marie was expecting something of the sort.

The little procession left the gaunt building at speed. First, there were four motor-cyclist of the escort ; then the Citroen with Irma Peterson, looking demure and attractive in her magnificent mink coat, sitting next to Mat Harlow ; two more of the escort ; the semi-armoured prison van containing Drummond ; and last a whole posse of the escort.

Mat Harlow glanced at Irma Peterson. She had shown no sign of recognition in that horrible first moment when they had met : but Harlow felt that he had been unduly apprehensive about it. She had only previously seen him for a few moments, pulling faces at her, in the Savoy in London, and in any case he looked very different now. She had accepted him without question, and Harlow felt profoundly grateful to the fetish of discipline demanded by the Nazi hierarchy.

The shooting started when they were about half-way to the airport. It came so suddenly that even Harlow was surprised. Jean-Marie had certainly kept his promise : all of armed Paris seemed to be on the spot. Mat Harlow found it difficult to keep the bargain he had made, not to move from the car. It was necessary to keep out of the battle, he knew, because of the uniform that he was wearing : there was too great a risk of being shot by a friend. But it was a desperately hard bargain to keep . . .

Harlow suddenly felt a slender hand in his : he looked round quickly. Irma Peterson was staring at him with wide eyes, no colour at all left in her face . . .

He laughed.

"You've got nothing to worry about . . . *yet!*" he said.

She gave one small gasp : then she acted with incredible rapidity. As Harlow, with a shock, realised that he had spoken in English, she had opened the door and was half out of it. He made a grab at her, but was too late.

Mat Harlow could have shot her. But, somehow, he could not pull the trigger . . . she vanished into an alley.

The firing died down as suddenly as it had begun. Harlow looked round. They were helping Hugh out of the disabled van, and towards him. German bodies and crashed motor-cycles, seemed to be lying everywhere . . .

With a smile, Harlow made room.

"Wotcher, cocky!" said Hugh Drummond. "You were at least forty-eight hours sooner than I dared expect you." He smiled cheerfully. "You haven't, by any chance, got anything liquid on you . . . ?"

Proudly, Mat Harlow produced Algy's flask, as the car darted forward.

"Thanks, Mat," said Hugh Drummond. "You're a real pal!"

XXXII

PHYLLIS GETS A PRESENT

"After that," said Hugh Drummond in the matter-of-fact tone of voice in which he had told the whole story, "we lay very low indeed. We saw, and were duly impressed by, the very careful precautions which were taken to make quite sure that no unauthorised person reached the meeting of the Council of Resistance, and that the meeting was not disturbed. And then . . . well, we just came home."

The Great Man who had been drawing on a sheet of paper throughout the recital, looked up with a smile.

"I should very much like to see Mr. Longworth . . ."

"At the moment," answered Drummond, "Algy is closeted with the War Office. But he has instructions to report to you directly they have done with him."

"Good." The Great Man paused for a moment, apparently consulting his designs as if to draw inspiration from them. "What it really boils down to—over-simplified of course—is that the French people as a whole are strongly pro-Allied, far more healthy mentally as a Nation than they were in nineteen-forty, and that those composing the Resistance Groups are potentially another Allied army?"

"And a particularly useful one," said Mat Harlow, "because they are already well organised behind the enemy's lines . . ."

"Yes." The Great Man looked up suddenly. "You . . . er . . . . you both agree about all this:"

"We had thought of making two separate reports . . ." began Hugh Drummond.

Mat Harlow finished the sentence for him.

"But there's no sense in it. We shall sign the same report."

"That is really splendid!" said the Great Man rather surprisingly: it was a great deal for him to say. "When can I expect the written details?"

"In three or four days." Hugh Drummond told him. "I'm taking Mat down to my farm in the country, where we can write in peace."

"I am, of course," said the Great Man a trifle awkwardly "most extremely obliged to both of you . . ."

The postman had been sighted, and Phyllis had gone to open the door to him. Harlow and Drummond were seated on either side of the fire and Peter Darrell was standing waiting to pass round the tankards which Algy Longworth was busily filling.

"Do you think, here in England, they'll read that report?" asked Mat Harlow.

"Oh, they'll read it all right." Hugh Drummond laughed. "Will they in America?"

"Yes, they'll read it. But will it make any difference?" Hugh Drummond lighted a cigarette.

"I dunno, old pal. Depends if it cuts across their

blasted prejudices too much. Anyway, it'll shake 'em. How about America ? "

" You bet it'll shake 'em ! And—maybe—they'll learn ! " There was a short pause.

" Why did Mr. Big seem so surprised we were going to sign the same report ? " asked Harlow suddenly.

Hugh Drummond grinned.

" Professional politicians and diplomats," he said, " often like doing their own dribble, and kicking their own goals . . . it does, of course, improve the game—unless you're playing on the same side."

Phyllis came in cheerfully.

" Look, Hugh . . . a parcel ! "

" For me ? "

" No, for me ! I do believe it's a present ! "

She opened it. She took a bottle of Guerlain's *Vol de Nuit* from the box. Her eyes opened wide.

" How lovely ! Who on earth can it be from ? And how on earth did anyone get hold of *that* nowadays . . . ? "

" Can I see it, darling . . . ? "

Something in Drummond's voice made her hand it to him at once. She noticed that the others were watching him closely, that there was a sudden tension in the air.

Hugh Drummond examined the bottle carefully : then he looked at her.

" I'm afraid, my sweet, it's a practical joke . . . in very bad taste. Watch ! " He undid the stopper. As soon as the air reached the liquid, a blue flame rose from the neck of the bottle. Drummond quickly put it in the fireplace.

" Good gracious, goodness me ! " said Algy Longworth. " Fancy that ! But how useful if you wanted to destroy something . . ."

Hugh Drummond caught Mat Harlow's eye : he suddenly burst out laughing.

" I don't think it's funny at all ! " said the disappointed Phyllis.

" I'm sorry, darling." Hugh Drummond lifted his tankard. " It depends on how you look at it . . . well, chaps, here's to the next time ! "